Not Quite a Mom

Also by Kirsten Sawyer

Not Quite a Bride

Not Quite a Mom

KIRSTEN SAWYER

KENSINGTON BOOKS
http://www.kensingtonbooks.com

KENSINGTON BOOKS are published by

Kensington Publishing Corp.
850 Third Avenue
New York, NY 10022

All Kensington titles, imprints and distributed lines are available at special quantity discounts for bulk purchases for sales promotion, premiums, fund-raising, educational or institutional use.

Special book excerpts or customized printings can also be created to fit specific needs. For details, write or phone the office of the Kensington Special Sales Manager: Kensington Publishing Corp., 850 Third Avenue, New York, NY 10022. Attn. Special Sales Department. Phone: 1-800-221-2647.

Kensington and the K logo Reg. U.S. Pat. & TM Off.

ISBN-13: 978-0-7582-1664-9
ISBN-10: 0-7582-1664-5

First Kensington Trade Paperback Printing: February 2008
10 9 8 7 6 5 4 3 2 1

Printed in the United States of America

To Eleanor
for napping just enough to let me write this book.

~1~

"He finally did it!" I squeal with excitement into my black cordless phone.

"He" is my boyfriend of seven (*and a half*) years, Daniel McCafferty. "It" is a proposal. I guess now he is technically my fiancé, since I am wearing a stunning 1-carat (.85 carat) engagement ring on my left ring finger. On the other end of the phone is my best friend (only friend), Courtney Cambridge.

"Oh my God, Elizabeth, congratulations!" she screams back at me, sounding as excited as I feel.

This is why I love Courtney. She is the kind of friend who *really* cares. She sounds as excited as I feel because she *feels* that excited. She's been like that since the day we met, in our freshman year at UCLA. Courtney and I were both cursed with horrible first-year roommates and so we spent most of the year in the mildew-smelling lounge eating vending machine food and trying to top each other with bad-roommate anecdotes. It created a bond that has lasted until now.

Now we are thirty-two. We have our own, roommateless apartments in Los Angeles and instead of spending our nights eating Kit-Kats in a dorm common room, we spend them eating Chinese take-out in our respective apartments on the phone.

"Tell me everything," Courtney demands.

As I begin to tell her, in specific detail, every event of the evening, I gaze happily at my hand. The evening had begun like any other. It's Saturday night, so of course Dan and I had plans to go out. Like almost every Saturday, he picked me up at 8 p.m. with a bouquet of roses in hand. We went to dinner at a new place on Beverly Drive and then decided to splurge on dessert. This is where the evening stopped being ordinary for a few minutes. When our crème brulée arrived, neatly wedged in the caramelized sugar was a ring. In utter shock, I looked from the ring to Daniel, still holding the spoon I had poised to dig in.

"Will you marry me?" Daniel asked, leaning over the table.

I looked once more from the bejeweled dessert into his eyes before responding, "Absolutely." Then I took the ring out of the custard, licked it off and slipped it onto my finger. On cue, the waiter brought two glasses of champagne. We toasted and then ate the dessert.

After we left the restaurant, the night pretty much returned to normal—except for my new accessory. We went back to my apartment, had sex, I faked an orgasm, and Dan smiled proudly. Then he got dressed, I wrapped myself in a pink silk robe and walked him to the door. Some nights Dan stays at my apartment, but if he has plans for early the next morning, like he did this night, he goes back to his own apartment to avoid disturbing me on a day when I can actually sleep in. The next morning, he was playing golf with a judge, so I kissed him at the door and watched through the window as he climbed into his navy blue Audi A4 with a glowing smile. As soon as he drove off, I lunged for the phone to dial Courtney.

Just as I get to the part with the ring in the crème brulée, my call waiting beeps.

"Ignore it," Courtney instructs.

"I can't!" I argue, "What if it's Dan?"

"Okay, fine," she concedes and I click over.

"Elizabeth Castle?" the voice on the other end inquires. It's obviously not Dan . . . it must be some stupid sales call.

"Speaking?" I reply in a clearly annoyed tone.

"Ms. Castle, I am calling in regards to your best friend."

I am distracted thinking about how soon I will be Mrs. McCafferty instead of Ms. Castle and so it takes me a second to process what the caller has said.

"Courtney?" I ask after a lengthy pause.

"Oh, um, no," I can tell the caller feels awkward, and my feelings of irritation begin to return. "Charla Dearbourne Tatham," he finally says.

He pronounces the last name as it's spelled, and instinctively I correct his pronunciation: "Dearburn."

It's like I'm instantly transported to the fifth grade, when Charla Dearbourne actually *was* my best friend and I had to stand up to every moron who pronounced her name incorrectly. At eleven years old, we were positive it was the people who were idiots and not the fact that her name was not pronounced the way it was spelled that was the problem. I probably haven't thought about Charla for a dozen years. All at once, I'm flooded with memories of my childhood friend, quickly followed by the disdain I feel whenever I think of my hometown.

I grew up in a small (pathetically tiny) town in Central California called Victory. Of the town's approximately seven hundred residents, 70 percent were rednecks and the other 30 percent were hicks. Basically the only thing Victory has going for it is that it's a bump in the road on the way to a posh ski resort. Granted, there are nicer bumps on either side of it where most people take their rest stops, but occasionally a yuppie couple will miscalculate the distance and end up stopping in Victory to refuel their Range Rover and have lunch at one of the "quaint" (crappy) local eateries. My childhood dream was for a wonderful, childless couple on their way to a lavish ski vacation to fall in love with me, adopt me on the spot, and take me with them. This never happened, so the day I turned eighteen, I burned rubber out of Victory and never looked back.

Charla and I had been friends since the day we started kindergarten, and we pinky swore up and down that we would remain best friends until the day we died. By high school, we both knew we were growing apart, but we still vowed to keep our schoolyard promise. Then, at seventeen, Charla made a mistake *very* common among the girls at Victory High . . . she got pregnant the night of our senior homecoming dance.

While I helped her decide between Tiffany and Debbie (after the beloved '80s pop stars Tiffany and Debbie Gibson) as the best name for her daughter, I also decided to make my life different. I kept my legs securely crossed while I anxiously filled out applications for every college I could get a scholarship to. In May, one month before graduation day, Tiffany Debbie Dearbourne was born (four other babies were also born to girls in our graduating class that month) and I announced my decision to enroll at UCLA for the fall and to get a jump on things by attending the summer session starting in just six weeks.

Charla was my biggest champion, and she promised that as soon as she got back on her feet, she and Tiffany would meet me in Los Angeles. We kept this dream alive until about halfway through my freshman year, when Charla informed me that her boyfriend, Clark Winters (*not* Tiffany's father), wanted to marry her. Even though part of me knew she was never coming, I was so disappointed in her that I not only didn't return home for her wedding, I never spoke to her again. I heard from my mother when three years later Charla went down to the courthouse with a black eye and filed for divorce. A few years after that my mother updated me that Charla was marrying Chuck Tatham, and while I didn't care enough to send her congratulations I was happy for her because I remembered Chuck from high school and knew him to be a nice guy.

"What about Charla?" I ask the caller, wondering why this person, and not my own mother, is calling to share Charla gossip with me.

"I'm sorry to inform you, Ms. Castle, that Mrs. Tatham has passed away."

At first his worlds don't register or make sense. "Mrs. Tatham?" The only people in our small town who went by Mr. or Mrs. were teachers at the school. Mrs. Tatham wasn't ringing any bells. Then it hit me like a bucket of ice water.

"Can you hold on a moment?" I politely ask and I hit the "flash" button on my phone before he can answer. "Court, I have to call you back," I say, my mouth feeling filled with sawdust.

"Everything okay?" she asks.

"Yeah," I reply without meaning it. "I'll call you right back." And then I click back over to the stranger waiting on my other line. "I'm back," I tell him.

"I'm sorry to bring such bad news," the caller apologizes. "Mrs. Tatham and her husband were driving home early this morning when their car swerved off the road. Unfortunately the style pickup that Mr. Tatham was driving had actually been recalled many years ago on account of the gas tank being underneath the passenger cab and the risk of explosion upon impact. They were both killed immediately."

I can picture the kind of pickup they were driving as if it were sitting in my living room. The rusted old trucks are common in Victory—I think my own stepfather drives one.

Thinking of Russ and his hunk-of-junk car makes me think of my mother. I haven't talked to her in some time, but I'm certain that she and Charla's mother are still friends. Why didn't she call me? Then I remember—my mother and stepfather are away at a bowling tournament this weekend.

Russ is a big bowler in the Victory league and he and my mother often travel to compete. Charla's parents are in the same league.

Suddenly my heart fills with sadness. For the first time since the day I loaded all my worldly possessions into my old green Datsun (a car I thankfully no longer own) and left Victory, I feel a pang of homesickness and a longing for my mother.

"When will the funeral be?" I ask, trying to focus on the details in an effort to avoid the pain.

"No arrangements have been made yet, Ms. Castle. Mrs. Tatham's family is out of town at the moment—"

"Thank you for the call, I will keep in touch with family in Victory to get the details," I say, cutting him off.

I hang up the phone before he can get another word out, and I immediately pull the cord from the wall. I wonder for a split second who the person on the other end was—he never did identify himself, but the truth is that I don't care. I am flooded with conflicting emotions. This was the happiest night of my life and now the joy has come to a crashing halt. Suddenly I am heartbroken over the loss of a friend I haven't even thought about since I was in my twenties.

"Humph, some friend," I say to myself as I swallow four Nyquil with the glass of water that has been on my nightstand since yesterday. Still in my shiny pink robe, I curl up on the slightly tangled sheets left from my tryst with Dan and close my eyes tightly.

~2~

I awake the next morning with a mind-blowing hangover. It takes me a minute to remember that I got it from the four little green pills and not a night of fun. It takes me a second after that to remember why I overdosed on cold meds when I don't even have the slightest sniffle. When I do remember, I roll over and plug the phone back into the wall. Then I return to my back holding the handset and dial my mother's phone number. She answers on the fourth ring.

"Hello?" she says, and from the mumble I can tell a cigarette is pursed between her lips as she speaks.

"Mom, it's me. I heard about Charla."

"Oh, baby doll. I've been trying to reach you all morning. You know your phone was disconnected?"

"I know. Someone called me last night."

I roll on my side and catch a glimpse of the clock beside my bed: it's almost noon. I'm surprised (and a little hurt) that neither Daniel nor Courtney has broken my door down with a fireman's axe.

"Look sweetie, Margie's over here now and I'm helping her fix up the funeral arrangements. You think you'll be able to make it home?"

Margie is . . . was . . . Charla's mother. I can picture the two of them sitting in my mother's kitchenette smoking Kools in their dingy white Keds with their ratted, teased, and Aqua-Netted hairdos. Victory is in a bit of a time warp. My mother was quite beautiful when she was young. She was even Miss Central California as a teenager, which gave her celebrity status back in Victory. Now you can see the traces of her beauty, but you have to look through the skin grayed by years of nicotine and under the pounds of pancake makeup.

"Of course," I say, and I mean it even though every time until now I have come up with a last-minute excuse to avoid returning to Victory. "Send Margie my sympathy," I add.

"Will do, sugar, I'll talk to you in a bit."

With that she hangs up, but I don't move until the "beep, beep, beep if you need help, please dial the operator" lady comes on the line. Even then, I listen to her prerecorded message several times before finally clicking the phone off. I don't set the phone down, though. I immediately dial Dan's cell phone. No answer, so I dial Courtney's and she picks up.

"What happened to you last night!" she demands before even saying hello. The caller ID has clearly given me away.

I take a deep breath, "Do you remember my friend Charla, from home?"

Courtney and I were bonding right around the time that Charla and I were officially coming to an end. Court spent many nights listening to me complain about the rednecks from my hometown, specifically Charla, whom I felt extremely abandoned and betrayed by.

"Yeah, the girl with the teen-pop baby?" she asks with a giggle. We took to calling Tiffany Debbie the teen-pop baby in our Victory/Charla-bashing sessions.

"She died yesterday," I say, my voice as flat as a board.

"Oh God, Elizabeth, I am so sorry," she says, her voice filled with horror. "I thought you were going to say she was coming to L.A."

"Nope, definitely not coming to L.A.," I say, and even I can't help but giggle at my horrible joke (lack of a joke).

"Tell me how you're feeling," Courtney commands in a soothing voice, which I affectionately call her "therapist voice."

Courtney had quite a bit of trouble finding her true calling. At UCLA, while I stayed firmly focused on journalism (whole lot of good it did me career-wise), she flopped around in every major from Chinese landscaping to nursing, including an entire year as a psychology major which she thinks makes her Dr. Freud's equal. She eventually landed in English, with plans at graduation to become an acclaimed novelist. Courtney spent the summer working on her book, which I think never got past page 23, before deciding that going to law school and becoming the attorney general was her definite calling.

Showing more drive and dedication than I had expected, Courtney graduated from law school, passed the bar, and got a job as an assistant D.A. in Beverly Hills. This is where she met Dan and introduced us. Less than a year after beginning her legal career, she realized she hated the law. She quit her job, intending to pursue acting, actually explaining to me with a straight face how she thought her experience in the courtroom really made her perfect to star in an *L.A. Law*–type drama. At the same time, she started gluing rhinestones on everything from cell phones to Ugg boots to sell to rich people. Then, by some miracle, *InStyle* magazine called her accessories "musthaves," and ever since then her business, SparkleCourt, has been her main focus, but she still considers herself something of a psychology expert and a qualified therapist.

"I dunno, Court," I admit, letting her play shrink, since I definitely need the help. "Conflicted?" I offer.

"Um-hum," she replies, and I have to stifle a giggle.

Courtney does her best to counsel me for the next hour

before getting off because she is late for a party at the home of Debra Messing, who is apparently a huge SparkleCourt fan. When we hang up, I'm relieved that our session is over and that Courtney has settled into only helping people through retail therapy. She's well intentioned, but there certainly isn't a hidden talent there.

I glance at the clock again and decide to call Dan ... maybe he has been trying all this time and there is something wrong with my call waiting? His cell phone goes straight to voice mail and I click off dejectedly without leaving a message.

I wander into the kitchen to find some food and am spreading peanut butter on white bread when the phone rings again. I drop the bread and knife in mid-smear and trot to the phone, so confident that it's Dan that I don't even bother to look at the caller ID.

"Hey," I answer the phone, picturing Dan's sweaty head under his plaid visor and his wide, toothy smile. Instead of hearing his warm voice, I hear the same stranger's voice I heard last night.

"Ms. Castle, this is Mr. Platner. We spoke last night regarding Charla Tatham," he reminds me.

Oh, so that's who last night's caller was. If memory serves, all the sons of the Platner family are attorneys in Victory. They are a strange family that for generations has left Victory to attend law school and then—here's the strange part—*returned* to Victory to practice in the same dumpy office the generation before had used. I'm wondering which Platner this is. There was one a year above me at Victory High, but Buck Platner always seemed a little dense.

"Is this Buck Platner?" I ask, unable to fathom the football playing meathead who took me to his senior prom as an attorney.

"Yes, Lizzie, it is," he says as if he doesn't want to admit it, and my temper flares internally as he uses my childhood nickname.

"It's Elizabeth now," I correct him, coolly, trying to quash a swell of anger, "or Liz."

"Oh, well, sorry about that Lizzie . . . I mean Elizabeth," he stutters. "Look, Liz, you hung up so fast last night and your line has been busy ever since, except when there was no answer at all."

"Well, what is it Buck?" I snap as my concern that something is wrong with my call waiting is confirmed. I need to get off this stupid call quickly since Dan is probably trying desperately to get through.

"Look, Lizzie . . . Liz . . . Elizabeth, Charla had a last will and testament. My father was actually the one who drew it up for her," he drawls, and my mind goes back to Victory.

I am 100 percent, or if it's possible to be more than 100 percent certain, that's what I am that Charla did not have any great fortune that she left to her long-lost best friend. In fact, I am pretty certain that all she had was a crappy old Victory house and maybe a crappy old compact car, and since the truck clearly would not be getting handed out to survivors I didn't see any loot I'd be interested in.

"Well, she named you guardian of her daughter, Tiffany Debbie Dearbourne."

Again he pronounces the name the way it's spelled, and again I correct him, but this time with a bit less patience.

"It's *Dearburn*," I bark. "You ought to know . . . you went to high school with her."

"*Dearburn*," he repeats, without making any apologies for his mistake. "You're her guardian."

I'm so focused on thinking about how even though he's now an attorney it is clear that Buck Platner is still dense that I don't hear him.

"So we'll need you to sign some papers," he continues.

"Sign what papers?" I ask, not getting over my annoyance easily.

"The guardianship papers," he explains, and then goes on in depth about some sort of process, but again, my mind is not with him.

"Guardianship papers?" I ask, feeling that perhaps there is something wrong with my whole phone and not just the call waiting, since Buck and I seem to be carrying on two separate conversations.

"Lizzie . . . Liz, I just explained that you are to be guardian of Tiffany," he says sounding exasperated and probably thinking that I am the dense one.

As his words finally penetrate, I feel a tightness in my chest and a spinning in my head. I can't breathe well—short snips of air are escaping out of my chest, but I can't seem to draw a good breath in. As my head grows lighter, I am somehow able to rationalize that this is a panic attack. I had one once before when my hairdresser and I had a major failure to communicate and I had to attend my college graduation with a permanent wave.

"Relax," I command myself, but apparently I say it out loud and Buck thinks the command is intended for him, which leads to more confusion between us.

I grab an empty paper bag which was used to bring take-out moo shoo into my apartment yesterday and breathe in and out, hardly noticing the lingering smell of hoisin sauce. My heart starts to slow down, and suddenly my head rationalizes that "guardian" in this case obviously doesn't mean what I think it means.

"What do you mean by guardian?" I ask, eager to get the misunderstanding cleared up. "Doesn't a person have to agree to be a child's guardian? Wouldn't I have had to sign some sort of legal document?"

"Jesus, Lizzie," he says, forgetting to correct himself, which is okay since I'm too distracted to notice his mistake, "I thought your folks said you went to *UCLA*." He pronounces my alma mater in what I am assuming is his attempt at a hoity-toity voice. "By guardian I mean you are her legal guardian—you have custody. Charla is dead and her will states that if that happens, you raise her kid," he finishes in a huff, forgetting his professional manner and not bothering to sugarcoat a thing.

I have a horrifying flashback to a conversation in Charla's dingy bedroom, shortly after she realized she was pregnant, where I wholeheartedly agreed to be the unborn child's god-mother. Does that hold up in a court of law?!?

"But I can't be a guardian," I argue. "I'm only thirty-two years old!" I whine, sounding like a twelve-year-old.

"Well, guess what, Lizzie, so was Charla," he snaps. "Look, what do you want me to do about this? You are who she picked, which I assume means she thought you would be good . . . although it seems likely she hadn't dealt with you recently," he adds under his breath.

His scolding shuts me up. "What am I supposed to do now?" I ask in a pout, my eyes filling with tears, and the panic attack that had subsided returning in full force. I am partially wondering what the legal procedure to come will be and partially wondering about my life.

"You need to sign these papers ASAP, and then Tiffany will be yours," he says it as if he has just sold me a new hatchback. *Just sign these papers and a 2004 Honda Civic will be yours!*

"Okay," I say, highly aware of the fact that I don't have a choice. "Send the papers to my office on Monday," I instruct, giving him the phone number to call to get the mailing address from my assistant.

"Thank you, Ms. Castle," Buck says, returning to his professional attorney persona. "Again, I am terribly sorry for your loss."

"Thanks, Buck," I mumble, not wasting time or energy on being formal or polite—even bordering on cynical, before clicking the phone off and setting it on its base with shaking hands.

Another world away, Buck Platner hangs up his old beige phone before slamming his fists and then his head down on his scratched desk. That hadn't gone anything like he had planned and neither had the night before.

The night before, Buck had been sitting home alone with his golden retriever, Wildcat, when his own phone had rung. His nights were usually pretty quiet (boring) and so the ring had startled both Buck and Wildcat, who had been relaxing on the couch, Buck with a Hungry Man TV dinner and Wildcat with a fresh pig ear.

"Hello?" he answered.

"Son," his father's gruff voice boomed through the receiver. "We're having a bit of an emergency situation down at the office. I need you here."

Buck quickly agreed and rose from the couch, not bothering to turn off the television or throw away the remains of his microwave meal.

He stood almost six feet five inches in his bare size 13 feet. As if these kind of calls were the norm, which they certainly were not—he had never received one before—Buck slid his feet into a well-worn pair of Adidas sandals and brushed the crumbs off his belly before grabbing his shoddy, faux-leather briefcase and keys and heading out the door.

Besides the tacky attaché case and in spite of the spots of Hungry Man gravy on his belly, Buck looked sexy in his Levi's and white cotton T-shirt. His skin was tanned from spending time outdoors, his athletic physique was clear under his clothes, and his blond hair was neatly buzzed an inch from his scalp. Climbing into his new black F150, he rubbed his blue eyes and looked at the clock on his cell phone. He had definitely never been called to work at this hour before.

The office was only a few blocks from Buck's home, and within minutes he was parking next to his father's Cadillac and climbing out of the truck. Hurrying inside, his stomach tightened with worry about the "emergency" inside.

Once in the office, he found his father, the image of Buck but thirty-five years older, sitting at his desk, rubbing his own blue eyes. Sitting across from his father was a teenage girl dressed in what looked like pajamas, but these days what kids wore to school and to bed looked very similar. Her eyes were red, and clearly she had been crying.

"Buck," his father said glancing up and looking grateful to see his younger son, "This is Tiffany Dearbourne."

"*Dearburn*," the girl, Tiffany, said miserably.

"Hello," Buck said stiffly, feeling as uncomfortable as he always did in front of clients of the legal practice.

"You went to school with her mother, Charla," his father went on to explain. "Sadly, Charla and her husband, Chuck Tatham, were killed in a bad car wreck earlier this afternoon."

Buck's mouth fell open slightly in shock. Back in high school, he'd known Charla Dearbourne as the best friend of his senior prom date and the one girl he thought about consistently, even though it had been a dozen years since he'd seen her face.

"Tiffany's mother was a client of ours, I drew up her will many years ago," Buck's father, Larry Senior—called Larry S—continued. "There aren't any real assets . . . a house here in town not worth too much, a 1989 Toyota compact. Obviously, the truck is no longer included. She assigned a guardian for her daughter here though, another gal you went to school with, so I thought maybe it would be best if you contacted her about all this. Let's see, what's her name?" Larry S asked himself as he shuffled through the manila file folder containing Charla's papers. "Ah, here it is: Elizabeth Castle."

Elizabeth Castle? Buck's heart skipped a beat—that was the girl.

"Um, sure, Dad. I can contact her. Do we have a phone number?" he asked trying to play it cool with the same butterflies in his belly he'd felt before calling her and asking her to be his date to the dance.

His father scribbled the number on a yellow Post-it note and handed it to Buck, who headed for his private office. Once inside, with the door closed, he sat behind the desk preparing what he would say.

His heart was racing with anticipation—in just a few minutes he would be speaking with Lizzie Castle. He had taken Lizzie to his senior prom when she was a junior, but just a few weeks after that he had gone off to Arizona for football preseason practice. Because of the football schedule, he hadn't gotten back to Victory for Christmas that year and had joined a bunch of guys at Lake Havasu for spring break. When summer finally rolled around, Buck had been eager to return home to see Lizzie but had learned that just days before his homecoming, she had headed to Los Angeles to get a jump on her freshman year at UCLA. She hadn't returned to her hometown after that, but over the past years Buck had thought about her often.

Lizzie was the only girl who had ever resisted Buck, and that intrigued him beyond belief. As an attractive athlete, Buck had never had to work hard with members of the opposite sex; it seemed that there were plenty of girls who wanted to go out with him—or just have sex with him—simply because he played football. Lizzie Castle was the only girl who had ever seemed immune to this. Buck had always found her lack of interest in him irresistible.

Feeling ashamed that he felt excited to be placing a call of such a depressing nature, he carefully dialed 9 for an outside line, followed by 1-310, and then the phone number his father had scrawled out for him. She picked up quickly, and Buck figured that she must have been on the other line.

Instead of saying what he had planned, the words that came out of his mouth sounded like they always did when he was trying to deal with clients—completely dense. The call was over in a matter of seconds, and only after he heard the dial tone return did Buck realize that not only had he failed to identify himself, he had also failed to impart any of the information he was supposed to.

He thought about dialing her number again but thought again, deciding that he needed the evening to compose himself and would give her the night to collect herself as well before calling again in the morning. Dejectedly, he opened the door that joined his office to his father's and walked back in where the aging Platner and Charla's daughter sat uncomfortably. As he entered his father looked up, glad to see him.

"Well, everything settled?" he asked, a little too eagerly. "Is she on her way here now?"

"Not exactly," Buck said, uncomfortably.

"Are you driving her down to L.A.?" his father asked, his eyes narrowing as he motioned toward Tiffany.

"Not quite. She just needed the evening to collect herself," Buck offered, aware of how lame it sounded.

He saw his father's face flush slightly. "This girl's a minor. She cannot spend the night alone, and her grandparents are out of town."

Buck felt the disappointment he always felt oozing out of his father whenever he tried to handle something around the office. The fact was that although he was a good attorney,

Buck was horrible at handling anything to do with the clients or the business side of the practice.

"She can spend the night at my place," Buck offered pathetically.

"Well, I guess there's not really another option now, is there," his father said, rising from the desk and closing a briefcase as ugly as Buck's but much more worn. "Be sure to connect with this Ms. Castle first thing tomorrow so this girl can get down to L.A. Miss Dearbourne," he said looking at the miserable young girl as he crossed his office, "I am sorry for your loss. Things will get straightened out in no time."

"I don't want to go to L.A.!" Tiffany called out, her eyes filling with tears.

"Well, I'm afraid there's not much choice. We have to follow your mother's wishes here," his father said as he squeezed past Buck with a glare and stepped into the office's small reception area.

Before either Buck or Tiffany could say another word, his father was out the door and the two of them were alone in the office. The room was so still they could hear the quiet buzzing of the old copy machine that their secretary, Doris, had forgotten to turn off—again. The silence was only broken by occasional sniffles from Tiffany while Buck stared down his chest, unsure of what to do next.

Seeing the gravy spots on his belly, he looked up. "Have you had your dinner yet?" he asked kindly.

Although upon first appearance, Buck looked more like a fighter than a lover, he had a truly kind heart, which easily shone through his rough exterior as soon as he opened his mouth—as long as he wasn't with a client. Tiffany, not looking up, shook her head no.

"Well, come on, let's go get something for you to eat."

~4~

A few hours earlier, fifteen-year-old Tiffany Dearbourne had been pedaling her old purple bicycle as fast as it would go toward home. She'd been at her friend Laci's house and hadn't realized the time . . . her mother would be home any minute. Normally it wasn't a big deal for Tiffany to get home after her mom, but right now she was grounded and shouldn't have been out at all. After spending most of the weekend cooped up inside the stuffy house, Tiffany decided that if her mother couldn't bother to stay in town and uphold the punishment that she didn't need to obey it.

It really was a stupid punishment anyway. Tiffany had returned home twenty-seven minutes past curfew the weekend before. Her mother, Charla, had gone down the warpath and had grounded Tiffany for the next three weeks. Obviously an overzealous punishment, but since her mother had gotten pregnant her senior year of high school, she was convinced Tiffany's fate would be the same.

The ridiculous thing was that while Tiffany had been with a boy—her boyfriend of four months, Red Richley—she was not going to make the same mistakes her mother had. Instead, she was determined to follow in the footsteps of her Aunt Lizzie and get the hell out of Victory. Lizzie wasn't actually Tiffany's aunt, but rather her mother's best friend in the whole world. Tiffany hadn't seen Lizzie since she was a little baby because Lizzie had hit the road and attended college in Los Angeles, where she was now a successful career woman.

Sure, Tiffany had been at the lake (dried-up lake bed) with Red in his father's green Chevy, but she never had and never would let him move below her waistband. Unfortunately, Charla didn't believe Tiffany's pleas of innocence. Tiffany didn't let the punishment get her too far down, though. She just kept counting the days until her high school graduation, when she could make her own exit from Victory. Until Sunday afternoon, that is, when the boredom had gotten to her and she'd ridden her bike the three and a half blocks to Laci's house.

The girls had just watched MTV and drunk Cokes—in actuality, all things Tiffany could have done from her own house. It was just more fun to do them with Laci. As her legs shook from the power required to move the old bike at the speed Tiffany needed to get home, hopefully unscathed, she seriously doubted how worth it the afternoon with Laci had been.

As she rounded the final corner and was only a few houses from her own, Tiffany sighed with relief that her stepfather's pickup wasn't in the driveway. The relief lasted only a few seconds before she realized that a black-and-white police car was there instead. She was done for now . . . her own mother had called the police because she'd broken a punishment that was stupid to begin with?!?

With each pump of her legs on the rickety old pedals, Tiffany prayed that the cops were there for some other purpose and that she would get away with her outing. As she curved into the driveway, one of them called out to her.

"You Charla Tatham's kid?"

He was a stereotypical Victory cop, bursting out of his uniform because of too many hours spent eating Dunkin'

Donuts and not enough chasing criminals. In fairness, there weren't a whole lot of criminals to chase in their town. He looked older, probably close to retirement, with graying hair and wrinkled eyes. He mopped at his sweaty brow with a dingy handkerchief. The other cop looked like he was probably a rookie. His uniform was starched to perfection and he kept looking to the other for approval.

"Uh, yes, sir," Tiffany replied, in her best ass-kissing voice, which was quite shaky at the moment. In her head she was saying, "Oh crap."

The older officer looked at his partner and nodded, then back at Tiffany, who was leaning the rusted bike against the side of the house.

"We've got to talk to you. Can we go inside?" the young officer asked.

Tiffany's fear had morphed into outrage that her mother would treat her like this. She felt so stupid and childlike . . . and the fact that the policemen were being so nice to her only reinforced her belief that they felt sorry for her that her mother was such a lunatic as to call the police over because her grounded teenage daughter had ventured out from under their roof.

"Sure," Tiffany replied, red-faced from both the heart-pumping ride home and embarrassment.

Tiffany untied her key from the drawstring waist of the pajama pants she hadn't bothered to change out of to go to Laci's and stuck it in the front door. She quickly opened it and walked in, followed by the officers.

"Look, I know what this is," Tiffany said, staring at them defiantly.

Again the officers looked at each other. The fat one pulled uncomfortably at his shirt collar—the house was stuffy.

"This is about your mother," the young officer said.

"Just let me have it," Tiffany said, deciding to roll over

and take what she had coming . . . she *had* broken her punishment, even if it had been stupid to begin with.

"We're sorry to have to tell you that your mother and stepfather were involved in an automobile accident this afternoon. They were both killed."

The words hit Tiffany so hard she actually had to look down to be certain that the officer hadn't drawn his weapon and shot her in the stomach. How could this be true? Thirty seconds earlier, she had been cursing her mother's insanity, hoping that the police were at her house for some other reason than to bust her, and now all she wanted was to hear Charla screaming at her for sneaking out.

"I snuck out—I'm grounded," she said to the officers. She'd meant to speak it, but it came out in a whisper that made her throat ache as her eyes filled with tears.

"That's all right, dear," the fat officer said and came toward her with his arm out.

She knew this was a kind gesture, but his fat white arm, shiny with sweat, and the smell of his body odor made her turn away. He didn't seem to take it as a personal offense, and simply patted her back instead.

"We're going to need to take you with us," the young officer informed her. This was the first time he'd had to deliver bad news in the line of duty, and he was finding it more difficult than he had expected.

"Where?" Tiffany asked, desperately wanting to stay in the house she'd been itching to escape from earlier that day.

"Your mother had a will drawn up by Larry S. Platner. He has your guardian information."

Normally, Tiffany was a feisty teenager. This weekend wasn't the first time she had been grounded, and the offenses ranged from her messy room to her "smart" mouth. Normally, she would have put up a fight that included four-letter words and door slamming. Right now, she didn't have it in her. She just nodded her head and followed the two strangers out of her home. She then climbed into the backseat of their cruiser, where criminals sat, and stared out the window as they backed out of her driveway. As they drove down her street, Edison Way, she saw neighbors coming to their front windows to look out. It was uncommon to see a police car in their neighborhood, but she was sure that more than one of them wasn't surprised to see her in the back of it. If only they knew . . .

~5~

Now, many hours later, Tiffany found herself climbing the front steps of Buck Platner's house. As Buck held the door open for her, she assumed that his wife must be inside waiting for them because all the lights and the television set were on; instead, a golden bear of a dog greeted them.

"This is Wildcat," Buck explained, affectionately scratching the dog behind the ears.

Tiffany gave the dog a polite "hello" pat, which he seemed to appreciate wholeheartedly, and then scanned the room she was standing in.

Upon inspection, it couldn't have been clearer (even to a fifteen-year-old girl) that Buck was single. The living room was a mess. The coffee table was littered with old newspapers, beer cans, and what looked like the remnants of a Hungry Man turkey dinner. The walls were bare, and the mantel was decorated with football keepsakes from Buck's illustrious past.

Although Tiffany had never actually met Buck Platner, her mother would point him out around town over the years as if he was some sort of a celebrity. She guessed he was a bit of a Victory celebrity—he had been the star of their high school football team. That alone was enough in this town, but on top of it, he had been recruited to play football on a full scholarship at a university in Arizona . . . maybe the University *of* Arizona, she couldn't remember. After that, he had gone to law school. All of these accomplishments: sports, more sports, a college degree, and a graduate degree were enough to get a statue of yourself in the town square. Tiffany also remembered her mother boasting that her aunt Lizzie had gone to Buck's senior prom with him. She could tell that her mother felt this connected her to the celebrity, even though she had never seen them exchange more than a simple hello if their paths happened to cross directly.

Tiffany couldn't help but notice with irony that her mother would have been overjoyed by an invitation into Buck Platner's home, and now here Tiffany was.

"Lemme find something for you to eat," Buck said, quickly trying to gather as much trash from the cluttered coffee table as possible before ducking into a room off the living room. After a few minutes, he stuck his head back through the door. "Um, is there anything in particular that you like?"

Tiffany tried to muster a smile at his gesture and headed into the kitchen to find something, although she wasn't feeling particularly hungry. In the end, she settled for a bowl of Lucky Charms cereal. Buck's kitchen looked like a child's fantasy. Nothing green, lots of cans, and plenty of sugar. On a normal day, Tiffany could have gone crazy stuffing her face with junk food, but tonight she felt that the knot in her stomach was taking up any room that could have been used for food.

Tiffany and Buck sat on the living room couch—a couch Tiffany noted was extremely ugly but exceptionally comfortable—watching TV in silence for most of the night. Finally, at almost midnight, Buck suggested that he show Tiffany to the guest room.

Buck rose from the couch and led Tiffany down the hallway, where he opened the only door on the right. Inside was a perfectly comfortable guest room/home office combination. On one side of the room was a corner desk with computer gear and stacks of paper. On the other, a double bed with a plain black comforter. Like the living room, the only decorations were items that Buck had held on to from his football career.

"Sorry it's not much," Buck offered.

"No, it's fine," Tiffany said, realizing she should have been more polite but not having the energy.

"The bathroom is down the hall. There's only one, so you go ahead and use it first." Buck motioned to the door at the end of the hall.

Tiffany nodded and headed down the hall, nervous about what she might find. In her experience, men were not the nicest people to share bathrooms with . . . at least her stepfather, Chuck, was not. At home, the toilet seat was always up, with spots of pee along the rim. There were always globs of toothpaste in the sink, and short, dark, curly hairs along the edge of the tub. With great trepidation, Tiffany pushed open the door and turned the light on. Immediately she let out a sigh of relief. The bathroom appeared to be the one place where Buck was extremely neat. The toilet seat was down, the lid closed, and both the sink and the floor were clean. On one side of the counter was a single blue toothbrush and an electric razor, on the other, a bar of white soap sitting in a plain white soap dish.

It wasn't until she was actually standing in front of the sink that Tiffany realized she didn't have any of her own toiletries. She could see them sitting in the disgusting bathroom at home. She rinsed her face off, not even bothering to wait for the water to warm up, then dabbed it off with the black hand towel hanging on the bathroom wall.

As she quietly stepped out of the bathroom, Tiffany found an anxious looking Buck waiting in the hall for her.

"Are you all right?" he asked nervously.

"Yeah. I just realized that I don't have my toothbrush or anything with me."

"Oh," he breathed a sigh of relief. "We can go over to your place tomorrow and get your belongings before we head to L.A."

"Right, to L.A.," Tiffany replied oddly before opening the door to the guest room and walking in. She avoided making eye contact with Buck as she shut the door behind her, mumbling "good night" as she did. She didn't look at him because she didn't want him to see her cry, but once alone in the guest room, Tiffany lay down on the bed and sobbed silently into the pillow. She only stopped for a second, holding her breath, as Buck tapped on the door and instructed her to wake him if she needed anything during the night.

Tiffany doubted she would be able to sleep at all, but much to her surprise her crying soon quieted into exhaustion, and before she knew it, it was morning. She woke up because she thought she heard the door to her room opening. Her mother, a chronic "morning person," had a nasty habit of continually looking in on her all morning until she was finally awake. Tiffany opened her eyes expecting to see her mother's face in the doorway. Instead the door was closed and it wasn't her room. In an instant, the previous day's event flooded back into her head and numbed her entire body. She decided to lie in bed as long as she could—no need to get a jump on the misery she knew lay ahead.

Buck's night had not been as restful. He'd spent most of it thinking about what he would say when he talked to Lizzie. For hours, he had the conversation over and over in his head; and then when he was able to doze off, he dreamed about messing it up and woke up in a cold sweat. His anxiety over the impending conversation was compounded by the fact that soon they would be face-to-face.

At nine o'clock on the dot, Buck decided that it was a reasonable hour and picked up the phone beside his bed. Normally he would place a call like this from his office, but after sneaking a peak at Tiffany, he was relieved to find the teen sleeping peacefully. All his muscles tense with anticipation, he dialed the number from the yellow Post-it note, which was now crumpled beside the phone; busy signal. The letdown made his head spin for a second. Dejected, Buck headed to the kitchen to make coffee, pulling a pair of Arizona sweatpants over the boxers he normally wore around the house. Every fifteen minutes he hit the redial button on the phone and waited, paralyzed, hoping to hear ringing. For almost two hours, he only got beeping . . . and then suddenly, on his seventh attempt, it rang. The change of sound was enough to make his heart race as he lumbered back to his bedroom where his notes were laid out on the unmade bed.

As the phone rang, Buck went over in his head what he had rehearsed all night. Unfortunately, as soon as Lizzie answered the phone, he lost his train of thought and nothing came out right. Instead of the connection he had envisioned, where he said, "Lizzie, this is Buck Platner," and she said, "Oh, Buck, it's been way too long," he once again fumbled his way poorly into "professional lawyer" speak and screwed up the whole thing. Like an idiot, he pronounced Charla's last name wrong, again, then Lizzie—Elizabeth now—seemed confused about the whole guardian thing, causing him to get impatient, and finally—the cherry on top—he agreed to send the guardianship papers to her on Monday rather than arranging to see her today with Tiffany. The whole thing could not have gone worse—he didn't do his job right and he didn't handle his grand reunion with Lizzie/Elizabeth well either.

Things actually went even worse than Buck realized because Tiffany was standing silently in the hall outside his room the entire time, listening to the conversation. Although she heard only one side, she heard enough to know that her "Aunt Lizzie," as her mom had always referred to her, wasn't running to her rescue. In fact, from Buck's end of the conversation, it didn't sound as if she wanted anything to do with Tiffany at all. It was clear that the call didn't go as Buck had intended, since upon setting the receiver down he quietly said "Shit" under his breath while shaking his head.

~6~

"Shit" I say as I set the phone back in its cradle. I quickly snatch it back up again and dial Dan's cell phone number, pressing each digit as hard as I can and holding it down as if this will impart that this is an emergency and prompt him to answer the call. For the third time this morning, it goes straight to voice mail. I consider leaving a message, but what would I say?

"Dan, my childhood best friend who I haven't had anything to do with in the entire time we've been together has sent us an early wedding present!" That doesn't really explain things. *"Dan, great news! We aren't even married yet and we already have a teenager!"* That would be ridiculous. *"Dan, apparently my friend Charla doesn't update her will very often because she named ME as the guardian of her daughter!"* The truth sounds just as absurd.

"Oh, God," I say as I set the phone down on the cradle and mindlessly return to the half-made peanut butter sandwich on the kitchen counter. I feel like vomiting, but I don't know what else to do, so I complete the sandwich and stuff it in my face and then meticulously clean the entire kitchen, leaving no signs that the room has even been entered let alone used for food preparation and consumption. As I clean the knife, I consider taking my own life as an out but realize that it really isn't feasible with a butter knife. *This cannot be happening to me.*

I had a plan. Getting out of Victory was step number one, but it wasn't the entire plan. During the four-hour drive from Victory to Los Angeles the summer before my freshman year, I laid it all out in my head. It included graduating in four years, pursuing a successful career in broadcasting, marrying an attorney (or a doctor), having first a daughter and then an adorable son. There isn't any room in the plan for a fifteen-year-old girl at this time in my life and there isn't a contingency for something like this.

Still feeling like I've been socked in the chest, I wander around my apartment; my mind is racing around looking for an exit. As I pace, I straighten. I align the picture frames on my mantel, I confirm that my CDs are in alphabetical order, and I fluff the pillows on my Pottery Barn couch. I like things to be perfect. I thrive on perfection . . . that's why I'm so good at my job as a fact checker on *The Renee Foster Show!*. Okay, I admit that putting my degree in journalism to use confirming what color underwear Jennifer Aniston wears (white) and how John Travolta orders a steak (rare) isn't *exactly* what I'd planned on, but it includes a brief (sixty-second) on-air segment every single day (Monday–Friday), and being on air really is my dream. Plus it's a whole lot closer to perfection than a fifteen-year-old Victory teenager under my guardianship. I look at the photo exactly centered on my mantel; it's a shot of Dan and me at his parents' house last Christmas. I love this picture because we look like the ideal couple—faces squished together, smiling broadly in front of his mother's uniformly decorated tree.

The first Christmas I spent with Dan's family, I felt as if I'd died and gone to holiday heaven. Unlike the dusty, hot Victory Christmases I'd grown up with—the ones where my mother had brought the fake, color-not-found-in-nature-green tree in from the garage and not bothered to remove all the cobwebs before hanging mismatched glass balls and plastic Baby Jesuses all over it and plopping a supermarket ham on our regular dinner table—the McCafferty family Christmas was like a postcard. From their long mahogany dining room table, you can see the twelve-foot Douglas fir, decorated with matching gold balls and red bows on one side, and the front yard covered in a flawless blanket of snow on the other. Their mouthwatering homemade dinner is served on Wedgwood china, and everyone gathers around a baby grand to sing carols after dessert. Like I said, Holiday Heaven.

"Oh, God," I moan to the perfect couple in the picture. I pick up the phone and dial Courtney's cell phone. Debra Messing will have to understand—this is an emergency.

"Hello!" Courtney booms into my phone and her voice is so upbeat it almost makes me feel better . . . *almost*. I can picture her sitting in Debra Messing's backyard, surrounded by Hollywood's elite and talking on her perfectly rhinestoned flip phone.

Courtney is gorgeous. Way back when we first met, I was pretty sure that somebody like her would never want to be friends with a Victory girl like me. Courtney's father is Bennett Cambridge, the head of the Watson Bros. movie studio, and her mother is Alana Russo Cambridge, a former movie star turned executive housewife. Executive housewife is a term Courtney penned for her mother, since she doesn't actually do anything that a housewife does. She simply overseas the staff that does it in their Bel Air mansion, which is so big that it has its own bowling alley—which, Courtney often boasts, has two more lanes than the Spellings'.

Courtney is the spitting image of her glamorous mother, and the two are featured in every single Hollywood mother-daughter photo shoot alongside duos like Blythe and Gwyneth and Goldie and Kate. She is tall and slender, with curves in all the right places. Her curly blonde hair is always just on the complimentary side of bed head and her brown eyes are so dark that they look almost black. You never know from one day to the next if she'll be in a tailored Armani suit or a sari that she actually got in India while chasing down the "love of her life," of which there have been quite a few.

She is the most dramatic and impulsive person I know, the type of girl who can turn lemons into lemonade effortlessly and even make you forget you had lemons to begin with. Prime example: following Ajay Dhir all the way to India, determined to show him that they were meant to be together. When he finally was able to convince her that they were not (something, in Ajay's defense, he had been trying to do for three months in Los Angeles before traveling home for his grandmother's funeral), Courtney turned it around and made the trip one of the most fabulous shopping sprees I've ever heard of. If anyone can prevent me from becoming suicidal over this, it's Courtney. Plus even though she's not practicing, she did graduate from law school and pass the bar, so she should be able to figure out how to get me out of this mess from a legal standpoint.

"Court," I say, feeling both relieved to have connected with her and terrified that by speaking the words aloud my situation will somehow become more real than it already is. "Something awful has happened."

"What's wrong?" she asks, and I know that even surrounded by a designer lunch and countless celebrities, she is giving me her undivided attention.

"Remember I told you about Charla?" I confirm, because while Courtney is brilliant and wonderful, she is known to have her share of "blonde moments."

"Right, the dead girl," she says in the same tone a person might confirm a girl had brown hair or was in dental school.

"She left me her daughter," I spit it out. I don't know how to sugarcoat it and there is no point beating around the bush.

"Oh my God!" Courtney exclaims, and I feel comforted that her sentiment is the same one I've been having since

Buck Platner hung up the phone. "That's so exciting!" she continues, and I am momentarily shocked before quickly realizing that she is in fact having a *major* blonde moment.

"No, Court, I am this kid's legal guardian. I don't have the papers or anything yet, but I'm pretty sure I have to raise her."

"I'm so jealous!" Courtney continues, and I realize that she must be talking to someone at the party and not to me.

"Courtney!" I command—whatever starlet she is talking to is going to have to wait. "I need your undivided attention right now!"

She is the only person I can talk to. Besides Courtney, I don't have many other friends. I'm friendly with people at work—like the days that I actually have the time to take a lunch break, if I'm not racing around to the dry cleaner or eyebrow waxer, I don't have to eat alone; but there isn't anybody else who knows about Victory. I've even been vague on the details with Dan. Needless to say, it's a past I've worked all of my adult life to overcome and not something that I'm very happy to share with the world.

Daniel McCafferty is exactly the type of person I have always wanted to marry and I never wanted to take any chances with the relationship. He grew up in an affluent midwestern family and then followed his two older brothers to Princeton. After Princeton, he went to USC law school because he knew he wanted to practice in Los Angeles. Now he is an assistant district attorney and living in Beverly Hills. The apartment is in 90212, not 90210, but that's because he has chosen a life of service as an ADA. Honestly, he would be making so much more money if he were working in a private firm, but he likes to give back to people. I know he wants his wife to be a certain type of person—to fit a certain image—and I'm not sure that person comes from Victory. I've simply said that I grew up in a small town and I'm not that close with my family. It's all true, it's just not very detailed, and thankfully that doesn't seem to bother him, since we are officially engaged now. The plan was really going so well up until now. Our engagement arrived exactly when I wanted it to—give or take eight months—but if we plan the wedding in one year and then are married for a year and a half (instead of two years) before getting pregnant, we can catch up and be right on schedule. Dan and I may not have the passion or the sex life of fairy tales, but he is exactly what I have always wanted and I am positive (I really am) that I will be happier with him than with someone who can give me an orgasm—I can do that myself.

"Can I tell you, I was *just* thinking about getting inseminated," Courtney starts chatting. "I've been playing with little Roman and thinking to myself, 'Courtney, this is what life is all about. The children really are our future,' but then I started getting freaked out about stretch marks and labor. You are so lucky. This is ideal!"

I'm about to explain to Courtney how far from ideal my situation is when my pacing takes me by the window and I see Dan getting out of his car. "Oh my God," I exclaim, looking down at myself and realizing that I am still in pajamas. "Dan's here!"

"He's going to be so excited!" Courtney cheers.

"I'll call you back," I frantically explain, not even taking a second to clue Courtney in about how far off base she is.

I glance out the window and see Dan making his way around the front of the car, stopping briefly to rub a spot on the hood with his elbow, before running to my bedroom to put myself together.

In record time, I am able to get dressed, brush my hair and teeth, and make my bed, and I am just placing the final decorative throw pillow when Dan knocks at my door. I take a deep breath to try and calm my heaving chest before answering his knocks. When I open the door, Dan is leaning against the sill with a bouquet of pink tulips in one hand and the broad grin that melts my heart on his face.

"For my fiancée," he says, handing me the bouquet.

See? I am the luckiest girl in the world. Clearly, he is the most wonderful man ever to walk the face of this earth. I am so taken with him at this moment that I am able to put the Tiffany situation out of my head and wrap my arms around his slightly sweaty neck.

"How was golf?" I ask, heading into the kitchen to get a vase for the flowers. My Saturday night roses are always in the center of my dining room table in a vase from Baccarat, but luckily I have a plain vase I got at Crate & Barrel to give a girl at work as a wedding present before realizing that I wasn't invited to her wedding. I unwrap the vase, feeling grateful that I hadn't gotten around to returning it yet, and arrange the tulips.

"Golf was golf, Elizabeth." Dan launches into an anecdote about his game as I return to the living room and set the flowers in the middle of the coffee table, moving this month's *InStyle* and a stack of coasters out of my way to do it. "But enough about golf," Dan says, turning to me and smiling. "I want to ask you something . . . something important."

"Don't you think you've asked me enough important things this weekend?" I tease, flirtatiously.

"Elizabeth, let's move in together. What do you think?"

I smile, a smile reminiscent of the smile that spread across my face when he proposed, and say, "Definitely."

"Excellent!" Dan booms. "Because here's what I'm thinking. We're engaged, but there's no reason to rush to the altar. Right?"

"Right," I agree wholeheartedly, but I start to feel a little confused by the direction of our conversation.

"So we'll move in together and then when it feels right, we'll start thinking about setting a date. Marriage definitely isn't something we want to rush into."

"No, of course not," I say, but my mind is thinking that an

engagement generally means the time feels right to start planning a marriage.

"And kids are *so* far off. I mean, you're young, I'm young; we both have careers. Of course we'll have two kids down the line, but not for quite a while. Am I right?"

"You're definitely right," I say, the smile on my face starting to feel plastic and pinched.

"So, I think you should just move into my place since I'm in the 90210," Dan says with an enthusiastic grin.

"90212," I correct him. My heart is sinking all the way down to my stomach, causing the feeling of extreme nausea I suffered from most of the morning to return with a thud.

"You know what I mean. I'm going to jump into the shower and then I think we should celebrate this 'next step,' " Dan says looking at me with one eyebrow up, a look I know means he wants sex.

I couldn't be less in the mood for the three minutes of uncomfortable poking that Dan considers foreplay and the seven minutes of thrusting that Dan considers making love, but I smile seductively and say, "We should definitely celebrate."

I concentrate wholeheartedly on not vomiting until I hear the shower water, and then I pick up the phone and dial Courtney's cell phone again.

"Is Dan so excited?!?" she answers.

"Oh my God," I moan for the umpteenth time since Buck Platner's call this morning. "It's so much worse than I even realized."

"Shit," Buck says again, this time out loud. "What am I gonna do now?" he asks Wildcat, who is still asleep on the unmade king-size bed.

His first problem is the now homeless teenage girl asleep in his guest room. The second is explaining his repeat bungle to his father. Not to mention the fact that he, once again, screwed up with Lizzie Castle. While trying to think of ways to put a positive spin on this to both Tiffany and Larry S, he stands up and heads to the door of his bedroom. Much to Buck's surprise (horror), Tiffany is standing in the hallway.

She jumps slightly at seeing him, and Buck can tell that her brain is trying to calculate if he has seen her or if she can duck back into the guest room. It's obvious that she had been listening to his conversation.

"How'd you sleep?" Buck asks, deciding to pretend that the awkwardness that accompanied him into the hallway doesn't exist.

Tiffany does not follow his lead. "She doesn't want me, does she."

It's a question, but she says it like a statement. Unfortunately, it's a statement Buck knows for certain to be true.

"That's not true at all," Buck lies, hoping Tiffany can't see through him. "She's so concerned about you and your well-being. She just needed the weekend to collect herself."

"I thought she needed the evening to collect herself." Tiffany counters.

This is why people hate teenagers, Buck thinks to himself. This is also why he shouldn't lie. "The evening, the weekend . . . it's like twenty-four hours' difference. Let's have some breakfast." Buck quickly changes the subject and lumbers down the hallway toward the kitchen.

The house is small—too small for a wide receiver like Buck Platner, but technically big enough for one person—and since Buck couldn't justify a bigger house for just himself, he squeezes himself in like Alice in the rabbit hole. Once inside the messy kitchen, Buck opens the old refrigerator in hopes that fresh food has magically appeared overnight. No such luck. Starting to live like a grown-up is constantly on Buck's list of things to do . . . it just never gets done. Instead of containing breakfast staples like coffee and Nutri-Grain bars, Buck's shopping cart always ends up with marshmallow cereal, which he often has to eat dry since it seems his milk is perpetually past its sell-by date. To say that this home needs a woman's touch is the understatement of the year.

Buck peers into the fridge, easily looking through the sparse contents—beer, mustard, and leftover pizza—and finding himself face-to-face with the buzzing old light bulb. He looks sheepishly over his shoulder, hoping he is alone, but finds Tiffany standing behind him looking skeptical.

"Okay, here's what we're going to do," Buck quickly decides. "We're going to go out for breakfast, go to your house and get your stuff, and then you're going to spend the night here. Tomorrow morning, we're going to drive down to L.A. and Lizzie is going to be thrilled to see you." Buck says each step with such conviction that he even has himself believing in this plan.

"Where are we gonna go for breakfast?" Tiffany asks, and

Buck breathes a sigh of relief that she is on board with the plan or at least not putting up a fight.

He quickly thinks about her question. His father always goes to Sunday breakfast at Denny's in the next town over with his mother after church. "Mug's," Buck answers definitively.

Tiffany nods her head and walks out of the kitchen saying, "I'll get my shoes," as Buck breathes a sigh of relief that a plan is now in action.

~8~

Sitting in the cracked brown vinyl booth at Mug's, Tiffany can't help but think about how her stepfather, Chuck, loves (loved) the crummy coffee shop. Normally, whenever he suggested it, Tiffany put up a fight to go to Denny's instead. Denny's benefited from the power of the parent company and undoubtedly has better food. Mug's, so named because of the owners', sisters Mildred and Wilma Appleby, mismatched collection of mugs in which they serve everything from coffee to clam chowder, is substandard on a good day. Today, though, Tiffany didn't have the strength or the will to argue. She doubted she'd be able to eat anything anyway—which she was proving true as she shoved the runny scrambled eggs around her plate and took tiny sips of watery hot chocolate from a Shepherd and Moore Insurance Agency mug with a smiling yellow sunshine on it.

Buck had laid out a plan: breakfast, going home to collect her belongings, and then, in the morning, going to L.A. to deliver her to her aunt Lizzie. She could tell that Buck had tried hard to sound convincing when he told her about her aunt Lizzie's concern for her and about how happy she would be to see them when they arrived. She had quelled her normal teenage defiance and let him believe that she believed it.

"Eggs okay?" Buck asks with a look of true concern.

"They're a little runny," Tiffany admits, taking a bite of overly buttered wheat toast midway through her answer. "Toast's good, though."

"Yep, they make good toast here," Buck agrees, taking a bite of his underbuttered raisin toast and thinking that his eggs seem runny enough to be a salmonella risk.

They finish what they can manage to stomach of the putrid breakfast before Buck puts a single twenty-dollar bill on the table and doesn't wait for change.

"Ready?" he asks politely, signaling to Tiffany that it's time to get up and go.

As she stands up, her flannel pants stick to the sweat the vinyl booth created on the backs of her legs. She looks down as she peels them loose and realizes for the first time—or maybe just caring for the first time—how stupid she looks out in public in the same pajama pants she has had on since she went to bed two nights before. Tiffany stares at the green-and-navy plaid as she makes her way out of Mug's. She also notices that as she passes by the booths and tables and walks toward the door that people are whispering. Victory is a small town, and in small towns word travels fast.

"They all know about my mother," she thinks as she pushes the restaurant door open and hears Wilma Appleby mutter "Poor thing" from behind the old register.

Out of the corner of her eye, she sees Buck nod at the beehived restaurateur as he holds the door and follows Tiffany out. In silence, they climb into his truck and the engine starts with a roar. Chuck's truck is (was) an older (*much* older) version of the same Ford. Tiffany takes notice of all the improvements the manufacturer has made—most noticeably the difference in the starting sound. Buck gives his key a slight turn and the truck eagerly turns over. Chuck would have to hold his key for seconds while the old engine begged for mercy before accepting defeat and grumbling to attention. The blue oval with *Ford* in script in the middle of the steering wheel is identical, though. Tiffany finds herself wishing that Buck's truck was a piece of shit like her own family's simply so that she could find some comfort in something familiar. For as long as she could remember, Tiffany had complained about her boring life. Now, her life had suddenly become much more exciting, and she wished with all her might that it was back to the mundane existence she had formerly despised.

A few seconds go by before Tiffany realizes that they are still sitting in the parking space in Mug's cracked-asphalt parking lot. She looks over at Buck, who is watching her, looking afraid to speak—like she is counting something important and one word could cause her to completely lose her place. When they make eye contact he uncomfortably asks, "Where is your house?"

"Oh," says Tiffany, feeling stupid for not realizing that of course he doesn't know where she lives (lived). She gives him simple directions to her house, which is only a few miles away, and then settles back in the passenger seat, her wish for familiarity coming true as they travel the well-known route.

In a few minutes, Buck's truck is in her driveway, perfectly centered over the oil stain Chuck's truck had left behind. He puts the car in park and then turns the engine off, but he doesn't make a move to get out.

"Do you want me to come in with you?" he asks, clearly unsure of what he should do.

"No, that's okay," Tiffany says, trying to sound nonchalant . . . the way she would have this time last week. Of course, this time last week, Buck Platner wouldn't have been driving her home from breakfast, and *if* he had, her mother would have been running outside, bursting with excitement, to greet him and invite him in for a cold Coke.

Buck nods, giving the key a half turn in order to lower the power windows. He then leans his head against the back of the seat and instructs Tiffany to take her time.

She hops out of the truck and makes the same walk up the driveway that she has made thousands of times. When she gets to the front porch and stoops to retrieve the emergency key—which is actually the only one they ever use—from under the doormat, she realizes that her legs are shaking.

With uneasy hands, Tiffany puts the key in the lock, turns it, and then puts it back beneath the mat. She opens the door and steps inside, and can hear her mother hollering, "Tiffany Debbie Dearbourne, I pray to God you've wiped your feet!" That was how her mother always greeted her. Charla wasn't a religious woman; in fact, the only thing she ever prayed for was for Tiffany to wipe her feet. Nine times out of ten, Tiffany lied about having used the key-hiding mat to clean her feet.

Today, she steps back outside and wipes her fake-Ugg clogs on the mat. It's a mat she has always despised. It says, "Never mind the dog; beware of the owner!" Chuck thought it was the funniest thing he'd ever seen. Tiffany hates it passionately, especially since they don't even have a dog. Once her feet feel sufficiently clean, she steps back in the house and takes a deep breath.

The house reeks of its normal stale cigarette and beer smell. It's a scent that's both sickening and comforting to Tiffany, but today it's a bit different. Oddly, it seems that being left empty just overnight has added a musty stuffiness to the small house. As Tiffany walks through the living room, she finds the silence deafening. She looks into the galley kitchen on her way through and sees Charla's coffee cup from the morning she left still sitting on the counter.

It's a stained and chipped mug that says "World's Best Mom." Tiffany had bought it for $4.98 and given it to her mother for Mother's Day approximately five years ago. Tiffany and Charla both knew that Charla was not the world's best mom, but Charla loved the mug and used it every single day. Tiffany walks the five paces it takes to cross their kitchen, which is really just a strip of linoleum surrounded by counters and cupboards at the edge of the living room. She peers into the mug and sees an inch of coffee sitting in the bottom. Her mother always drank her coffee black with four teaspoons of sugar. Occasionally Tiffany would take a sip and always regretted it because the normally bitter liquid was sweet enough to rot your teeth on contact.

Tiffany pours the remaining coffee down the drain and carefully washes the mug, then sets it upside down on the drying rack under the window. Looking at the silly mug causes tears to well up in Tiffany's eyes, so she quickly exits the kitchen and hurries down the carpeted hall to her own bedroom. Once inside with the door closed behind her, she falls face forward on her unmade bed and cries.

After just a few minutes, she stands up, wipes her eyes, and retrieves a large overnight bag from beneath her lumpy twin bed. In it she packs all her favorite designer knockoff clothes. She knows that her aunt Lizzie is a successful career woman in Los Angeles and she wants to fit in as much as she can. Once her clothes are packed, Tiffany places a ratty stuffed frog, Mr. Ribbit, into the bag. She has slept with Mr. Ribbit since before she can remember, and while she would be mortified if anyone knew about it, she would also be devastated to leave home without him. Tiffany lugs the bag across the hall to the bathroom, careful to avoid looking toward her mother's bedroom.

Inside the grimy bathroom, Tiffany packs her toiletries in a clean, gallon-size Ziploc bag. Like any teenage girl, she owns gobs of products—Noxzema cleanser, Stridex pads, Maybelline cosmetics. She takes them all and stuffs them into her bag. She takes one last look around the bathroom, which smells of Chuck's Old Spice and her mother's Aqua Net, and then glances in the mirror. For a second, she doesn't recognize her own reflection.

Tiffany is a pretty girl and she knows it. She knows that

she is one of the prettiest girls at Victory High. Her hair is L'Oréal Preference "Extra Light Natural Blonde," and her eyes are turquoise blue, like her mother's. She is skilled at applying makeup and almost never leaves the house without a generous application of Maybelline Great Lash mascara in "Very Black." Her clothes are always fashionable and too tight in the right places. Today, none of this is evident.

Her hair is a greasy mess, piled on top of her head in a lumpy bun, and her mascara is hanging in dark circles under her eyes; there is also a red pimple blemishing her heart-shaped chin. For a second she is mortified and considers getting into the soap scum–encrusted shower but decides that when Buck said to take her time, he probably didn't mean that much. She makes a guttural sound of disgust before walking out of the bathroom. She starts down the hall toward the front door, then drops her bag and turns around.

Tiffany walks briskly to the end of the hallway and into her mother's bedroom without breaking stride until she stands in front of her mother's worn oak dresser. She opens the top drawer, which contains her mother's faded cotton underwear and torn underwire bras. In the back of the drawer is a small black velvet jewelry box. Tiffany knows that there isn't anything of any value in it, but these are the pieces that her mother cherished. Inside are the tiny diamond earrings that Chuck gave her as an anniversary gift, the gold cross that her grandparents gave her as a high school graduation gift, and a tarnished sterling silver heart on a matching chain that Tiffany had given her for her thirtieth birthday. Chuck had actually purchased the necklace, but the gift card hadn't given him any credit. Tiffany acknowledges that her stepfather was a good man as she tucks the little box under her arm and walks out of the room toward the front door.

The house is basically a long hallway leading to her parents' room, with her room, the bathroom and the living room/dining room/kitchen branching off. Tiffany walks straight to the front door, hardly stopping as she stoops to pick up her bag. Once outside on the front porch, which is cluttered with dying potted plants, Tiffany removes the key from beneath the stupid mat. She locks the door and bends halfway down to put it back before she changes her mind. She stops mid-bend and instead palms the key, squeezing her hand tightly so that she can feel the metal cuts digging into her palm as she walks back toward Buck's truck. She can hear Green Day playing quietly on the stereo, but Buck looks like he's fallen asleep with his head tilted back.

The sound of the door opening makes him jump slightly, and he opens his eyes and turns the stereo even lower in one movement.

"Everything okay?" he asks, looking like he feels guilty for having dozed off while Tiffany collected her things.

"Yep," she answers, but they both know it's not the truth.

~9~

That morning when my alarm goes off at six thirty, I am snapped out of a dream. A dream where I am dressed in a Vera Wang wedding gown I once tried on at Neiman Marcus in a fit of fantasy—a dress with a price tag close to that on my used BMW convertible—standing in line at the Wal-Mart in Victory to buy condoms. For once, I am grateful to hear the piercing beep from my Sony Dreamcube.

I quickly stop the *beep, beep, beep* before rolling over and looking at Dan, who is still halfway asleep. He looks so sweet and innocent in the blue poplin pajamas he keeps at my house. The night before had been a bit of a roller coaster. Dan's announcement about his desire to move in together but not get married and definitely not have children for a while had thrown me . . . especially in light of the fact that much to my dismay I had just inherited a *teenage* child. But after that, he had been so sweet. We'd "celebrated," and then Dan had ordered my favorite Chinese food to be delivered and we spent the night on the couch, cuddled up watching repeats of *The West Wing*. Around eleven thirty, he turned off the TV and kissed my forehead, which I thought was a signal that he was leaving, but instead he said, "Let's go to bed." I'd fallen asleep, wrapped in Dan's arms, and hadn't stirred until my alarm rescued me from my strange dream.

"Good morning, sleepyhead," I coo at my wonderful fiancé in bed beside me.

"Five more minutes?" he begs me without opening an eye.

"I'll take the first shower," I tell him and slide out of bed and into my robe, hoping that his eyes are still closed and that I am covered before he sees the bony structure that is my body. I sneak a peek back at him as I walk around the bed toward the shower and am relieved that his eyes are shut and his breathing is the heavy, borderline snore that means he is asleep.

Once safely locked inside the bathroom, I neatly hang my robe on the hook behind the door. I wash off the previous day's makeup—this is something that I normally do before going to bed, but when Dan spends the night, I always keep it on, lest he see me au naturel and go running for his life. After a shower, I carefully reapply the makeup as well as moisturize every square inch of my body and tend to my hair with a dryer and a round brush before removing the robe from the hook, putting it back on, and exiting the bathroom, which now feels about 95 degrees.

"Okay," I say to Dan, who is now sitting up in bed checking e-mail on his BlackBerry.

He nods, gets out of bed and heads into the steam-filled bathroom without taking his eyes off the little blue device.

After I hear the water being turned on, I again remove the robe and toss it into a white wicker hamper in the corner. I stop to examine my body in the full-length mirror on the wall. I am so skinny . . . not good skinny, like thin and petite . . . I am bony and undernourished skinny. And believe me, I'm not undernourished; it's just how I am. I have ribs that stick out, angular hips, and birdlike legs. I look okay in clothes because it can all be camouflaged, but naked it is not so flattering. I quickly dress for work in the secondhand Seven jeans I got on eBay and a shirt from Target. I once read that if you have one expensive piece of clothing on, people assume everything you wear is designer. Every day I count on this being true.

I am filling my travel mug with coffee by the time Dan emerges from the bathroom, which now resembles a sauna.

"What time do you have to be in court?" I ask, as I add raw sugar and organic milk to my drink.

"Not until the afternoon," he says, pouring himself a cup in a ceramic mug and drinking it black.

"I'm sorry, I have to run. We're shooting two shows today," I explain as I kiss him good-bye and collect my bag.

I struggle out the door, careful not to spill coffee on myself, and down to my car, hoping that there wasn't any middle-of-the-night rain, since the car's convertible top has a tendency to leak and I have forgotten to bring a towel down with me. The car gives me plenty of trouble, but I always dreamed of driving a BMW and I absolutely adore it. I set the metal container in the center console's cupholder and put my bag on the seat next to me. I take a deep breath before starting the engine and placing my hands on the black steering wheel. My engagement ring catches my eye and I can't help but smile . . . things are still going according to plan . . . for the most part.

~10~

The walls of my office are glass, and before I even enter the room I can already see the pile of work waiting for me. It's a two-show day, which means it will be nonstop. I've been working at *The Renee Foster Show!* for all of the show's eight seasons. I'll admit, it's not exactly what I thought it would be. After graduation, I got my first big (mid-size) break in journalism as a runner at the Los Angeles ABC affiliate, KABC. Renee was coanchor of the 7 p.m. and 11 p.m. newscasts and, obviously, she was my idol. Not only did she hold one of the most coveted positions at KABC, she is happily married to her college sweetheart and has two adorable little boys. Her life is perfect, and following in her footsteps would be ideal. After two years I'd worked my way from glorified go-fer to second assistant to the news director. I still wasn't exactly putting my education to good use, but I was getting closer. Then Renee made her big announcement: she was leaving the news desk behind to host her own daytime news magazine show. When she offered me the chance to come with her as a junior fact checker, I jumped on it.

At the time, I was under the impression that a daytime news magazine show would be what it sounded like . . . like *60 Minutes* or *20/20*, just during the day. The show turned out to be much more like *The View*, with more celebrity gossip than actual news, but eight years later I am the head fact checker and am generally able to convince myself that I am working in journalism and that someday this job could lead to my dream job as a news anchor . . . plus as head fact checker I get to do a brief on-air segment called "That's the Facts." For approximately sixty seconds, the camera pans over to me, seated behind a desk, and I give Renee a rundown on celebrity facts. I supply her with bullets of information on celebrity comings and goings, and then I say, "I'm Elizabeth Castle, and That's the Facts, Renee." Everybody's got to start somewhere.

I take a deep breath as I set my bag under my desk. I don't bother to sit down, though. I grab the pile of manila folders on my desk and head down to the stage, looking through them and passing out assignments to the group of junior fact checkers who work in cubicles surrounding my glass office. The junior fact checkers are a peppy bunch of recent graduates with degrees in a host of liberal arts subjects. I both love and hate them because none of them is jaded yet and none of them thinks that eight years later they will still be working on this show.

By the time I have made my way through the department, my arms are empty except for the red plastic clipboard that accompanies me wherever I go. I slip a headset over my mousey brown hair, which would be pathetic if not for a ridiculous amount spent on highlights every six weeks, and struggle to attach the transmitter to my waistband. The headset is a direct connection to my assistant, Hope. From the stage, I keep in constant communication with her, and she farms out all fact-checking requests on my behalf.

"Hope, are you there?" I ask as I clunk my way down the metal staircase that connects our offices with the show's stage. As I wait for a reply, I enter the cold soundstage and see that the audience for the first show is already seated. I cross through the show's set, a space that is part home living room and part home office. The home office part houses the desk I sit behind for my on-air segment (seconds).

"Good morning Elizabeth," Hope chimes through the headset.

"Good morning. Do we have any messages?"

Hope rattles off a list of calls, most of which need returning but none of which are pressing enough to send me back up to my office this close to show time or even inspire me to have Hope connect me through my headset. In fact, most of the messages don't even get my attention, except for one.

"A Buck Platner called asking for our address here. Do you know who that is, Elizabeth? Can I give him the address?"

A sick feeling shoots into my stomach as I answer, "That's fine, Hope. Call him back whenever you get a chance and give him the address. No rush," I add hoping that she won't get around to it for days or even weeks, but knowing that Hope is far too responsible to wait any length of time. Part of me had hoped that perhaps my out-of-sight, out-of-mind approach might rub off on everyone else involved, causing them to forget about the whole guardianship issue; then it would all just disappear as if it had never existed.

"Wishful thinking," I mutter to myself as I approach the hair and makeup area where I see the back of Renee Foster's head in big rollers. "Good morning, Renee," I say and make eye contact with her unmade-up face in the light-framed vanity mirror.

"Oh, Elizabeth, thank God you're here," she says, as she says every morning. "It says here that Halle Berry's dog is a Lhasa Apso," Renee says holding up the thick stack of papers that are her show notes, "but I saw it in the hallway and it looks more like a Shih Tzu to me."

"Lemme find out for you, Renee," I say calmly as the show's makeup person starts applying a thick coat of foundation to her face. In need of the day's second cup of coffee, I walk over to the craft services table. "Hope?" I say into my headset.

A few seconds pass before she says, "Sorry, Elizabeth. Buck Platner called again and I was just giving him our address."

"Crap," I think to myself, but I say, "Can you confirm what breed Halle's dog is?" "Crap," but this time I say it out loud and Guadalupe, our caterer, thinks I am referring to the coffee. After reassuring her that my crude behavior has nothing to do with her, I take a big sip of the coffee; it is crappy and it burns my tongue.

I'm thinking about the papers that will soon be on their way to me when Hope's voice booms in my right ear, "Halle's dog is a maltese." I'm picturing Buck Platner, exactly as he looked in high school, wearing a letterman jacket, laughing as he puts the papers in a manila envelope and telling the postman to rush them to me. "Elizabeth!" Hope calls, and it jerks me back to reality. "Did you hear me? The dog's a maltese."

"A maltese? Are you sure?"

"Positive. I just got off with her manager's assistant who conferenced me in with Halle's dog trainer. The dog is a purebred maltese."

"Who was on that?" I ask, needing to know which member of my staff ineptly supplied Renee with the wrong dog breed.

"Christy," Hope answers

"I knew it," I seethe, and with that, my mind is one hundred percent on my work and I take off to give Renee the correct information.

I sit down in the empty salon chair next to Renee and go over all the information for the entire show, including everything I will be sharing with her during "That's the Facts, Renee." When I share them with her on-air, she will act interested and surprised, but in fact not a single item will actually be news to her. We have spent the past week deciding together exactly which facts will be announced in today's rundown.

"Okay, Elizabeth, sounds good," Renee says as she rises from her chair with flawless hair and makeup and removes the black drape that had covered her from the neck down, revealing a black velour Juicy warm-up suit. "I'll see you out there," she calls over her shoulder as she heads to her dressing room.

I watch her for a second and then look back down at my clipboard as a loud voice booms overhead, "FIVE MINUTES TILL SHOW TIME."

"Okay, Elizabeth, let's touch you up," Marcela, the makeup artist, says to me.

I nod appreciatively, and she dabs powder on my T-zone. I receive only a fraction of the makeup that Renee does, but Marcela is so talented that it does wonders for my appearance. When she is finished, the voice booms, "ONE MINUTE TILL SHOW TIME."

As I head back to craft services for another cup of coffee, I hear the audience-warmer introducing Renee and the audience going wild with excitement. With another crappy although now not as hot cup of coffee in hand, I head to the wardrobe room, where I have my choice of the items from Renee's last-season wardrobe that she didn't like enough to take home with her. I select a black-and-white tweed Moschino jacket with silver buttons and put it on over my T-shirt. Since I sit behind a desk, there is no need to change anything from the waist down.

From the wardrobe room, I can hear Renee's opening monologue and the enthusiastic laughter of the audience. I know that I have about five minutes while she banters with the show's DJ, Karl, until I need to be in my seat behind the desk. I grab another cup of coffee from the craft services table and test it against my lip to be certain it has cooled down considerably before chugging the entire cup, while awkwardly bending forward in order to avoid dripping on the jacket. Caffeine is my lifeblood, especially on two-show days. As I swish cold water from the Arrowhead cooler in my mouth to remove any coffee from my teeth I hear Renee.

"And now let's check in with the Fact Mistress, Elizabeth Castle."

"Shit," I say wondering how the ridiculous banter session was over so quickly, spilling water out of my mouth while ripping my headset off. Hoping my hair doesn't look too horrible, I dart to my desk while the audience is maniacally laughing at Renee's stupid "fact mistress" joke. Before the gigglefest has ended I am seated in the black Aeron chair that lives behind my stage desk, which is covered with charming prop-desk trinkets and looks nothing like a desk that anybody would actually use. Camera three rotates around, and before I have totally caught my breath it is staring me in the face with a brightly burning red light.

"Well, Elizabeth, what's new and exciting?" Renee asks before taking a sip from *The Renee Foster Show!* coffee mug that I know contains room-temperature water (people have been fired over water that is too cold or too hot).

"So much is going on in Hollywood, Renee. Everyone is all abuzz over Jack Flight and Auburn Smith's recent engagement. Not to mention the drama on the set of *Desperate Housewives!*" I enthusiastically reel off a handful of information about Hollywood's hottest stars before ending with, "and that's the facts, Renee. Back to you."

"Wow!" Renee responds, and I am quite certain that she did not listen to a single syllable I have spoken. "Thank you, Elizabeth."

I smile once more and watch as camera three moves away from my desk before I stand up and head back to the wardrobe room to hang up the blazer and retrieve my headset. I replace it over my head and reattach the transmitter to my belt.

"Hope," I say into the headset, since I can tell by the audience warm-up guy's voice on the stage's PA system that the show is on a commercial break. "I'm off-air now and if you need me, I'll be in the producer's booth for the rest of the show."

A split second goes by before Hope replies, "Actually, Elizabeth, I need you up here now. Buck Platner is waiting for you in your office."

While he waits for Tiffany to collect her belongings, Buck sits in his truck and fiddles with the stereo preset buttons until he finds a station without idiotic DJ banter or an annoyingly long commercial break. He had offered to accompany the teenager inside and would have graciously done so, but he was more than a little relieved that she preferred to go alone. Buck had laid out a plan for Tiffany that culminated in their arrival in Los Angeles. She had gone along with the plan, and now he had some major thinking to do.

First, he has to figure out his professional and legal responsibility. His father's instructions had been to summon Elizabeth Castle to Victory to sign papers and take custody of Tiffany. Buck's conversations with her had clearly not gone according to plan, and Lizzie's homecoming wasn't happening. Instead, Buck's new plan was to show up at Lizzie's door with Tiffany in tow. He knew he was going to be blindsiding her and he hated to do it, but he really had no choice. The second thing to figure out was how he was going to handle himself when he saw Lizzie for the first time in so many years. His demeanor during their phone calls was never what he hoped it would be, and Buck was acutely aware of the risk that he would once again come off like an oaf when he was face to face with Lizzie.

"Elizabeth . . . not Lizzie," he reminded himself under his breath and then closed his eyes and laid his head back against the truck's black leather headrest, listening to Billie Joe Armstrong's voice.

A split second later, the passenger door to the truck opened, startling Buck. He jumped to attention, turning down the radio volume and wondering if it was disrespectful of him to listen to music while Tiffany retrieved her things from her dead parents' house. Too late to do anything about it, Buck confirmed that Tiffany was okay and she was polite enough to lie to him. He turned over the truck's powerful engine and backed out of the driveway, being careful not to crush any of the Tathams' dying plants under his tires.

It was Sunday afternoon now and Buck suddenly saw a flaw in his plan. He and Tiffany weren't scheduled to go to Los Angeles until the next day, and aside from avoiding his father, Buck didn't have a clue what to do the rest of the day.

"Are you hungry?" Buck asked Tiffany, who was gazing mindlessly out the window.

"No, not really," she answered without turning away from the window.

"Me neither," Buck confessed, still feeling the parts of the Mug's breakfast he was able to get down sitting in his stomach in a pool of grease. "What about a movie?" he offered, seeing the benefits of sitting in darkness and not having to talk.

"Nothing good is playing," Tiffany informed him.

Feeling at a loss, Buck tried again, "Is there anything you want or need to get done?"

"Nope, not really," she answered and then sat silently once more.

Buck nodded slowly, racking his brain for ideas and coming up dry. They drove a few minutes in silence before Buck realized that the truck was heading back to his house. Not having any reason to fight it, they completed the route without exchanging a single word and too soon were sitting in Buck's driveway under the huge oak tree whose roots caused his sinks to back up twice a year.

Buck sighed to himself as he unbuckled his seat belt and climbed out. Tiffany followed him, without a word, onto the front porch and into the house. It was going to be a long, quiet night.

Of course, as has always been the case for Buck, when he is unprepared for something, time flies at an alarming rate. If he has nothing to do on a weekend, the time drags on while he sits alone and watches ESPN. If he has something, like a court appearance to prepare for, Monday morning arrives before he has even had a chance to crack a file. So, the long, quiet night he was counting on to figure out exactly how to handle things in Los Angeles flies by. Buck and Tiffany watch TV and eat dinner, exchanging very few words, and yet it was not the horribly uncomfortable evening he had anticipated. It is a relief to Buck that she seems to enjoy the same television programs he does, laughs at the same stupid jokes and is willing to eat the same pineapple and pepperoni pizza that he loves and most others despise.

Buck's first impression of Tiffany had been that of a typical sullen and difficult teenager. Obviously, she deserved some space in light of the fact that her mother and stepfather had just been killed, but nonetheless, he didn't think much of her. After last night, however, Buck is starting to realize that deep down, underneath the silly teenage clothes and the sulking demeanor, is a special kid. Now he just hopes that Lizzie will be able (willing) to see it, too.

Buck awakes with a start on Monday morning, hearing footsteps in the hallway outside his room. It takes a second for him to remember his houseguest and more than a second for his heartbeat to slow down to its normal pace. A quick glance at the clock shows it to be after seven, and Buck sits up with a feeling of dread in his gut. Today is the day . . . the day that he will be face-to-face with Elizabeth Castle, and as much as he is anticipating their reunion he is also dreading it.

He steps out into the hall and startles Tiffany as badly as she had startled him a few minutes earlier. They exchange awkward good mornings and then go their separate ways— she to the bathroom and he to the kitchen to make a much-needed pot of coffee. Their paths cross a handful of times until they both end up at the front door ready for the drive to Los Angeles.

On her shoulder, Tiffany holds the duffle bag she had carried out of her house yesterday. Buck carries his briefcase as he would on any Monday morning, but unlike other Monday mornings, he is dressed casually in jeans and an untucked button-front shirt with the sleeves rolled up. Although his clothes look like something he might just throw on, a great deal of thought had actually gone into it and although he felt stupid changing his shirt three times, he feels confident about the blue stripes he has settled on because a girl in a bar had once told him that the stripes really brought out his blue eyes, and then she went home with him.

"Ready?" Buck asks Tiffany, holding open the front door for her to walk through.

"Ready as I'll ever be," the girl confesses, and Buck feels a sharp pang of sympathy for her, vowing to think a little less about himself than he has been. "Nice shirt," she adds, and he takes one more second to think only about himself and feel pleased with his final choice.

They pile into the truck and, after a quick stop for gas, are on the highway (really, they are on the highway all along, since it runs right through the middle of Victory—the signs simply change to "Main Street" and the speed limit is 30 miles per hour instead of 65, but it's not like you take an exit or anything to get there). Buck had at least counted on traffic and more silence from Tiffany so that he could have ample time to gather his thoughts, but instead there are hardly any cars on the road and the teenager has suddenly become chatty.

While they "shoot the breeze," as his grandfather would have said, Buck learns that Tiffany is a cheerleader; didn't care much for her stepfather, Chuck, although she does feel "real bad" he is dead; and always dreamed of getting out of Victory. She talks a little about her mother, and Buck feels a bit ashamed that he doesn't have much to contribute, since his interaction with Charla since their high school graduation had been limited to vague nods and waves around town.

Buck decides to take advantage of Tiffany's new openness and see if he can gather some information about Lizzie that will help him when they arrive in Los Angeles.

"Actually," Tiffany tells him, "I don't even ever remember meeting my aunt Lizzie! I don't think she and mom had talked in ages."

The knot in Buck's stomach grows larger. Lizzie is the guardian for a kid she's never even met?!? Things are going from bad to worse, and they are barreling toward Los Angeles at 80 miles per hour.

When they are just outside of town, Buck and Tiffany stop at a McDonald's to grab some lunch. While Tiffany is inside getting Big Macs and chocolate shakes with the twenty-dollar bill Buck gave her, he places his second phone call of the day to the work number that Lizzie had given him on Saturday. The first time, he'd been able to sneak the call while Tiffany used a gas station bathroom, but he'd only gotten a secretary, who was unwilling to give him their address without Lizzie's consent. Thankfully, this time the secretary was able to give him the location. After hanging up, Buck flips through the pages of his old Thomas Brothers Guide map and is both pleased and horrified to see that they are very close.

Buck glances up and sees Tiffany walking across the parking lot with a big bag boasting golden arches, so he quickly stashes the map under his seat and greets Tiffany with a smile as she hands the food bag across the front seat to him before hoisting herself up into the cab.

"We're almost there," he cautiously informs her, paying close attention to her reaction.

"Awesome," she replies, managing to sound completely confident and utterly terrified at the same time.

Buck envies her being able to sound at all confident as he shovels in french fries at breakneck speed. Before he has even finished his lunch, the heartburn kicks in, and Buck pops a couple of antacids as he maneuvers the big truck around the few miles of overpopulated Los Angeles land between him and Lizzie. All too quickly, they are parking in a spot labeled "The Renee Foster Show! Guest Parking," and he and Tiffany are climbing out of the truck and walking toward a large, almost industrial-looking building.

Silently, they make their way through the chaotic offices until at last they reach a glass room surrounded by chest-high walls that make up a number of cubicles. There is a plastic sign stuck on the side of the door jamb that reads "Elizabeth Castle—Head Fact Checker," and Buck can't help but feel a swell of pride that Lizzie is doing so well. Before he has a chance to figure out what to do next, a pretty red-haired girl calls to him from her cubicle.

"Can I help you?"

"Oh, uh, yeah. We're here to see Lizzie—Elizabeth Castle."

"Do you have an appointment?" the girl, who only looks slightly older than Tiffany, asks while expertly opening a scheduling program on her iMac.

"No, not exactly," Buck admits. "I'm Buck Platner—"

"Oh, right. Hi, Mr. Platner. I'm Hope, Elizabeth's assistant. We spoke on the phone earlier."

"Oh, Hope . . . hi," Buck says uncomfortably. There is a

momentary pause while nobody says anything, so Buck asks, "Is she here?"

"Elizabeth's actually on-air right now. It's a two-show day, so things are totally hectic."

"On-air?" Tiffany pipes up, finally showing some interest in the conversation.

Hope looks at the teenager and then again at Buck, wondering who they are. They must be father and daughter . . . or brother and sister? Buck looks to be about Elizabeth's age, so he's probably too young for this girl to be his daughter. Hope secretly hopes that he's not someone Elizabeth is involved with, because he is extremely good looking and she is feeling extremely single these days.

"For her segment, 'That's the Facts,' on *The Renee Foster Show!*" Hope explains to Tiffany, but her eyes seem stalled on Buck's pecs. "Why don't you have a seat in Elizabeth's office and turn the monitor to channel 28. That's the direct feed from the studio, so you can watch what's going on."

Tiffany eagerly heads into Elizabeth's glass office and Buck follows after nodding a "thank you" to Hope, which she returns with a flirtatious smile.

~12~

"Buck Platner is in my office? BUCK PLATNER IS IN MY OFFICE?!?" I ask myself over and over hoping that I misunderstood Hope completely; each time the question becomes more frantic. My lungs sting and my head feels like it's in a beehive as I thunder up the metal stairs. Once on the office floor, I try (fail) to catch my breath as I make my way to my office. I can see the outline of Buck's blond, buzzcut head through the glass wall and all attempts at composure are lost. From here he looks exactly like he did standing on my parents' front porch waiting to pin a corsage on me, and I feel the same nausea.

I slip into the office and close my glass door quickly behind me. Neither Buck nor the person he has brought with him realizes I have entered the room. They are staring at the television monitor, which is tuned to the direct stage-feed channel.

"What are you doing here?!?" I gasp as my chest rises and falls. No hellos, no niceties . . . I have to get Buck and whoever this other person is out of here immediately.

"Lizzie—Elizabeth," Buck says, scrambling to his feet as quickly as he can, clearly caught off guard by my entrance. The girl, who looks around sixteen, stares up at me. She looks vaguely familiar and I wonder if she is a fellow Victory loser who is Buck's assistant or maybe even an intern, since she looks so young. Probably his girlfriend, I think, feeling disgusted.

"Hi," she says quietly, but it's clear that under normal circumstances she is a confident girl.

I ignore her greeting and again look at Buck. "Well?" I ask tapping my foot with impatience.

"Lizzie, you look great," Buck says crossing my small office in two steps. "We saw you on the TV," he says, motioning at the small Panasonic. I see that Renee is back on her cream sofa with Halle Berry's dog sitting on her lap while the Oscar winner smiles from a floral chair strategically positioned to look the way the furniture in your living room might be arranged while ensuring that every celebrity's "good side" is clearly visible to the three large cameras that roll back and forth across the stage floor.

"Shit," I say, "I've gotta get back down there," knowing that if that show cuts to commercial and I'm not there to answer any stupid question Renee has about anything in the world that it will get ugly. "What are you doing here?"

Buck looks slightly puzzled for a beat before turning back toward the teenage girl and saying quietly yet firmly, "This is Tiffany."

"Tiffany?" I peek around Buck's lineman frame for a second glance at the girl. Now I know why she looks familiar. She looks like Charla—or more specifically, like a prettier version of the Charla that I vaguely remember from high school.

"Hi," she says again, adding a little wave and losing what little confidence she had in her first greeting.

I straighten my body and look up, directly into Buck's blue eyes. "I cannot do this now," I tell him through a clenched jaw, then I hold my breath and wait for him to bulldoze me.

Instead, he says—no asks, "We could come to your house tonight?" sounding as nervous as a high school nerd inviting a cheerleader on a date.

"Perfect," I say, relieved that this means they will be leaving my office now. "Hope will give you my address. Be there at eight," I tell Buck as I turn toward the office door. Before he can respond, I'm heading down the hall feeling relieved.

I enter the stage just as the voice from the booth booms, "THIRTY SECONDS!"

I hustle over to Renee and ask, "Everything okay with you?" to which she answers, "Why wouldn't it be?" while looking at me as if I just landed in a spaceship. Gee . . . maybe because it never has been in the history of this mindless show? "Just checking," I say smiling like an idiot and walking away, simultaneously relieved that she wasn't having a meltdown while I was upstairs, offended that I wasn't desperately needed, and generally sickened about Buck's visit to my office and his impending visit to my home.

~13~

My mind is a complete blur for the remainder of the show. My body stands in the producer's booth like a lifeless wax statue while my mind runs a marathon. Buck Platner and Tiffany Dearbourne are going to be at my house tonight at eight . . . TONIGHT AT EIGHT. He's probably going to make me sign these papers he keeps mentioning and those papers probably make me the legal guardian of Tiffany. And then what will happen? He'll leave . . . walk out the door and leave me there with a fifteen-year-old kid? Again, my head feels like a beehive—but now the bees are swarming and my entire body buzzes with panic.

As soon as the director yells "CUT!" I'm summoning Hope through my headset.

"Hope? Are you there?" I ask, silently praying that she isn't away from her desk. A split second later, I breathe a sigh of relief.

"I'm here, Elizabeth."

"Thank God," I say to myself, and, "I need you to get Courtney Cambridge for me," to Hope. I know it sucks to make her connect me on a personal call, but this is an emergency. "Try her home, office, and cell," I instruct.

Before my call can be connected, though, I hear Renee calling, "E-liii-zabeth," drawing out the second syllable of my name just long enough that it starts to sound like nails on a chalkboard.

"Shit. Hope, find Courtney and tell her she has to be at my house at seven thirty tonight," I quickly tell her. "Wait, no. Tell her to be there at seven. She *has* to be there."

"Sure thing," Hope replies as cheerfully as ever.

I take a deep breath. Hope will take care of it. She has to. Courtney has to be there because she is pretty much my only hope to get out of this mess. She was an attorney. She will find a legal loophole or an expired statute of limitations or something that will nullify Charla's entire will. I take a deep breath and try to relax. If Hope tells Courtney seven o'clock, she'll be there at seven thirty . . . that will give us thirty minutes to figure out a strategy before Buck shows up.

"Please God, let us figure out a strategy," I pray to myself as I hear Renee's shrill, "E-liii-zabeth!" once again. "Coming," I reply, gathering all my strength and adding a wish for patience to the holy request.

The rest of my day is hectic enough that I am able to put my problems about halfway out of my head. I deal with Renee's complaint that mentioning Prince Harry's date with a pop star is "too political," and her confusion over how to say Ralph Fiennes's name, while watching the clock spin out of control toward eight o'clock and the doom that awaits me.

At about six twenty-five I finally return from the stage to my office, where Hope confirms that she got in touch with Courtney, who has promised to be at my apartment at "seven, sharp." I breathe a sigh of relief as I finally sit down at my desk and turn on the futuristic iMac that sits on top of it. The stack of folders I removed this morning has somehow regenerated, and my e-mail inbox mockingly flashes "48 new messages." I breathe a sigh of resignation and glance at the clock on the desktop: 6:37 p.m. I dart my mouse toward the once-bitten blue apple in the upper left-hand corner of the screen and scroll down to "Shut down," like a kid sneaking money from his mother's purse. I hold my breath until the screen flashes to black, and then bend over to retrieve my bag from the spot where I haphazardly tossed it this morning. When I sit back up, Renee Foster is standing at my door with Hope standing behind her mouthing, "I'm sorry."

"You're not leaving, are you?" Renee asks in her I-work-twenty-four-seven-and-*that's*-why-I'm-a-success voice.

"Actually, I have something I need to take care of tonight," I offer, trying hard to keep my voice strong. I cannot let her bully me into staying right now. I have to get home to meet Courtney. I sneak a glance at my wrist: 6:39 p.m.

"Well, I really need to go over a few points for tomorrow's show," she says expectantly.

I straighten my spine, hoping a taller posture will give the illusion of confidence. "We'll have to do it in the morning. I cannot be late for this appointment," I say hoping that if it sounds official enough, Renee will not question me.

"Fine . . . be in my office at nine o'clock on the dot," she says, and I silently rejoice. "What's this super-important meeting?" Renee questions, and the rejoicing comes to a screeching halt.

Not sure what to say, I pathetically explain, trying to sound like I really wish I could tell her, "It's a personal matter."

"Anything to do with that darling little diamond you're sporting?" she asks in a tone that would seem like girl talk if it were not so demeaning.

My face flushes with anger and embarrassment at the way she has referred to my beautiful engagement ring, but I swallow it all and simply answer, "Unfortunately not," even though the truth is that in a way tonight has *everything* to do with my engagement. If I do not get home and come up with a way to keep Tiffany Dearbourne away, my engagement, marriage, and entire life could be over.

"See you in the morning," Renee says coolly as she turns and walks out of my office.

Relief floods me until I glance at my watch, which shows the time to be 6:42. Panic takes back over and the knot in my stomach tightens as I hike my bag a little higher on my shoulder and hustle out of the building. I keep my head down and my pace brisk until I reach my car. Once inside, I start the ignition and speed out of the parking lot as quickly as I can. Of course the speed doesn't last long because two short turns later and I'm sitting in the rush-hour parking lot that Olympic Boulevard turns into nightly.

"Come on," I plead with the wall of cars I am facing. "Go!"

Normally the traffic of my relatively short commute doesn't bother me. Normally I am so exhausted from my workday that I almost enjoy sitting and staring mindlessly at thousands of shining red lights. Tonight, I don't have time—or really the ability—to relax. With each red light, my blood pressure increases, and by the time I pull into my carport parking spot behind my apartment, I feel like I'm about to have a stroke. It's 7:12.

I know that I am not going to find Courtney waiting loyally at my front door, but I still can't help but feel disappointed when I arrive and there is only a stack of supermarket circulars jammed halfway through the mail slot. I grab the junk mail and open the door, using the papers to flick on the light switch. The dome light above the entryway/dining room illuminates and I do a once-over of my apartment. My perfect apartment . . .

I still remember the day I signed the lease like it was yesterday. It was the single most exciting day of my life (before getting engaged, of course), and even though that was two years ago, I still get a surge of joy every time I walk through the door. When I got promoted to head fact checker, I was finally earning enough money to get my own place. I had suffered through countless horrible roommates—my freshman year of college was only the beginning. The bad luck continued for years to come. There was the kleptomaniac who stole my Prada loafers, the refrigerator labeler who threw an apple at me for accidentally eating a container of her yogurt, and the nymphomaniac I caught having sex on my bed. Each one was more traumatic than the next, and finally being able to live on my own was tremendous.

Besides the joy of solitude, the apartment is also a gem. The location, off Third and Fairfax, couldn't be better, and the charming details like wainscoting and leaded glass won me over immediately. Plus, the girl who owns it was moving out to live with her fiancé, so I felt it had a good vibe or aura or karma or *something* like that (not that I really believe in any of it). At first the apartment was almost completely empty. Since I had always lived with a roommate, I didn't own very much furniture, but I felt it was better to have nothing than to have something cheap and temporary. Over time, my savings grew, and eventually each room was filled with coordinated components I had selected from pages in the Pottery Barn and Crate & Barrel catalogs.

A wave of sadness washes over me as I think about leaving this apartment to live with Dan in his considerably smaller place off Doheny Drive. I quickly suppress the sadness, though, with a vision I often have of the home that Dan and I will buy after we are married. I take a deep breath . . . I cannot let that three-bedroom/two-bathroom dream slip away. Where is Courtney?

I grab my phone off the breakfast bar and hit speed dial #4 to connect me to her cell phone. She answers after three rings and I hear the stereo in her Range Rover blaring Gwen Stefani before I hear Courtney's voice.

"I'm five minutes away," she says, not sounding at all sorry or even aware that she is already fifteen minutes late.

"Okay . . . hurry," I implore her, relieved that I created the thirty-minute time buffer.

"What's all this about anyway?" she asks.

"I'll explain when you get here," I tell her. I think doing this face-to-face is probably better, especially since Courtney's driving is distracted on a good day and I really don't have the time or energy for her to have another fender bender tonight.

We hang up and I do what I always do when I'm anxious— I tidy. I walk around the apartment, changing the water for my flowers from Dan, fluffing pillows, and straightening pictures. The truth is that the water was fresh, the pillows were fluffy, and the pictures looked like a level was used to arrange them, but it's almost a compulsion for me.

Twenty—not five—minutes later I hear a roaring engine on the street and look out the window to see Courtney flattening a trash can in an attempt to parallel park. Finally she gets upstairs and I start explaining the reason for her emergency visit. Mostly, I am reiterating the information I have already shared—about Charla dying and leaving me her teenage daughter—and trying to impart to Courtney that this is not a good way to have a child without getting stretch marks. I haven't even gotten to the part about Dan and the fact that he doesn't want to have any children for years and years when I hear another car roaring down my normally quiet street. I look out the window and see Buck and Tiffany getting out of a black truck.

"Oh my God, they're here," I almost shriek in panic.

Courtney crosses from the kitchen, where she was searching through my almost empty refrigerator to the window where I am sitting.

"Oh my God," she echoes me and I feel a second of relief that she finally understands the severity of the situation. "That is the Victory attorney guy?" she asks.

"Yes," I confirm with disgust.

"He is HOT," she almost growls.

I turn and look at Courtney, who is staring at Buck Platner crossing the street like a lioness hunting her prey.

"I'd take the stretch marks to have his babies," she says without taking her eyes off him.

Despair washes over me. I'm done for; I'm a goner. Courtney was my only hope—my last resort; but now that her hormones have entered the scenario, they will take over. I am totally screwed.

~14~

Needless to say, the visit to Elizabeth's office was almost a complete disaster. The only saving grace was that Buck managed to arrange to see her again at her home after work. As he and Tiffany sit in traffic on the 405 freeway, he replays the meeting again and again. They were sitting there watching the talk show Elizabeth works on and then suddenly she was in the room, obviously unhappy to see them. Nonetheless, Buck's heart soared. She was everything he remembered and had aged as beautifully as he would have expected. Her light brown hair is blonder now, probably from living so close to the beach, but her green eyes are exactly the same. When she looked up at Buck, her glare so narrow she was almost squinting, his heart felt like it would leap free of his chest.

She had practically thrown Buck and Tiffany out of her office . . . well, she *had* thrown them out, but somehow Buck had coordinated his brain and his tongue—with great effort—to arrange to meet again that night. Now he had the rest of the day to really pull it together. No more winging it. This time he was going to have a speech prepared—word-for-word—leaving nothing to chance and no space for anything to go wrong again. Not only would he take care of the custody situation he had come to town to resolve, he would win her over and show her what a catch he is.

"What are we going to do all day?" Tiffany asks, snapping Buck back to attention. In his mind, he was standing in Lizzie's home, delivering a cinematic legal speech and she was gazing at him in awe.

"Oh, um . . ." he had been so focused on the evening's plans that he failed to think about the hours to fill in between. "I don't know. Anything you want to do?"

"Go to the beach and get coffee from Starbucks," Tiffany answers quickly while staring at a woman in a Hummer talking on a cell phone one lane away. She had clearly been thinking about this.

Starbucks coffee is kind of a big deal in Victory. Needless to say, the coffee empire does not have a chain in the small town. Most of the town's residents would be beyond outraged at the thought of having to pay upward of three dollars for their plain black joe and would be confused and repulsed by mochas, gingerbread lattes, and double espresso shots. For the younger, striving-to-be-hip residents, though (definitely the minority), Starbucks coffee is a sought-after commodity. Unfortunately, it's quite a trek away and few people have gotten to experience it. Buck can't help but smile that it's right up there with seeing the Pacific Ocean for Tiffany.

"Sounds like we've got ourselves a plan," Buck says, smiling at the back of Tiffany's head.

"Does she look famous to you?" Tiffany replies, still staring at the woman in the Hummer.

Buck glances to his right . . . the woman is tiny, or at least looks tiny behind the wheel of the enormous car. Her stripy blonde hair is pulled into a messy looped ponytail, and the sunglasses on her face are almost as big as the car. As he looks, she shuts a rhinestoned flip phone and lifts a Starbucks cup to her lips.

"Oh my God—she's drinking Starbucks," Tiffany gasps. "She must be famous."

Tiffany stalks the woman for miles of bumper-to-bumper stop-and-go, until she finally exits the freeway.

"Is that the exit for Beverly Hills?" Tiffany asks as she watches the tank-size car barrel down the off-ramp.

"I'm not sure," Buck admits as he tries and fails to squeeze his big truck over toward the 10 West, since the sign indicates it is the exit for Pacific Coast Highway.

Eventually, Buck is able to fight his way off the 405 and onto the 10, which is moving slightly better. He carefully watches the signs and follows them to the end of the freeway, which turns into Pacific Coast Highway. There on their left is the Pacific Ocean. Even though he was born and raised in California, he has seen this ocean only a handful of times. Buck peers over the tops of the squished-together, run-down beach houses and through the tiny spaces in between the brand-new-looking beach mansions at the golden sand and blue-green water.

The sand is scattered with people, and bouncing up and down in the water are surfers with wet blond hair and black rubber body suits. Buck stares for a second, feeling an uneasiness in his stomach that this is probably the kind of guy Elizabeth dates now that she lives in Los Angeles. He wonders about taking up surfing, but even only seeing them from the waist up as they sit straddled across their surfboards, Buck knows he isn't built like these guys. He's built to hold back an aggressive offense on a football field.

"Have you ever seen the Pacific before?" Buck asks Tiffany without taking his eyes off the water.

"Nope," she admits.

He breaks his stare for long enough to glance across the car at Tiffany, expecting to see a look of awe on her face. Instead, she is looking out the right side of the car toward a little outdoor shopping center.

"A Starbucks!" she exclaims pointing up about one hundred yards.

Buck can't help but smile even though he feels a little disappointed that she isn't as excited about the ocean as she is about the coffee shop. Nonetheless, he turns his attention back to the road and they quickly arrive at the Starbucks. Outside, there are four little black metal tables with two matching chairs at each table; only two of the tables are occupied: one by an unshaven man in a tattered Lacoste shirt typing on an Apple laptop, the other by two teenage-looking girls both dressed in velour warm-up suits and suede boots with fur inside. One girl has a bubblegum-pink bag at her feet that says "Juicy," and from the top of the bag a tiny, almost rat-size dog is poking its head up to receive bits of blueberry muffin from its owner.

Buck watches Tiffany gape at the girls as she enters the store. She tries to play it cool and act like she's a regular, but she looks much more like a child entering a candy store with a "Free Candy" sign out front. Tiffany stares at each person seated inside the small establishment and Buck knows she is trying to see if anyone is famous. Her stare stops a particularly long time at a blonde girl in black sunglasses and a hat reading *Us Weekly* and is startled when the surfer-looking man behind the counter in the dark green apron asks, "Can I get something started for you?"

Tiffany whirls around and stares at him shocked for a split second before regaining her composure and trying to play it cool.

"Oh, um . . ." she fumbles, staring up at the menu of drinks with names like machiatto and Frappuccino. "What do the famous people get?" she finally asks the barista.

He stares back at her for a split second, with a look that combines pity and amusement before smiling kindly and lowering his voice to say, "Courteney Cox comes in here a lot and she always gets a venti mocha."

"That's what I'll have," Tiffany tells him confidently. "Buck, you want a venti mocha too, right?" she asks with a tone that says, "Anybody who's anyone drinks a venti mocha."

"Sounds good," he says and hands a five-dollar bill to the green-aproned employee. The barista punches some buttons on his computerized cash register and says, "That'll be nine sixty-five."

"Nine sixty-five," Buck repeats, a little shocked. The citizens of Victory *definitely* wouldn't respond well to paying ten dollars for two cups of coffee. Although, it's not just coffee . . . it's a venti mocha . . . Buck reminds himself, wondering what a venti mocha is as he pulls another five out of his worn wallet.

Even though Tiffany insists they will have a better chance of spotting celebrities if they sit at one of the tables outside the Starbucks, Buck drags her across the street to sit on the beach, where they drink their enormously large and extraordinarily sweet beverages. An hour later, they are both shaking from the caffeine and the beach is starting to get cold. Buck feels wimpy unrolling his shirtsleeves while the surfers continue to run in and out of the waves. He and Tiffany leave the beach and head back to the car. He decides that they have time for dinner before they need to be at Lizzie's and thinks twice about asking Tiffany what she wants to eat, knowing that the answer will be some bizarre place she read about some celebrity going in a magazine.

Sure enough, she is certain that sushi is the ticket to star sightings, since Starbucks didn't really pan out. Raw fish isn't exactly Buck's idea of a good dinner, but he obliges, and the two set out in search of sushi. He really can't keep from enjoying himself on this adventure with Tiffany. Her enthusiasm for finding famous people in Los Angeles is entertaining at worst and infectious at best. Buck finds himself peering into restaurant fronts trying to see someone he recognizes from television or movies, grateful to be thinking about something other than their upcoming appointment with Lizzie.

~15~

Before I can even compose words to try to bring Courtney back to reality and convince her that Buck Platner is not her soul mate, he is knocking at my apartment door and Courtney is undoing the top button of her blouse and pulling her boobs into place as she crosses to answer it. She gives me an excited smile, which I return with a tortured gag before pulling the door open.

I am positive that the reaction she receives from Buck is not what she had hoped for. Instead of the instant connection I know Courtney had envisioned and expected, she is met with a look of surprised confusion. First Buck swings back to check the number on the outside of the apartment and then he looks directly over Courtney's head into the apartment, scanning across it until his eyes land on me, cowering by the window.

"Oh, Lizzie, there you are," he says with relief.

"I'm Courtney Cambridge," Courtney offers, smiling flirtatiously.

"Buck Platner," Buck says professionally, extending his right hand to Courtney, but hardly glancing at her, let alone noticing her recently arranged breasts. "Lizzie—er, sorry, Elizabeth, I have the custody papers here," he says stiffly, holding up a manila envelope.

"Courtney is my legal counsel," I inform him defiantly.

"It's so great to see you. You look wonderful," he says, without acknowledging my words. It's as though he is reciting a planned speech. A split second later, his brain processes what I have told him and he repeats, "Legal counsel?"

"Yes," I say coolly, careful to avoid Tiffany's gaze, which I feel directly on me.

"Oh, um, okay." He stumbles over the words uncomfortably. "Well, Ms. Cambridge, what we have here is pretty standard. My father actually wrote up Mrs. Tatham's last will and testament—"

"Oh my God, you *have* to call me Courtney," she says, grabbing his biceps and playfully shaking Buck's large frame.

"Okay, right, Courtney," he continues looking even more uncomfortable now that Courtney is holding him halfway in an embrace. "Like I said, my father prepared these documents, but I think you'll find that everything is in order. Oh, this is Tiffany," he says trying to motion to the blonde girl standing behind him but having trouble because Courtney still has a grasp on him.

"You must work out," Courtney says sounding like an idiot rather than an attorney, and as I wince, I notice that Buck has the same reaction.

"Um, yes . . . so if Elizabeth signs all the places that are marked, I think we will be finished with this matter."

"Courtney has to go over all the papers . . . every word!" I practically exclaim, hoping to snap Courtney's brain back into place and jog her memory that she is here to save my life, not to open another chapter of her love life.

"Yes!" Courtney jumps in, and I feel a split second of hope. "Let's give them a look over dinner. Do you like sushi?" Courtney asks, grabbing Buck's lower arm and turning his body toward the still-open front door.

"Oh, um, we actually ate already," Buck says politely.

"Then let's go get a drink. I'm parched," Courtney says, unphased by the attempted rejection.

Before Buck can formulate another response, she is dragging him down the hall and I am left alone in my apartment. I stare out the door for a few seconds before realizing that I am not alone . . . it's even worse . . . I'm with Tiffany. I realize that she is also staring down the hall looking as abandoned and shocked as I feel. I take a breath and then another . . . they'll be back soon. They just went for drinks. How long can drinks take? A voice in the back of my mind is reminding me that Courtney could turn running out for milk into a four-hour excursion, but I quickly quiet the voice. I have to be positive; I have to believe that they will be back soon and that Courtney will have come through for me.

An hour . . . they'll be back in an hour. *Oh God!* the voice in my head screams. *What am I going to do with this kid for an hour?!?* I take another breath.

"So, hi," I say to Tiffany, breaking the trance that held her staring out the door. I cross the room and gently close it.

"Hi," Tiffany says uncomfortably, taking a sideways step a little further into the apartment.

She's dressed in the same jeans and pink top she was wearing earlier in the day. Her straight blonde hair is now pulled into a messy looped ponytail and she is wearing a fresh coat of sparkly pink lip gloss. She looks a lot like her mother did when we were in high school, with her petite frame and button nose—like a young Meg Ryan. Charla was always the most popular girl in our class, and I was her best friend—that was my claim to fame. It was Charla who was captain of the cheer squad and gave me a place on it, and Charla who got invited to school dances and made one of her date's friends take me. Until the day that Charla got pregnant, she had never made a false move. Everything she did was perfect and everything I did was second best. In spite of this, there was never any jealousy between us because Charla didn't have a competitive bone in her body. She never made me feel inferior and was always my biggest fan. I wonder if Tiffany is like this, too, and I feel a wave of sadness for the friendship I let go of and the friend who is now gone for good.

"I'm sorry about your mom," I say, and I genuinely mean it.

"Thanks," she says in a tone that I have trouble reading.

"I'm sure they'll be back soon and have all this squared away," I say trying to sound reassuring. I mean honestly, I'm sure Tiffany wants to be here as little as I want her here. She has a life in Victory—she probably has a best friend and a boyfriend . . . and her grandparents. Why would she want to live with a perfect stranger? "Would you like a glass of wine?" I offer, suddenly realizing that I am in desperate need of a large helping of the Charles Shaw "two-buck-Chuck" chardonnay chilling in my fridge.

"I'm fifteen," she says, with a look that implies she thinks I am the dumbest person in the world.

I feel like the dumbest person in the world. "Right, sorry," I say, wondering if it would be rude of me to still have a glass. "Can I get you anything at all?" I ask, silently hoping that she asks for water, since besides the cheap wine that is all I have.

"I'm fine," she answers.

Relieved, I offer her a seat on the pristine sofa, which she accepts with a shrug. I perch on the cushion next to her and we sit in awkward silence for what feels like an hour but is more like fifteen minutes. There are a few awkward exchanges between us, but things remain unbearably uncomfortable as the minutes tick by. At last I hear a car out front and I spring with uncontrollable joy from the couch toward the window.

"They're back!" I exclaim gleefully before looking down at the street, where there is no sign of Courtney's black Range Rover.

Instead, I see Dan's blue Audi parallel parking in the spot left vacant by Courtney. Absolute terror washes over me. Dan's here. Dan is here. DAN IS HERE and Tiffany is here. This is an enormous, gigantic problem, since Dan was never, ever supposed to know about the "Tiffany situation," or really about Tiffany's existence at all. I stand for a split second, paralyzed in fear, before Tiffany's hopefully confirming "They're back?" breaks my trance.

"You have to hide!" I shout with desperation.

"What?" she asks, confused.

"You have to hide, quickly," I say, standing and opening the perfectly organized closet in the apartment's entrance.

Before she can ask another question or put up a fight, I am cramming her into the tiny space between my J.Crew pea coat and jean jacket. I close the folding door a centimeter from her nose just as Dan knocks on the door.

I feel like I might throw up as I open it and put on a surprised smile for my fiancé.

"Surprise!" he says with a smile as I throw the door open.

"Dan! What are you doing here?" I ask, trying to sound happy, not horrified.

"A guy can't surprise his fiancé?"

"Of course you can," I say trying to figure out what to do. As far as I can tell, there are two options. Number one: get rid of Dan by sending him away. Number two: get rid of Dan by leaving with him. Okay, so really there is only one option—get rid of Dan—just two options to accomplish this by.

"Sweetheart, could you go pick up some mint chip? I am desperate for ice cream," I say with the sweetest smile I can muster.

"You want me to go pick up ice cream? What, are you pregnant?" he says with an uncomfortable laugh.

Oh God! This is backfiring.

"No, are you kidding? Definitely not, I'm just starving for ice cream. Could you go?"

"Lemme sit down for a few minutes. Then we can go get some together. I could go for some Rocky Road."

Okay, we're going to default into Option Number Two. No problem at all. We'll sit for a minute and then we'll go. Yes, I will be leaving a fifteen-year-old girl locked in my closet, but I'll send her a note once she's safely home in Victory explaining the whole thing and I'm sure she'll understand. Dan kisses me gently (blandly) on the lips as he crosses through the living room to the couch. I stand frozen in fear as he passes in front of the closet, but Tiffany seems to be staying silent. Maybe I'll send the explanatory note with some flowers or a basket of muffins.

We sit down on the couch and Dan picks up the remote control from the coffee table. He leans back and puts his feet up, but before he can press the power button, I'm on my feet again.

"Come on, let's go get ice cream before we start watching TV," I implore as I take the remote out of his hand and lay it back on the coffee table perfectly centered on my *Vanity Fair* coffee table book.

Dan groans a little but starts to lift himself off the couch. "All right, you win," he says with a sweet smile.

Relieved, I return his smile and take his hand as we head toward the door. My hand is on the knob and I feel like I'm home free when Dan pulls my other hand back.

Motioning at the closet where Tiffany still stands, he says, "Aren't you forgetting something?"

I fill with panic. He knows Tiffany is in the closet! "What?" I ask, realizing only after the word is out that it escaped about an octave higher than it should have.

"Elizabeth, you're always cold and you want to eat ice cream without a jacket on?" he says smiling fondly at me.

A jacket . . . he thinks I'm forgetting my jacket. Of course he doesn't suspect I have a teenager locked up in there.

"Actually, I'm warm tonight. I've been hot all day. That's

why I want to eat ice cream," I explain, feeling confident that this explanation will get us out of the apartment.

He shrugs and then opens the apartment door, holding it for me. I feel the cold air rush into the room immediately and wish I could get a jacket out, but I have no choice. I have to tough it out. I am over the doorjamb and he is about to follow when I hear voices coming down the hall. Really only one voice—Courtney's—going on and on about who knows what. I feel like a deer in headlights or a bear in a trap. My only hope is that some miracle will happen and Courtney will completely cover for me. My prayer is not answered. As soon as Courtney sees Dan she exclaims, "Daniel McCafferty! Big news, huh? Congratulations."

Dan assumes she is talking about our engagement and graciously accepts her congratulations. I am feeling a glimmer of hope that we might get away.

"We're going to get ice cream. Be back soon," I say to a confused-looking Courtney and an even more confused-looking Buck. I start down the hallway when Buck asks, "Where's Tiffany?"

I spin on a dime, but can't move another muscle. I look at Dan in horror.

"You named your ring?" Dan asks, thoroughly amused.

"Oh, ha-ha, yes." I pick up the ball and run with it. "Tiffany is right here, where she always is," I say, holding up my left hand for everyone to see. "Let's go."

Nobody seems to have heard me. Instead of Dan following me down the hall, he stands right there in the doorway while Courtney says, "So, you're gonna be a proud papa," to Dan and then turns to me and says, "Everything in these papers is in perfect order." She smiles, looking pleased with herself for a split second before seeing the horror on my face and the terror on Dan's.

"You *are* pregnant!" Dan spits out.

"Oh my God, you're pregnant!" Courtney exclaims at the

same time a disappointed sounding Buck says, "You're pregnant?"

"No! No! I'm not pregnant," I confirm.

"I don't get it," Dan questions. His confused eyes dart from me to Courtney.

I stare down at my shoes. I have no idea how I am going to get out of this. There is no escape.

"I thought Dan was here to meet Tiffany?" Courtney says, and she slowly seems to be realizing that nobody is on the same page right now.

"You thought I was here to meet the ring that I bought for her?" Dan says, his confusion turning into annoyance.

"Where is Tiffany?" Buck Platner asks again. God, I hate him.

Dan looks at Buck like he's an idiot. "Who are you?" he asks, and I can see anger starting to build up inside him.

I have seen Dan lose his temper only once before, but when he is pushed too far his temper is totally catastrophic.

"She's in the closet," I mumble, still staring at my shoes. I notice a scuff on the right toe that hadn't been there earlier and for a second my mind wanders to thinking about how I might have gotten it.

"What?!?" Buck and Courtney exclaim at the same time.

They rush into the apartment and Courtney pulls open the closet door to reveal poor Tiffany still standing there.

"Hi," she says dryly.

"Who the hell is this?" Dan asks, angrier still.

"This is Tiffany," I offer meekly.

"Elizabeth. What the fuck is going on?" he asks, and I wince because I have never heard him curse before.

I have no choice. I am trapped, stuck in a corner between a large, sharp rock and a cold, dark, hard place. I quickly explain to Dan who Tiffany and Buck are and why they are at my apartment.

"So you're her guardian?" Dan asks, glancing briefly at Tiffany before turning his fiery gaze back to me.

"Courtney is going to take care of it," I almost whisper.

"Elizabeth, there's nothing to take care of. Everything's done. When you sign these papers you will have custody," Courtney says, cautiously motioning to the envelope Buck Platner holds under his arm.

"When did you find out about this?" Dan asks me sternly.

I tell him the truth and wince before he even has a chance to reply.

"You knew about Tiffany when we had our talk about moving in together and not having children and you didn't mention it?"

From the corner of my eye I can see Courtney, Buck, and Tiffany staring at me in shock. I can't bear to look straight at Dan because I know his look is far, far worse than shock.

"I was taking care of it," I say pleadingly.

"I don't know what you were doing," he says in disgust. "I can't deal with this . . . with *any* of this," he says, making a sweeping gesture with his arm. "I'm outta here."

He starts to walk down the hall and I run after him, tears starting to sting my cheeks.

"I"ll take care of it," I tell him trying to sound reassuring but sounding desperate instead.

"I don't really care what you do," he spits out angrily, without even turning around.

"Wait! " I beg.

"No, you don't get it. The engagement is off. We are off. I'm outta here *for good*."

"Dan!" I call after him. His words haven't hit me yet. I hear Courtney gasp sharply behind me, but it still doesn't register. He's angry. He doesn't want children and he thinks I'm going to have this teenager—but I'm not. Courtney *is* going to take care of this, and the plan can get back on track.

Suddenly Dan turns around and relief fills my heart. I start to run to him, but he puts his hand up. "Mail the ring back," he says coldly.

"What?" I ask, looking down at my hand. When I look up again he is gone—for good.

~16~

Tiffany stands in the hallway of Lizzie's building with Buck on her left and Lizzie's friend, Courtney, on her right. The scenario playing out a few feet in front of her is one she normally would have been enthralled to witness—a breakup, and a particularly nasty one at that. Unfortunately, she isn't able to relish the entertainment of this lovers' quarrel the way she normally would. Normally, Tiffany was the kind of teenager who would linger in a restaurant booth eavesdropping on a couple arguing, or "lose" something in her backpack or locker so she could hear a couple breaking up in the hall after school, but this breakup was horrifying. She couldn't even look directly at them—this breakup was *because* of her.

A few minutes earlier, Tiffany had been pretty convinced her life couldn't possibly get any shittier. Her mom and step-dad were dead and the person who was supposed to become her guardian had hidden her in the coat closet. Although Buck had denied it, Tiffany had gotten the feeling that her "aunt" Lizzie wasn't exactly thrilled to be reunited with her long-lost best friend's daughter. This had created a fair amount of apprehension on her part, but Tiffany had done her best to relax.

The meeting at Lizzie's office hadn't gone well, but Buck had been a real sweetheart and the day in Los Angeles had turned out to be a lot of fun. They'd gotten Starbucks at the same place Courteney Cox does, sat on the beach, and had a sushi dinner. Then things had taken a turn for the worse. They'd arrived at Lizzie's house and instead of the warm welcome that Tiffany had convinced herself would be waiting, Lizzie was there with a girl she claimed to be her attorney in order to get out of being her guardian altogether.

This would have been bad enough, but the girl had taken Buck and left Tiffany alone with Lizzie. They sat there in a horribly awkward silence until Lizzie realized that her boyfriend was outside and stuffed Tiffany into her tiny coat closet. There she stood between coats that smelled heavily of Chanel Coco Mademoiselle—a perfume she knew well by the samples ripped out of every magazine she could get her hands on. Dizzy from the scent, Tiffany listened as Lizzie unsuccessfully tried to get rid of her boyfriend and then as Courtney and Buck returned and the entire story—which Lizzie had apparently been trying to keep from the man—came out.

Suddenly, the closet door was thrown open and there she stood, cheeks burning with humiliation. It was the second most embarrassing time she had been discovered in a closet. The first had been at Rachel Roman's fourteenth birthday party. There had been a game of spin the bottle and Tiffany had been more than happy when her spin landed directly on Ryan Quinn. The two were herded into a closet almost as crowded as Lizzie's, but smelling of mothballs instead of expensive perfume. Ryan had his tongue down her throat and his hand under her bra when Rachel's mother had thrown open the closet door. Apparently during their "seven minutes in heaven," Rachel's parents had caught on to what eight fourteen-year-olds do in a furnished basement and had broken up the party.

It was Courtney who pulled open the closet door with a look of horror upon actually finding Tiffany standing inside. Tiffany stood as still as a statue, her checks scarlet red.

Courtney whispered, "Oh my God," as she pulled Tiffany by the wrist out of the closet and into the hall. By the time Tiffany arrived and her eyes adjusted to the bright light of the hall after being in the closet's blackness, Lizzie and her boyfriend were halfway down the hall and Lizzie was crying. What felt like a split second later, he was gone. He'd dumped Lizzie—broken off their engagement—and Tiffany stood motionless in the hallway, knowing it was all her fault, as Courtney went to the sobbing Lizzie and Buck looked on in shock.

As Courtney put her arm over Lizzie's shoulders and guided her inside the apartment, Buck turned to Tiffany.

"Are you okay?" he asked, his voice a combination of concern, confusion and what, oddly, sounded like hopefulness.

"Yes," she said, her own voice heavily laced with humiliation.

Tiffany wished she could be anywhere in the world but at Lizzie's apartment. The room was frighteningly perfect. It literally felt like walking into a page of the Pottery Barn catalog. It was clear that no drink had ever been set down without a coaster and no foot had ever made its way onto the couch. She thought back to the ugly plaid couch in her own living room; like almost everything in that house, she despised it. Like the stupid doormat, it was another item that Chuck adored, and while even Tiffany would admit that it was comfortable, it was not comfortable enough to make up for how hideous it was. At this moment, though, Tiffany longed to sink into the burgundy velour and cover herself with the itchy blanket her mother had made during a crochet phase.

Buck put his hand sympathetically on Tiffany's shoulder, but the kind gesture almost made her feel worse. Really, things were bad enough without people pitying her—more than they already were anyway. A feeling of hate for Lizzie swelled through her and Tiffany enjoyed a small moment of spite where she silently congratulated the man who had stormed down the hall for getting away from such a bitch. But then almost as quickly as it came, it went away, and the feeling of guilt returned. Tiffany was the reason that Lizzie's life was in shambles, and while Lizzie certainly wasn't the only one, Tiffany felt responsible. Buck's hand stayed on her shoulder and gently guided her into the apartment, where she could see Lizzie and Courtney sitting on the pristine sofa.

Courtney looked up from consoling Lizzie and rose from the couch to meet them halfway between the door and where Lizzie continued to sit, sobbing. There the three of them stood, in a little huddle in front of a small, round bistro table that sat in the apartment's entrance/dining room.

"She's ready to sign the papers," Courtney said quietly, looking up at Buck.

"Are you sure?" Buck countered, sounding uncertain that this was the right time.

Tiffany silently prayed that Lizzie would refuse to sign the papers tonight—or maybe altogether—and she could go back to Victory and stay with Buck. Maybe Buck Platner would agree to be her guardian? Tiffany was positive that her mother would have been perfectly happy with the idea. I mean, who wouldn't want their child raised by a celebrity in their absence? "Please don't make me stay," Tiffany silently begged whatever higher power might be listening.

"There's no time like the present," Courtney said lightly, slowly blinking her long eyelashes at Buck.

Buck shrugged, still looking very unsure, but he turned and lifted his worn old briefcase onto the empty bistro table. He opened it and handed a stack of white papers held together with a large binder clip to Courtney. Sticking out from the papers were a number of red "sign here" tabs stuck on to ensure that Lizzie didn't forget to dot an i or cross a t.

"Do you have a pen?" she asked.

Buck reached back into the surprisingly well-organized case and retrieved a blue Bic, which he handed to Courtney.

She crossed back over to where Lizzie was holding her head in her hands. Tiffany noticed the pretty diamond on her left ring finger and immediately recalled Lizzie's boyfriend instructing her to send it back. His words stung in Tiffany's memory so harshly that she couldn't even imagine how they must feel being played on repeat in Lizzie's.

Only once in her fifteen years had Tiffany had the displeasure of being dumped (rather than doing the dumping). The dumper was Scott Marshall. He was actually the boyfriend Tiffany had before her current boyfriend, Red. Red was undoubtedly a rebound and Tiffany didn't have any real feelings for him. Scott had been another story. He was a senior, captain of the baseball team, and without a doubt the most handsome boy at Victory High. He and Tiffany dated for nine months, at which point Tiffany's "everything but" policy became an impassable problem.

It was the night of Scott's homecoming dance (coincidentally the same dance night that her mother had gotten pregnant fifteen years before) where he laid it out: have sex or break up. Unlike with every other boy who had laid down the same ultimatum, Tiffany seriously considered Scott's case. With the others, Tiffany had either walked away or simply refused and the ultimatum had gone away without being enforced. It was different with Scott, though, because Tiffany actually thought she loved him and that he might in fact be "the one."

Obviously, it was pretty unrealistic to find "the one" as a high school sophomore, but in her head she had it all figured out. She could get a promise ring after Scott's graduation and would wait for him while he went away to college (an ambition he never actually held), then upon her own graduation they would get engaged and have their wedding after she finished college. It really could have worked, and she tried to explain it to Scott, including the pledge to go all the way with him once she had the promise ring on her finger. Scott pretended to agree to the plan and in exchange received a blow job. Before she could even swallow, Scott harshly said that her plan was actually incredibly stupid and that if she wasn't willing to put out, he would easily find someone who would.

Five months later, she still felt the sting of Scott's words and the sick feeling of beer and his cum sitting in her stomach. Two weeks later, Scott was already dating Amanda Ruth, a girl well known for being an easy slut. Every time she saw the two of them together, Tiffany felt the sickness surge, so when Red Richley sweetly asked her to get a Coke after school one day, she readily accepted and had been with him ever since.

Lizzie wiped her eyes with the back of her hand and took the pen in her right hand. Without reading, or even really looking, she signed next to every single red tab until the end of the thick document had been reached.

"Okay," she said weakly putting the cap back on the pen and laying it across the stack of papers.

Courtney gave Lizzie a sympathetic pat on the shoulder before picking up the bundle and crossing back to Buck, who stood frozen in front of his open briefcase. His face registered shock, and perhaps a little disappointment.

"Okay," Courtney echoed as she handed the stack to Buck.

He nodded stiffly in response and then turned and looked at Tiffany. The girl could only blink rapidly in an effort to hold back tears. Lizzie had signed the papers and was now officially her guardian. That meant she had to stay here . . . here with a person who did not want her, with a person who probably hated her, since she had just ruined Lizzie's relationship with her fiancé.

"So we should go," Courtney said to Buck, and if Tiffany had not known how wildly inappropriate it would be, she would think that there was a suggestive tone to Courtney's statement.

"I guess so," Buck said tiredly, looking sadly in Tiffany's direction. "Will you be okay?" he asked her.

"I guess," she managed to squeak out, her throat straining from holding back tears.

Buck crossed to Tiffany and gave her a warm hug. "I'll come down this weekend to see how things are going." He almost whispered the promise into her ear. She only nodded and buried her head against his hard chest. Strange to think that forty-eight hours ago, Tiffany Dearbourne and Buck Platner had been strangers and now she felt so close to him . . . and yet he was leaving and she was staying.

Buck acted like he didn't want to leave. He was looking from Tiffany, who was screaming, *Don't go!* at top volume in her head but standing silently looking at her feet, to Lizzie, who sat silently on the couch with fat tears rolling down her thin cheeks while she looked at her own feet. Then Tiffany heard a soft coughing sound from the door and all three looked up to see Courtney looking directly at Buck and holding the door open.

He looked surprised but quickly took his hand off Tiffany's shoulder and crossed to his open briefcase. He snapped it shut and then looked again in Tiffany's direction.

"Bye, Tiff," he said softly, and then he looked at Lizzie. Awkwardly, he turned and took a step toward her, then decided against it and took the step back. "Uh, good-bye Lizzie— Ms. Castle. Again, I'm sorry for your loss," he said stiffly. Then he shook his head as if disappointed with himself as much as with the situation and walked out the door, followed by Courtney.

Tiffany just stood there in horror as the door closed behind them and she was left alone with "Aunt" Lizzie and her new life.

~17~

It is pitch black in my room, it must be the middle of the night, but I can hear my cell phone ringing from my bag in the living room. It's probably a wrong number . . . no way am I getting out of bed to answer a wrong-number caller in the middle of the night. Finally, the ringing stops and I close my eyes to go back to sleep. A split second later, the house phone starts ringing.

"Unbelievable," I groan to my empty room.

Before I can coordinate my brain and my limbs to get out of bed and answer the phone, the house phone goes silent and the cell phone starts ringing again. I get up, realizing that there must be a terrible emergency to evoke so many middle-of-the-night calls, but in the pitch blackness of my room I trip over something and land in a heap on the rug. Before I can get my balance and stand back up, the ringing stops and I hear a soft and hesitant "Hello?" in the hallway.

My heart stops . . . there is an intruder. Someone is in the house—probably to kill me. The caller is probably the intruder's partner, calling to coordinate the murder. Before I can rationalize that a murderer probably doesn't receive calls on the victim's house and cell phone, I hear the person who answered my phone say, "Actually, I think she's sick," and it all comes back to me.

It's not an intruder in the hallway—it's Charla's daughter, Tiffany. Still in pitch-blackness, I climb back onto my bed and across to where the alarm clock sits. It's 9:13 a.m., not the middle of the night; and I bet my life that the caller is from work, not the murder's accomplice, since I was supposed to be in Renee's office thirteen minutes ago. I throw my head facedown into the soft down pillow and for a split second wish that someone had come during the night and killed me.

I hear Tiffany promise to have me call whoever is on the other line as soon as I'm able and then sets the old-fashioned Pottery Barn phone's heavy handset back on the base. It's probably the third time the phone has ever been used. I bought it because it completes the look of my living room. It sits at the corner where the living room becomes the hallway to the bedrooms and looks perfect, but with its spiral cord and no nearby seating, it never ended up being very practical for everyday use. I sit like a statue in the darkness as I hear Tiffany's footsteps getting closer and closer to my room, and then she knocks very, very softly three times. My heart races, and I scoot myself silently under the fluffy down comforter. "Lizzie?" she whispers, and I concentrate on shallow, silent breathing. After a few seconds, she gives up, and I hear her footsteps disappear down the hall back toward the living room.

I roll onto my back, my chest rising and falling heavily as I try to regulate my breathing to its normal speed. My life has completely fallen apart. My plan has been destroyed. I try for a few seconds to figure out a way to put all the pieces back together, but there isn't one . . . it's impossible. I turn onto my side, my back toward the door, and I silently cry until I am asleep again.

My life continues like this for four days. I keep my black-out shades drawn to ensure round-the-clock pitch-blackness and I sleep off and on all day. When I wake up, I sometimes turn on the television and watch talk shows where people complain about their crappy lives. I have yet to find a show with a person whose life is as crappy as mine. I sneak out of my room in the middle of the night to get food (mostly dry cereal and ice cream) from the kitchen. By only leaving my room in the still of night, I make sure that I will not run into Tiffany. As I silently tiptoe across my apartment, I notice that she has been neatly stacking my mail on the dining room table, but she has also been sitting on the living room couch and not fluffing the pillows when she gets up. Obviously, I hate her.

I know I have sat in the dark for four days because I have watched Meredith Vieira and Matt Lauer happily banter four times and *Friends* sixteen times. I liked Katie Couric better on *Today*, and I hate all the episodes when Ross has the stupid monkey. I have also heard the phone ring four mornings in a row and Tiffany explain in a low voice that I was still very ill, too ill to come to work or even to call in. The phone has also rung five other times, but Tiffany's side of the conversation was always too one-sided for me to figure out who the caller was. On the fifth morning, the phone doesn't ring because it's Saturday, but at 10:06, Tiffany cracks the door. The sunlight from the hallway cuts across the blackness of the room, land-ing directly in my eyes from the spot at the head of the bed where I am curled around a box of Frosted Mini-Wheats.

"You're blinding me!" I shriek. "Shut the door."

"Sorry, Aunt Lizzie," she says quietly, but she doesn't make any motion to shut the half-open door.

"I'm not your aunt and *nobody* calls me Lizzie," I snap nas-tily.

There is a long beat of silence . . . long enough that a surge of guilt pulses through my body.

"Call me Elizabeth," I say, trying to lighten my tone a lit-tle.

"Look, Elizabeth," she begins, and now that my eyes have adjusted to seeing light for the first time in almost a week, I can see that she is wearing a black tank top and black knee-length skirt. As she talks, she stares at her toe digging into the pile of the carpet. "Obviously you and my mom weren't quite as close as she thought."

My first instinct is to snort, "Ya think?" sarcastically, but the mention of Charla sends a reminder flashing through my brain that this kid's mother just died. Obviously, I still hate her for ruining my life, but really it's more Charla's fault.

"Yeah, not really," I answer, also looking at her toe in the carpet.

"You've had some phone calls," she says, producing a pile of light pink Post-it notes that I recognize from my desk drawer.

"Did Dan call? You should have gotten me!" I say, suddenly certain that every single message is from Dan, begging and pleading to get back together.

"No," she says quietly, "he didn't call." Tiffany's words squelch my dream, but she doesn't seem to catch on because she starts flipping through the little slips of paper. "Courtney, Courtney, Hope, Renee Foster—that was kind of cool to talk to a celebrity—Hope, Courtney, Court—"

"Thanks, that's okay," I say, cutting her off.

"Look, I've been thinking about your situation and I feel responsible," she says in a single breath. It's clear she's been rehearsing whatever it is she's about to say to me. I'm about to agree that she is at fault for ruining my life, but something holds me back. "I want to help you get back together with your boyfriend. It's the least I can do. I have a lot of ideas of ways you can win him back," she says quickly.

Win him back . . . the words linger around my head like the smell of fresh flowers. I breathe it in deeply. It's brilliant. Dan broke up with me, but I can win him back.

"Win him back," I repeat, almost in awe.

I hadn't thought of it. I had simply accepted defeat and the fact that my life was over. Of course I had held on to a glimmer of hope that Dan would come back to me, but I hadn't thought of going out and getting him back. It's brilliant.

"Yes!" I say, suddenly realizing that the blinding ray of light Tiffany let into my room was actually a shining beacon of hope. "Let's start today," I say, knowing full well that this teenager might have had the luck to stumble onto the *idea* of winning Dan back, but that her help would be the last thing I needed to actually do it.

"I can't start today. My mom's funeral is today. Buck is coming to pick me up and take me home for it."

Suddenly the black clothes make sense, but the Buck part does not. "Buck Platner is coming to get you?"

"Yeah," she confirms, "he'll have to bring me back here tomorrow night, so we can start on Monday," she tells me matter-of-factly.

"Why is *he* coming to get you?" I ask.

"He's like the nicest guy in the world," she informs me.

"You're not *together*, are you?" I ask, repulsed at the idea of Buck's being involved with this teenager and also feeling another odd twinge of jealousy.

"Oh my God, gross! He's like twice my age."

A wave of relief washes over me, although I can't help thinking how the sixteen years between Tiffany and Buck is actually a small age difference compared to many couples in Los Angeles.

"He's just insanely nice and he's taking me to my mom's funeral. I'll be back tomorrow," she says and starts to close the door.

As she does, the room starts to get blacker, but before she can close it all the way, I hear myself saying, "Wait, he doesn't have to come all the way down here and get you. I'm going to the funeral. I'll drive you."

I'm a little shocked by the words coming out of my mouth. I have not set a foot back in Victory since the day I left. I told my mother on several occasions that I would be home for Christmas or Thanksgiving, but I always got out of it at the last minute. I didn't go home when my mother re-married or even when my paternal grandmother died. I once drove through Victory when a couple of college friends in-vited me to spend a weekend skiing at one of the girl's par-ents' cabin in Eagle Lake, but I slouched down in the backseat of her Grand Cherokee hoping that no one would see me and wave or offer any other sort of recognition. Part of me is un-sure why I have deemed Charla Dearbourne's funeral worth going back for, but the other part is confident that this is the right decision. I know deep down that Charla would have gone anywhere for mine. Plus, I'll be able to get the Tiffany custody issue officially taken care of. I'll personally deliver her to her grandparents or some other relative with whom it would make a lot more sense for her to be with rather than me.

"That'd be great," Tiffany says, "I'll go call Buck and tell him he doesn't need to come get me. He's probably already on the road, but it'll save him from having to make the whole drive."

For a second I linger over what a nice guy Buck Platner must be to drive over three hours to pick Tiffany up, but then a new thought edges that one out—I'm going back to Vic-tory. A sick feeling creeps into my stomach as I get out of bed. My legs are stiff from disuse, so I hobble toward the bathroom for my first shower since Monday morning. I'll just get through this weekend and then I'll come home—without Tiffany—and win Dan back, and life will get back on track.

~18~

Three and a half hours in a car normally feels like an eternity to me, but the drive to Victory goes alarmingly fast. I even endured many nasty gestures while maintaining 65 miles per hour in order to delay our arrival, but in what feels like the blink of an eye the highway speed limit has changed to 35 mph and the road sign says "Main Street." As we cruise past the sign boasting Victory, California, Population 734, the sick feeling rises from my stomach into my throat.

The funeral doesn't start for a while, so I decide that we should go to my parents' house, where we'll be staying, and drop off our bags. I even think about the notion of Tiffany staying with my parents permanently if no other relative is willing or able. Helping me out with this is the least my mother could do for me. About halfway through town, we come to Weber Way and I turn right. We pass ten identically shabby ranch-style houses before coming to the one I grew up in. In the fifties, a developer named Jeremy Weber (hence Weber Way) built three blocks of identical homes with matching two-car garages and window flower boxes. Now the majority of the homes have peeling paint and minimal landscaping. My mother's house is actually the exception—I am pleased to see a fresh-looking coat of yellow paint on the house and purple pansies that I know she planted herself in the window box. For a split second I feel nostalgic.

I park my BMW in the driveway and I am not unaware that it is the only BMW ever to park on Weber Way. Without saying a word to Tiffany, I turn off the car and get out, grabbing my outlet bargain Coach weekend bag from the backseat. She wordlessly follows my cue, grabbing her own duffel bag (I made sure that she brought *all* her possessions with her).

The silence continues as we walk up the driveway, and I take a quick pause at the door. Am I supposed to ring the bell? I know my parents are home, since my mother's Honda Accord and my stepfather's pickup truck are both parked in the open garage. I haven't lived here—or even been here—in a dozen years, but it's my house, so I forgo the bell, pulling open the worn screen door and then the front door. I take a step inside and it's like stepping into a time warp. I feel like I just got home from a day in the eleventh grade. My mom is sitting at the round kitchen table reading *People* magazine with a Kool perched between her lips, and my stepdad is comfortably reclined in a brown corduroy La-Z-Boy.

When my mother sees me, she does a double take before hollering, "Oh my God, Ray! Lizzie's here."

Her eyes fill with tears as she speaks, making me feel like a little kid. I drop my bag at the door and rush into my mother's embrace. For so many years the smell of cigarettes made me sick with memories of home, and yet right now, I breathe in the stale smoke from her clothes, hair, and skin with great fondness. Mom looks over my shoulder and sees Tiffany, who I am sure must be feeling awkward. She pulls back, grabbing my hand as she releases my body.

"Tiffany, sugarplum, you get in here."

She gives Tiffany a warm embrace, and I realize that my mother seems to know my former best friend's daughter fairly well.

"Oh, Ray, get in here and look at our Lizzie with Tiffany. It's like—" she breaks off as her eyes fill with tears, "well, you know . . . old times," she continues.

At this point, my stepdad comes into the room hollering, "What are you squawking about, Nancy?" as he moves. Once he sees me, his gaze softens and he whispers, "Well, would you look at that," before giving me a warm, welcoming hug. His flannel shirt reeks of Marlboro Reds. His tanned skin has aged considerably since I last saw him and now resembles leather. "It's good to see you, kid."

"How are you?" Mom asks, walking towards the kitchen. "Can I get you girls anything? How are you doing, Tiffany? What's new with you, Lizzie?"

My mom asks more questions than anyone I have ever met in my life. It's the same drive that forces her to read *People* magazine and *Us Weekly* every single week . . . she has to know everything interesting going on at all times. She's also probably the biggest fan of *The Renee Foster Show!*, and I'm pretty certain it doesn't have anything to do with my thirty-second spot.

"Lizzie, you're thinner than you look on TV," she continues. "Are you eating enough?" She gives my bony frame a once-over and her eye falls on my left hand, which still sports my engagement ring from Dan. I figured there was no point taking it off since we're getting back together next week. Mom gasps slightly. "You're engaged?!?"

She grabs my hand to inspect the ring, and I beam. I would never say it out loud, but my one-carat (.85 carat) diamond is a little small by L.A. standards. By Victory standards, however, it's a rock. "When do we actually get to meet the wonderful Daniel McCafferty? Have you met him, Tiff?" she says turning to Tiffany, whose cheeks flush slightly.

"Um, just briefly," she mumbles. "Could I get some water?" she asks, obviously desperate to change the subject.

I feel annoyed with my mother's constant questioning and

a little nervous because I recognize Tiffany's reaction. Charla was the world's worst liar. Just like Tiffany, her cheeks would flush scarlet red and her eyes would dart around the room as if looking for a place to hide. Her patented move, which she apparently passed on to her daughter, was the subject-change maneuver. I cross my fingers that my mother doesn't recognize the signs as easily as I have.

"Okay, enough questions," I announce. "I'm going to put my stuff in my room."

I retrieve my Coach bag and head down the hallway to my bedroom. Before I even open the door, I can picture the room in my head. I am positive that my mother hasn't touched a thing—that she's left it as a shrine to my childhood. The twin-size trundle bed where Tiffany and I will be bunking covered with a Laura Ashley knockoff pink-and-white floral comforter, the Michael J. Fox and New Kids on the Block posters on the wall, the little blue ribbons hanging above the white dresser for science fairs and spelling bees. I almost feel nostalgic as I open the door, but then the good feelings come to a screeching halt. I look back down the hall at my mother, who is quickly coming up behind me with an extremely guilty and uncomfortable look on her face.

The only thing in the room reminiscent of my childhood is the faded and peeling floral wallpaper. The posters, bed, and dresser are all gone. In their place stand an oak-colored desk and burgundy office chair, and a treadmill. On the desk sits an iMac, and across from the treadmill is a small Sony TV.

"What is all this stuff?" I ask in horror, "Where's *my* stuff?" I almost say "shrine" but realize in time that I'm probably the only one who thought of the room that way.

"Well, sorry, honey, you haven't been home in over a decade. And Ray needed a home office and I needed a workout space," she offers meekly.

"You needed an office?" I ask Ray, who has come up behind my mother.

"For my computer," he offers, sounding as lame as she did.

"Well, where the hell are we gonna stay?" I ask them pointedly.

They look at each other for a beat before turning back toward me. "There's a Holiday Horse Motel back out on the highway," my mother offers.

I let out an exasperated sigh. There is no way on earth that I am sleeping at the Holiday Horse. It's the kind of place that's boasts "HBO" on the sign out front and always, *always* flashes "Vacancy" in neon red.

"We can stay at Buck's," Tiffany offers from behind my parents.

"Oh, that's perfect," my mother says, sounding relieved. "Well, I'm going to finish getting dressed. We'll see you girls at the church at two."

Before I can protest, she hurries down the hall and into her own bedroom. I turn to Ray, but before I can get a word out he says, "Me too," and follows her.

I take another look back in the room that used to be mine, before giving up. "Okay, fine. Let's go to Buck's."

~19~

He knows it's wrong to be excited about a funeral, but part of Buck just can't help it—Lizzie is going to be there. His morning didn't start out so well, but just as he was climbing into his truck to travel hundreds of miles to Los Angeles so that Tiffany could attend her mother's memorial, the teenager called and told him there would be no need, that Lizzie was coming to the funeral and would drive her up. That's when things got better. Now, not only did Buck not have to make the drive, he'd get to see Lizzie. The last time he saw her, her head was buried in her hands sobbing because her obvious ass of a fiancé had dumped her, so he didn't get to say much. He had gained hope though that maybe they were meant to be together.

For a second Buck felt disgusted with himself that lately he was finding so much joy in other people's suffering— Lizzie getting dumped and Charla being laid to rest. Buck tried to quell the feelings of anticipation fluttering around in his stomach as he took his black wool suit out of the back of his closet. Buck only wore the suit for weddings, funerals, and court appearances. Since none of these events happened very often for him, the suit still seemed almost brand-new even though it was several years old. His father's law firm mostly handles family law cases, which tend to settle out of court. This is especially good for Buck, since his tongue tends to become paralyzed when standing before a judge. As for weddings and funerals, he just didn't happen to have too many friends who were getting married or dying.

As he fastened the pants around his middle, Buck's legs began to sweat. Even though the air conditioner in the house was on, the summer heat was starting in Victory and Buck knew that spending that day in the wool suit was going to leave him as drenched as if he'd stepped out of the shower. He couldn't help but feel a twinge of disappointment that he wouldn't look better for Lizzie but then quickly scolded himself for focusing on her and not the sadness of the day. Just as he was pulling a plain blue shirt from the closet, he heard a knocking at the front door.

Still in his bare feet and undershirt, Buck quieted Wildcat's barking and opened the front door. He did a double take, sure that the heat had already affected his brain when he saw Tiffany and Lizzie standing on his porch.

"We need to stay here," Tiffany informed him. "It's cool, right?"

Before he could answer, she was walking past him and heading toward the guest bedroom with the duffel bag she'd taken out of her parents' house a week earlier.

"Um, of course," he mumbled.

He watched Tiffany make her way down the hall. It's funny how quickly teenagers feel comfortable. A week ago they'd never met, and now she acted completely at home at his house. It made him feel good and it was nice for the house to feel a little fuller than just him and Wildcat. The comfortable feeling quickly vanished when he heard a rustle behind him and remembered that Lizzie was also standing on the porch. He quickly turned back to her.

"Here, let me take that for you," he said reaching forward for her overnight bag and almost punching her face in the process. His cheeks flushed red.

Lizzie returned the almost-decking with an annoyed smile but handed over the bag nonetheless. "Are you sure you don't mind?" she asked.

"Of course not," he replied sincerely as he took her bag, somehow managing to avoid doing anything else clumsy.

He led the way down the hall and could sense Lizzie looking his messy house up and down as she silently followed. Once inside the guest room, Lizzie said, "There's only one bed."

"Don't worry, I can sleep on the couch," Tiffany volunteered. Something in her voice told Buck she was anxious to make this arrangement work. She probably feared that Lizzie would drive her back to L.A. tonight if they didn't have somewhere to stay. Buck wondered about Lizzie's relationship with her parents and why they weren't staying there.

"I have an air mattress," he said. "I'll blow that up if you girls don't mind sharing the room."

"I don't mind," Tiffany quickly replied, looking at Lizzie, who only muttered, "It's fine."

Buck went to the hall closet to attempt to extricate the deflated air mattress from under the piles of stuff—coats, athletic equipment, a seldom-used vacuum cleaner—while the wool pants stuck to his sweat-drenched thighs. Finally, he pulled out a blue plastic mass and set it on the floor. After the funeral, he'd find the compressor in the garage, which was as overpacked as the closet, but considerably larger.

He returned to his room and finished dressing. Although he felt as if he might pass out, Buck looked exceptionally handsome once his dark blue tie was around his neck and the four-button jacket was on. At least the jacket covered the large sweat circles on the light blue shirt. He walked into the hall, pausing under the air conditioner vent, and waited for the girls. A few minutes later, but feeling like only a few seconds, as Buck enjoyed the cool air, the girls, both in sleeveless black tops, came out of the guest room.

"Should we all just drive together?" he offered, silently praying that Lizzie would agree, since he was desperate to spend time with her.

"Sure." She shrugged, obviously not caring one way or the other.

Buck silently whooped that they would be driving together, then once again scolded himself with reminders that two people were dead and today was their funeral. In silence, the three walked out of the house and piled into Buck's truck.

~20~

So much had been going on that Tiffany was almost able to put out of her mind that today was her own mother's funeral. The week in Los Angeles had been one of the most miserable of her life. The misery her aunt Lizzie was creating almost matched the misery of losing her mom. Tiffany knew it was her fault that Lizzie's fiancé had broken up with her, but did she really need to rub her face in it so much? She took to her room for the entire week, never even checking to see if Tiffany was alive or dead. Nonetheless, having inherited her mother's unconditional loyalty, Tiffany lied to Lizzie's office every day about the horrible illness that was keeping her from her office and made every attempt not to bother her "aunt."

The fifth day of the silence was the breaking point for Tiffany. A survivor, she needed to figure out a way to make the best of her miserable situation, so she approached Lizzie with an offer to help her win her fiancé back. In Tiffany's opinion, a girl shouldn't want to marry such a prick, but since she knew she would take Scott back and immediately have sex with him if he offered, she couldn't judge Lizzie too much. Thankfully, Tiffany's plan worked—even better than she had hoped. Lizzie quickly accepted Tiffany's offer for help and was so uplifted by the idea that she would be getting back together with Dan that she decided to attend Charla's funeral back in Victory with Tiffany.

Tiffany still secretly held out hope that Buck Platner would insist on becoming her guardian and take her away from Lizzie, but since that wasn't very likely, she was prepared to help Lizzie, thereby helping herself. The drive to Victory felt even longer than usual, and Tiffany's legs twitched from being still for so long. Lizzie drove slower than her great-grandmother had before she had passed away a few years earlier. Tiffany thought she was going to go insane by the time they finally pulled into the driveway of Lizzie's parents' house, a house identical to her own except for its pretty yellow paint and living purple flowers.

Lizzie's parents had seemed happy to see her, and everything was going well until she had followed Lizzie down the hall to the bedroom in the same location as her own had been, to what had been converted into an office and exercise room. Tiffany feared it would ignite another meltdown from Lizzie and quickly offered Buck's house as a place to stay. Knowing her choices were Buck's or the Holiday Horse, Lizzie agreed to Tiffany's suggestion.

Even though she'd only been to Buck's house twice, it felt so good to return there, and she felt totally comfortable. The warmth and kindness of his personality radiated through his home. It was the kind of place where you could feel comfortable putting your feet on the coffee table after getting yourself a Coke from the almost empty fridge. She wished so much she could live there instead of in Lizzie's designer showcase apartment with the couch that looked like you weren't even supposed to lean back on the fluffed down pillows.

So happy to no longer be alone with Lizzie, Tiffany was almost caught off-guard when Buck pulled his truck into the parking lot of the Holy Lady of the Ivy where the marquee sign that normally boasted the week's sermon topic said "Memorial for Charla and Chuck Tatham" in the same black lettering that the movie theater used for the newest Jack Canton film. Suddenly it hit her like a bucket of cold water.

Stiff and silent, she followed Buck and Lizzie into the church. Her grandmother was the first to approach her and grabbed her in a secondhand smoke–filled embrace. Gran's eyes were red from crying . . . or maybe from smoking her "special cigarettes," as she referred to the marijuana her grandparents grew on their sun porch. Gran and Gramps were good people but wacky beyond belief, and as a result, Tiffany didn't spend too much time with them. They were also busy people, active in their bowling league and cross-country motorcycle club when they weren't harvesting mary-jane for their personal use.

Her grandmother's hug released her into another and then another, and before she knew it, she had been hugged all the way to the front of the church. Feeling as if she'd gone through the wringer, Tiffany sat down alone in the front pew and stared at the matching side-by-side wooden coffins her mother and stepfather presumably lay in. As she wondered which box housed her mother's remains, Buck slid into the pew next to her and whispered, "You okay?"

Without a word, she buried her head against his chest and cried, big and audible tears for the first time, not caring who saw or what they thought. Before she finished crying, the service ended and once again people were trying to hug her, shake her hand, or awkwardly offer condolences. Buck, sensing her discomfort, gently took her hand and led her out a side door near the front of the church. The two stood silently and watched all the cars file out of the parking lot and head to her grandparents' house for sandwiches and lemonade. Gran had made all the funeral arrangements and had decided she didn't want a bunch of people standing around watching her daughter be put in the ground, so the brief funeral didn't include any graveside service. As quickly as it started, it ended, and everyone followed the caravan in the direction of the refreshments.

It goes without saying that I am not an emotional person. I don't cry at weddings, movies, or long-distance phone company commercials the way that many girls do. A guy I dated for seven months in college actually called me a "frigid bitch," which I think was just his way of voicing his anger that I wouldn't have sex with him, but it maybe had to do with the fact that I was with him when I got the call that my grandmother had died and I didn't shed a single tear. Don't get me wrong—I was sad . . . of course I was *sad*, but I just don't cry very easily. In fact, the tears I shed over Dan were the first to flow from my eyes in quite a long time—probably years.

All this being said, I was shocked to feel tears streaming down my cheeks during Charla's funeral. It wasn't so much the words the pastor was sharing about a woman I didn't know and her husband—your typical funeral stories about how much they loved life and blah-blah-blah—but the stories about the Charla Dearbourne I spent my childhood with. My memories began on the grade school jungle gym, where Charla and I would spend recesses perched atop the metal web sharing Oreo cookies like the queens of the playground. Then we were in junior high, using our allowance to buy light blue eye shadow at the drugstore, and stealing liquid eyeliner and mascara from our mothers' makeup collections. As some member of Charla and Chuck's bowling team droned on about their "dedication to the lanes," I remember Charla in high school, her wavy blonde hair and blue eyes both looking so big on her petite frame, telling me her boyfriend wanted to "go all the way" the night of the homecoming dance. I'd listened intently as she'd described every detail of the night—part of me jealous, the other horrified—and I'd sat with her on the side of the tub as we waited for a little plastic stick to tell her her fate.

After I left for UCLA, I'd convinced myself that we'd grown apart, but the truth is that I'd pulled away. Sometime around the blue eye shadow days, when every teenager thinks she's hot stuff, I'd become convinced I was too good for Victory and nothing (and nobody) would keep me in the small town. Now, suddenly, sitting wedged between my own mother and Charla's, I'm realizing how much I lost (gave away). The pain stuck into my stomach like a knife. As the pastor completed the eulogies and everyone stood up to greet those around them, Margie, Charla's mother, turned to me.

"Charley (that's what she'd always called her daughter and I'd forgotten until this instant) always knew she could count on you. I'm so glad you have her Tiffany," Margie said with a sniffle.

It was like twisting the knife. Before I could respond, other people were there patting Margie's back and offering her tissues. Suddenly, I realize that Tiffany is my second chance with Charla. By getting to know the teenager, I can make up for lost time with my childhood friend. As I look around the church, I revoke my vow to find someone, anyone, in Victory to keep the girl. She is coming back to Los Angeles with me. She will help me win Dan back and it will be just like the days when Charla and I would scheme and scam together.

Unfortunately, Tiffany is nowhere to be seen, which I

guess is for the best, since it would be awkward to explain that my plan had been to ditch her but that a sudden surge of feeling has prompted me to do the right thing . . . especially since no one really knew about my goal of getting rid of the teenager. My parents usher me toward their car, and before I can locate my original carpool, I'm in the backseat of my mother's Accord in the traffic of the funeral exit. My mother coos in the front seat about what a lovely service it was and how nice the flowers looked and asks my father if he thinks the wreath she sent looked nice enough. Their conversation is mostly background noise until I hear her mention Buck Platner.

"What's that?" I ask, realizing too late that my question came out far too eagerly.

Thankfully, my mother doesn't seem to notice, although I see Ray raise an eyebrow and look at me in the rearview mirror.

"I was just saying what a sweetheart he has been to Tiffany. Margie was telling me how she spent the weekend at his house when he had some trouble tracking you down, and there he was with her again today. I didn't even realize that he and Charla had been friends?" she says, never missing an opportunity to throw in any sort of question.

"Say, didn't you go to the homecoming dance with him?" Ray asks.

"I think it was a prom," I say, trying but failing to fake nonchalance. "The wreath you sent was lovely, Mom," I add in an attempt to change the subject even though I have no clue which of the dozen circles of carnations with gold cursive "Sympathy" across them my mother was responsible for.

"Oh, Lizzie, I'm so glad to hear you say that," she says and then starts bad-mouthing the other arrangements sent which were apparently completely inferior to her own.

I breathe a silent sigh of relief that I dodged the Buck Platner issue, but I can't help wondering why it was an issue to begin with. Before I had an answer, we were pulling up to the Dearbournes' house, one identical to my parents'. The Dearbournes' house is on Cheryl Court, apparently named for the developer's wife. It's around the corner from my parents, exactly 150 paces, which I know because every other week I "ran away" to Charla's bedroom; the weeks in between she ran away to mine.

The street is filled with old American-made pickup trucks and small imported sedans, with people dressed in their "best," which often only means a clean denim workshirt and boots, piling into the Dearbournes' home. I follow my parents up the steps and into the tiny foyer. The Dearbournes are kind of hippielike and their home is evidence. Above the dining room table is a purple peace sign that Margie crocheted, and a curtain of beads hangs at the entrance to the hall leading to the bedrooms. Margie always tried to make Charla wear hand-knitted sweaters and knockoff Birkenstock sandals, but Charla was much more interested in replicating the pages of *Teen* magazine.

Once inside, I again look for Tiffany, but I don't have any luck.

Oh well, I tell myself, *I'll see her tonight at Buck Platner's house.*

I still cannot believe I am spending the night there. I shake my head and throw a disgusted look toward my mother for the demolition of my childhood room. She mistakes the look for a sad face and returns by tipping her head to one side and making a frown. I turn away and then make my way through the crowd of people, who no longer seem like the forlorn crowd from the church, toward a plate of pressed ham and American cheese sandwiches on the table. I take one, as well as a handful of Oreo cookies. "Charla's favorite," I say to no one in particular as I set the plate down in order to twist the cookie apart and eat the white icing just like Charla and I used to do as kids.

~22~

Buck and Charla hadn't exactly been friends. They were *friendly* back when they both attended Victory High, especially when Buck had taken Lizzie to the dance, but in the years between that night and the day of her funeral, they had exchanged only one- or two-word greetings when their paths happened to cross. This fact wasn't lost on Buck as he sat in the front pew at Charla's funeral comforting her daughter.

In the past week, Tiffany Dearbourne, a girl he would have had trouble naming had he been face-to-face with her, was suddenly part of his life. As he sat in the pew, sweating profusely beneath his wool suit, Buck's mind wandered from the minister's eulogy. He thought about where he might be sitting right now if Charla had hired Frank Watson to write her will, or if she had named her mother, Margie, to be Tiffany's guardian. Maybe he would be sitting in a back pew somewhere with some of his Victory High classmates . . . or maybe he would be sitting at home on his couch watching a baseball game.

Buck's life had taken a quick turn down an unknown path one week ago when his father summoned him to the office. He now found himself front and center at Charla's funeral and reunited with Lizzie. He chastised himself for thinking about her during the funeral but continued to do it anyway.

He found himself straining to turn around discreetly and look for her in the crowded church—a difficult feat from the very front row. He couldn't see her anyway; people were packed in like sardines in a can. He did, unfortunately, catch the eye of his father, who gave him a questioning glare as Tiffany sobbed on his shoulder.

He hadn't thought about his father being at the funeral, but once he made eye contact it was obvious—Charla was a client, after all. Buck had been extremely vague and evasive when filling his father in on the details of Tiffany's transfer of custody. He certainly did not mention the extra days it took or that he personally drove her to Los Angeles. Buck knew his father would question him about how he had gotten to know Tiffany well enough in less than twenty-four hours to sit with her at the funeral, and Buck would have to figure out a way to avoid the explanation.

Just as Buck thought his skin would literally begin to melt, the minister finished speaking, and everyone else in the crowded church began. Tiffany was immediately accosted by aggressive condolence-wishers, and Buck couldn't help taking pity on her. He quickly ushered her out a side door of the church; it was a door he had walked through twice as a groomsman in the weddings of his high school buddies. One had gotten married in July, and Buck remembered standing on the side of the church feeling as though he might faint from the heat. The other had married in February, and Buck had stood in the same spot in probably the exact same rented tuxedo shivering from the cold. As Buck stood silently with Tiffany, he noticed that the paint that had been peeling badly the last time he'd been there had been replaced by a thick coat of yellowish white.

As hot as it was outside, it felt cool in comparison to the unair-conditioned church packed with people. He stood silently as Tiffany gulped to catch her breath and finally stopped crying.

"Thanks," she said hoarsely.

He simply nodded in response and kicked a small pebble off the walkway.

"What now?" Tiffany asked him, watching the pebble roll out of sight.

"Whatever you want," he answered.

He knew there was a reception—is that what you call it? Buck had always thought it a strange practice to have a party after a funeral. People are sobbing and depressed at the funeral and then fifteen minutes later are cheerfully eating tuna sandwiches with the deceased person's family—sometimes in the dead person's house. Anyway, he knew Charla's parents were inviting people back to their home after the funeral and he was torn about his desire to attend. Obviously, an opportunity to try to make a good impression with Lizzie was a top priority, but avoiding his father was another one. He suspected that his father, who was as big as he was and overweight on top of it, would be hot enough to swear openly as he mopped his brow with a handkerchief, but he also knew that his mother always did the "right thing," and going back to Margie and Gordon Dearbourne's house was probably the right thing to do.

"I wanna stay while they bury my mother," Tiffany replied.

Again Buck only nodded and then stood with Tiffany until the church emptied out. He stood silently by Tiffany's side as they put her mother's and stepfather's coffins on to little carts and wheeled them to the open and waiting graves. He kept his hand on her shoulder as they lowered the boxes into the ground, and offered her tissues as they filled the graves back up. When the ground was level and the workers were under a nearby tree wiping their sweaty foreheads and cracking open cans of Coke, Tiffany turned to Buck.

"I guess we should go to my grandparents' house now."

A surge of excitement mixed with dread pulsed through Buck. He hoped Lizzie would be there, but he dreaded what he would say to her if she was. Almost immediately he scolded himself for being so self-centered. He and Tiffany walked to the truck and climbed in. The black truck felt like an oven, and Buck kept the air conditioner blowing on them at full blast for the short ride to the Dearbournes'. It was too short a ride for the air to get cool, but at least the minutes of hot air blowing on his face were miserable enough to distract him from thinking about Lizzie.

By the time they arrived, many people had paid their respects and left. Buck was relieved that his father's Cadillac was nowhere to be seen as he expertly parallel parked the big truck in a space left vacant almost exactly in front of the house. They entered, and because of his height, Buck had an easy bird's-eye view of everyone in the house. His stomach flip-flopped when he saw Lizzie standing near the kitchen with a plate of Oreo cookies. His stomach flipped again when she looked up, saw him, and actually looked glad about it. Before he knew it, she had made her way through the crowd and was standing in front of them. Buck's shock was second only to Tiffany's when Lizzie threw her arms around the teenager and proclaimed, "I'm so glad you're here."

Buck was enamored with Lizzie, but he had to admit that until this moment she had behaved like a raving bitch to everyone around her. From Lizzie's tight embrace, Tiffany strained to give him a questioning look, which he could only return with a confused shrug.

~23~

The rest of the weekend in Victory feels like time spent in a time warp. Even though I haven't been home in so long, in some ways it feels like I've never left. Granted, this probably has much to do with the fact that little has changed in the small town. Besides the addition of a Subway, things are almost identical. Except now, instead of the hatred that used to surge through my veins at the lack of progress in the small town, I feel as if it is contributing to my second chance. It's the perfect setting to build a relationship with Tiffany that will make up for the one I lost with Charla.

Tiffany seems completely weirded out by my new attitude, but I'm not letting that dissuade me. I realize that I hadn't been exactly nice to her after she ruined my life—something that I now recognize wasn't even her fault—so I understand that the adjustment to the "new" me is going to take her some time. The truth is that she's a great kid . . . it's understandable how Buck could have grown so attached to her so quickly. She's so great, in fact, that I'm feeling pretty confident that when I win Dan back, he'll quickly grow to adore her, too.

Sunday morning I wake up to the smell of coffee brewing. For a split second before opening my eyes I think I am in my own bed and that Dan is making coffee in the kitchen. He has never made coffee before, but in that hazy place between sleep and waking I forget this fact. When I open my eyes, it takes me a beat to remember where I am. From the double bed, I can see Tiffany asleep on the air mattress on the floor below me. Saturday had been exhausting for her, and I am glad to see her getting some rest.

I silently swing my legs over the opposite side of the bed and tiptoe out of the room, which is very cramped with two beds, a desk, and our bags of stuff, in search of the coffee. Still not completely awake, I follow my nose directly into Buck's kitchen, pausing only briefly to pat the bear-size dog still asleep on the couch as I pad through the living room. I am inside the kitchen and eagerly staring at a full pot of black coffee before I realize that I am not alone.

"Morning," Buck says, and I visibly jump at the sound of his voice. My first instinct is a swell of disdain for him, but then I quickly remember my new life resolutions and my attitude softens—after all, I am in *his* house because he had been kind enough to invite us to stay after we showed up on his doorstep yesterday afternoon.

"Morning," I reply.

"Coffee?" he offers, and I readily reply, "Please."

He reaches into the cupboard above the coffeemaker to retrieve a mug, having to stretch over and around me in the process. He looks down as he effortlessly reaches and I suddenly feel self-conscious about standing in his kitchen in boxer shorts and a well-worn UCLA T-shirt. I pull the T-shirt down, avoiding his gaze, and when I look up, he is holding a cup of steaming coffee in front of me.

"Oh, um, thanks," I say, taking the black Fiestaware mug from him and thinking how his whole home is different than I'd imagined. It's certainly not well decorated, but it's also much more put together than I would have expected. I am secretly impressed with his matching dish set.

"Milk?" he asks, motioning toward the refrigerator.

"Please," I say, and then we both make a move and almost collide. Suddenly, we are caught in one of those situations where every time one of us moves, the other moves in the same direction, and we are trapped, unable to move in the opposite direction of freedom. After exchanging embarrassed smiles with each move, Buck finally puts both hands gently on my shoulders and says, "I'll get it."

"Thanks," I say with an embarrassed smile, and then, for some inexplicable reason, I move again and spill the hot coffee on Buck's bare foot.

"Aaargh," he grunts in pain.

"Oh my God, I'm so sorry," I gasp, setting the coffee on the counter and bending down toward his scalded foot.

"I'm okay," he says at the same time, also bending down.

Kneeling on the floor of his kitchen, we suddenly make eye contact, the burned foot between us and Buck's blue eyes twinkling as he says with a smile, "I'm gonna make it."

It is the strangest thing, because even though he is the injured one, my knees get weak and I am relieved to be so near the ground already. I return the smile, trying to remember if his dimples had been so pronounced back in high school. For a minute, or maybe just a second, time stands still and I think he is going to kiss me. I actually want him to. My lips are tingling with prekiss energy and I feel my head tip to one side.

Before I feel his lips on mine though, I hear a groggy "Morning" from behind me, causing me to jump farther than Buck's greeting had—in fact, causing me to jump so far that my head catapults up and into Buck's nose.

"My nose," he groans, grabbing his face as blood starts pouring out.

"He burned his foot!" I exclaimed to Tiffany, who hasn't asked what we were doing, and although she doesn't seem to care, I feel the need to explain. "Oh my God, you're bleeding!!" I practically scream, suddenly noticing the bright red blood covering Buck's face and chest.

I truly want to die of embarrassment. I have burned the man's foot and almost broken his nose, all within a few minutes—and thought that he wanted to kiss me in between! As he lies on the couch with a tissue clamped around his nose—a tissue that Tiffany has provided, since all I could do was stand there and shriek, "You're bleeding!"—I repeat, "I'm sorry, I'm sorry, I'm sorry," until he finally says with a smile peeking out behind the tissue, "It's okay." Except it sounds like, "Itch bouquet," because he has to keep pinching his nose to stop the bleeding. The sight of the dimples on either side of the tissue causes my knees to weaken again and I realize it is time to get out of Victory.

As Tiffany and I speed back to Los Angeles, the moment on Buck's kitchen floor plays over and over in my head. Was he going to kiss me? Did I really want him to? What would it have been like if he had? The thought of Buck's lips on mine sends an unexplainable shiver through my body.

"So, tomorrow you start the plan to win Dan back," Tiffany says from the passenger seat, breaking into my fantasy (by now Buck and I are doing more than kissing on his kitchen floor) and causing my cheeks to flush from being caught.

"Absolutely," I agree, pushing any and all thoughts of Buck Platner out of my mind.

Visiting Victory and making my peace with the town was one thing, but I can't abandon my plan altogether. Daniel McCafferty is the one I want—he is the one who fits into my picture of perfection. I have to focus on him and getting him back, I instruct myself, fighting not to think about Buck's big burned foot and the other things they say are big on a man with big feet. (Dan wears a size nine.)

~24~

We arrive back at my apartment Sunday night, and as soon as we walk through the door I am overwhelmed by how much I want—no, need—to get back together with Dan. What actually overwhelms me is the smell in the apartment. The roses from my engagement night, now over a week old, have rotted and filled the entire room with the stench of their decay. I remove the once crimson red roses that have turned black and drooped over, while making a dramatic connection in my mind that the roses represent my relationship with Dan. Unlike these blooms, though, our relationship will be glorious again soon.

I open the windows and light a pink, rose-scented candle to try to freshen the apartment's air. Since Dan is so good about bringing me roses, I am an expert; I know that they aren't as fragrant during some seasons as others. When they don't smell as good, I light the candle to assist them. I marvel at how lucky I am to have (had) a boyfriend so attentive that I am an expert on rose scents—I absolutely have to spend the rest of my life with him.

We aren't home fifteen minutes when Courtney arrives at my door. She had gotten wind that we are about to begin scheming, which is her number one hobby, and she refuses to be left out.

"Hello, team," she says, breezing in with a devious smile, dressed in a white tank top, floor-length peasant skirt, and gold flip-flops. Her curls are exceptionally wild and her thin arms are wrapped around two brown paper bags from Gelson's. "I've got supplies," she informs us, setting the bags on the table.

Tiffany immediately gets up and starts poking through them.

"There should be three pints of Häagen-Dazs in there," Courtney says, pointing to the bags.

"I'll put them in the freezer," Tiffany offers, and quickly separates the ice cream from the Pepperidge Farm Milanos, peanut-butter-filled pretzels, and Doritos.

"I thought you were going all organic," I say, surveying the feast of junk food. The last time I'd talked to Courtney she'd explained to me that her body was a temple and she would no longer pollute the temple with anything unnatural.

"Yeah . . . that was a pain in the ass. It was completely inconvenient to try to get to Whole Foods all the time, and Gelson's is, like, right around the corner . . . blah-blah-blah," Courtney says and shrugs. This isn't the first diet plan she's started and stopped. "So, how was the funeral, et cetera?"

"It was actually really good—obviously sad, but it was good for me to visit home," I say.

Courtney throws her head around, causing her curls to spring up and down, and gives me a look. "I've never heard you call Victory 'home' before."

"Well, it was different this time," I say, not really wanting to get into all the details right now.

Thankfully, Courtney's attention span is limited and there are other topics that interest her much more than my emotional growth.

"Did you see Buck?" she asks in a girlish way as Tiffany is walking back into the room carrying a bowl of dulce de leche.

"We stayed with him," she says nonchalantly, as she digs away at a caramel swirl.

"It was no big deal," I say, my cheeks flushing. "My parents turned my room into an exercise office and he has a guest room."

I quickly cross over to the partially unloaded Gelson's bag and busy myself pulling out more junk food in hopes that nobody will notice that I am bright scarlet.

"Soooo?" Courtney asks, dragging out the "o."

"It's no big deal," I reiterate, trying not to sound uncomfortable, but of course coming off like I'm extremely uncomfortable (which I am). Why did Buck Platner have to come up, and *why* is the thought of him evoking this type of reaction from me? Especially when I'm on the cusp of getting my life plan back on track!

Courtney looks confused for a split second before specifying her question. "Did he ask about me?!?" she practically shrieks as her own cheeks blush a pretty, feminine pink.

Oh God—I'd forgotten that Courtney had set her sights on Buck. Not only did I have an inappropriate almost-moment and mental fantasy about someone other than my ex/soon-to-be-reunited-with fiancé, I'd done it with the person that my best friend is interested in!

"Um, no . . . sorry," I say, not actually feeling sorry that this information wasn't what Courtney wanted to hear.

"Hmmm . . . he didn't? I wonder why not?" she asks out loud, but the question is probably directed inward. It is incomprehensible to Courtney that the person of the minute isn't as instantly infatuated with her as she is with him.

"You can ask him yourself, he's coming down this weekend," Tiffany says with a mouth full of ice cream.

"He is?!?" Courtney and I shoot to attention in unison.

Tiffany starts nodding "Yes" before moaning, "Brain freeze," and burying her head in her hands.

Seeming satisfied with the information that Buck will be within her clutches in less than a week, Courtney grabs a bag of Pirate's Booty. "I think these might be organic," she says, while shoving a fistful in. "Anyway, let's get scheming," she says mischievously.

Tiffany and I join her on the floor. Courtney pulls a yellow legal pad clipped to a SparkleCourt bedazzled clipboard from her black Furla bag and takes the top off a silver Tiffany pen.

"Ideas?" she asks looking around the circle.

I can't help but giggle because I feel like I'm at a meeting of the Baby Sitters Club or something; but then I quickly pull it together because this is actually of the utmost importance.

"I have some," Tiffany says confidently, and begins to list them. A handful I feel like she saw on the show *Friends*—although I'm not going to discount them, since Ross and Rachel *did* get together in the end. I certainly don't want to wait eight years or whatever it took them, but as long as I don't sleep with anyone else while Dan and I are on this little break, it shouldn't be an issue.

The thought of sleeping with someone else momentarily sends a flash of Buck's heart-stopping smile into my mind, but I chase it away with a thought of Dan's sweet grin and the house behind a white picket fence that life with him will provide. Life will be like it was in the beginning of *American Beauty* before everything got all fucked up, I promise myself. Now a vision of myself in Wellington gardening clogs from Smith & Hawken peacefully fills my mind. My attention is snapped back to the Baby Sitters Club when I hear Courtney explaining one of the many approaches she has used to get a boyfriend back.

"You know, after Pietro broke up with me, we not only got back together, we got back together with an engagement," she tells Tiffany with an all-knowing wink.

Before I can protest, since I already know the story of

Courtney and Pietro, she is explaining. Courtney met Pietro at Lake Como in Italy while taking some time off after her failed legal career and before her failed acting career. Supposedly Pietro's lineage was Italian royalty, but he had been educated in the United States since middle school and was also vacationing on Lake Como when he and Courtney met. As is always the case with Courtney, she was madly in love before she could pronounce his last name and spent four weeks having nonstop sex with him. At the scheduled end of his vacation, he said good-bye with little more than a pat on her head. This obviously devastated Courtney.

Apparently there had been quite a lack of communication between the two, since Pietro thought they were simply having a fling and Courtney thought she had discovered her soul mate. Pietro returned to New York City and the kind of life that Americanized Italian royals can live there, and Courtney returned to Los Angeles devastated and determined to show Pietro what she knew in her heart. A week later, she showed up in the lobby of his Park Avenue apartment house (how she got the address she has still never admitted) and announced that she was pregnant with his child.

As any noble, royal *Catholic* would do, he immediately proposed marriage, which Courtney gleefully accepted. She had already met with Mindy Weiss four times when Pietro figured out that she wasn't currently nor had she ever been pregnant with his child. The engagement didn't even last as long as the fling, but—and it's the end here that creates an aura of awe around Courtney Cambridge—when he confronted Courtney about the fake pregnancy, she became outrageously indignant, broke up with *him* and threw the seven-carat canary yellow diamond engagement ring he had given her out the window of her Wilshire Boulevard penthouse, screaming that it had "always looked like piss!"

That's a Courtney patented maneuver: she never gets dumped. The thing is, she actually gets dumped *all the time*, but always manages to get the dumper to take her back for just long enough so that she can dump him. Obviously, Courtney's version of the Pietro story is a bit skewed, and she is just getting to the part about throwing the ring out the window as a wide-eyed Tiffany stares in either horror or amazement (or maybe both). Finally I have to cut in.

"That won't work in this case," I say matter-of-factly, and Courtney shoots me a dirty look for ruining the climactic finale of her story.

"Why not?" she asks, annoyed.

"Dan broke up with me specifically because he doesn't want to have children and thought I was hiding one from him. I don't think saying I'm pregnant is going to make him come back to me. I think it's only going to reconfirm his suspicions and make him resent me more."

Courtney takes a second to process this information before nodding in agreement, "Okay, you're right. Let's start with one of your ideas then," she says, turning to Tiffany.

Tiffany smiles nervously at me and then the two girls explain step one in the plan to get Dan and me back together forever.

~25~

Buck was actually on the verge of giving up on Lizzie. Here he'd spent his entire adult life thinking about what he'd missed with her and how no woman could ever measure up—and then they were miraculously reunited and she turned out to have become a total bitch. The girl he remembered from high school was gone. Sure, Lizzie was beautiful back then and now, but there was something else about her that made her uncontrollably attractive to Buck. Unlike so many girls, she was confident and driven. She didn't sleep around—she didn't sleep with anyone, focusing instead on her dream of going to college and becoming a news reporter. She participated in life at Victory High, but almost as if she were a visitor to the campus, never fully giving herself to anyone or anything in Victory . . . except her best friend, Charla. It was her fierce loyalty that Buck admired most about her.

When Buck learned that Charla had named Lizzie as her daughter's guardian, he was impressed that even though (to his knowledge) Lizzie had never come back to visit her hometown, she and Charla had remained best friends. Obviously, he quickly found out that this was not the case. The Lizzie he encountered in Los Angeles was a shell of the person she had been, but Buck couldn't let go of his belief that the old Lizzie was still there.

After the funeral, Buck's faith was restored, as the Lizzie he remembered suddenly reappeared. Not only was it an enormous relief that she was finally stepping up to her role as Tiffany's godmother, it was a huge turn-on, too. Buck's feelings for her soared once more. Saturday evening, spent only eating pizza and reminiscing about Victory and their high school days, felt like a dream come true. Sunday morning there had been a moment in the kitchen when he felt like he and Lizzie were on the same page and he was about to kiss her, but when Tiffany walked in he couldn't do it. Now all he could do was wait until the following weekend when he'd told Tiffany he would come down to L.A. Obviously, checking on the teenager was important to him, but it was seeing Lizzie and hopefully getting a private moment (or more) to pick up where they left off in the kitchen that was at the forefront of his mind all week long.

~26~

I sit perched on the edge of the black Aeron chair behind my desk. My cell phone headset is on and connected to Tiffany, but my eyes intensely watch the clock in the upper righthand corner of the computer screen. Today is day one of the plan to get back together with Dan. *Plan A: the accidental bump-into.* Dan is an absolute creature of habit—one of the many traits I cherish about him, and extremely helpful in planning a "surprise" meeting. I know that every Monday night Dan leaves work at exactly six o'clock and goes directly to the Gelson's in the Century City mall.

I'll have to sneak out of work a little early to pull it off—not the best career move, given my mostly unexplained absence the week before, but I will make sure that I am grocery shopping at the same Gelson's at 6:20 p.m. when Dan arrives. Tiffany and Courtney have instructed me to arrive early and fill a cart with a list of items they have prepared. Then I just plant myself in the produce department and wait for the bump.

Wanting to have plenty of time, and knowing that in L.A. you can never count on traffic or parking to go your way, at 5:55, still on the phone with Tiffany going over final details, I shut down the computer and gather my belongings.

"Okay," I say, standing up from the hammock-looking chair, "I'm ready to go."

On the other end, Tiffany encourages me. "It's going to work . . . I can feel it. Don't forget to put the lip gloss on before you see him."

"I won't forget. I'll call you on my way home—or if you don't hear from me, assume it went well," I say with a surge of excitement. "Bye."

I press the button on the headset's base that ends the call before carefully removing it from my head and placing the headband on a black metal holder. I glance down quickly at the desk. It's as immaculate as you would expect—almost empty except for a black leather desk set and a pewter three-face clock from Pottery Barn displaying times for Los Angeles, New York, and London. In all honesty, I really only need to know what time it is in Los Angeles, but it feels like the kind of item a news reporter would have, so I bought it on clearance after Christmas last year. With a rush of guilt, I straighten the growing pile of papers in the inbox; it is highly unusual for me to leave the office when there is still work to be done, but I have to prioritize, and right now, getting back together with Dan is number one—I'm sure Diane Sawyer would do the same thing if she and Mike Nichols were on the outs. There is also a nagging fear that Renee, who hadn't exactly been understanding about the week of "illness," will find out I'm sneaking out.

"Hope, I'm still not feeling a hundred percent, so I'm going to head home a bit early today. You can reach me there if you need anything," I say, putting one hand on my stomach. I have already coordinated with Tiffany that if work calls the house, which I know is unlikely, she will explain that my fever has spiked again and I've gone to bed for the night.

"Poor Elizabeth," Hope says sweetly, "don't worry about work. Go home and feel better."

I smile weakly and feel another surge of guilt flip my stomach over, giving me a real reason to have my hand on my abdomen. I quickly exit the building, taking the back staircase instead of the elevator to reduce the chances of running into anyone. Once outside, I dart to my car and jump in. My heart races as I start the BMW's engine, saying a silent prayer that the car won't pick today to get fussy on me, and put it in reverse. I don't realize until I gulp for air as the car glides down the driveway that I have been holding my breath. I'm filled with relief that I'm officially off the property and that I noticed that the spot right by the door marked "R. Foster" was already empty.

I fly down Olympic and reach Century City in record time. I quickly park the car and walk briskly into the supermarket. Once inside, I retrieve Tiffany and Courtney's list from my purse and glance at my watch. It's ten after six . . . I have ten minutes to find—I hold the list up and count—eight items. I can do this. I feel like a preteen girl on a scavenger hunt. First on the list: "white wine—not too cheap," in Courtney's loopy writing. I have shopped at the market enough times with Dan to know where things are, and I quickly head toward the aisle filled with bottles of wine.

Three minutes later, the first three items (wine, Brie, and a long loaf of French bread) are in my cart. I lift the list out of my purse again and scan down to the fourth item—once again, it is written in Courtney's hand: "condoms." What?

I grab my cell phone and dial Courtney's cell phone. She answers almost immediately. "Condoms?!?" I ask.

"We want it to look like you're going to be entertaining," she explains shamelessly.

"Courtney! Do you really think he'll take me back if he thinks I'm already sleeping with someone else?" I ask, half disgusted at the thought and half thinking of my Buck Platner/kitchen floor fantasy.

"Jealousy is a very powerful tool," she informs me.

"He'd never believe it anyway . . . he knows me," I remind her.

Sex is not exactly something that I take lightly. I have only been with three people in my life, including Dan, and each of the three I believed was "the one," when I went to bed with him. The first had been my college boyfriend, Gary Kramer. We met in the fall of my sophomore year. Gary fit my profile: he was a handsome, well-bred midwesterner (or at least what a girl from Victory considered well bred—his parents were still married to each other), plus he was prelaw and a member of one of the campus's top fraternities. We met at one of my sorority "date dash" parties, where every girl brings a single male that she herself isn't interested in. One of my pledge sisters had dated Gary briefly before deciding that they were better as friends. One woman's trash is another woman's treasure. Almost immediately, I could picture myself getting pinned, engaged, and married to Gary. Still, I waited until our one-year anniversary to have sex. We stayed together until Gary, who was one year older than I am, suddenly dumped me before going off to law school.

The second had been Jeff Jones. Jeff and I met at the end of our senior year at UCLA in a journalism ethics class. Jeff wasn't an exact match for the part of my plan, which stipulated marrying a doctor or a lawyer, but since things had gone so wrong with Gary when he left to pursue his higher education, the thought of someone not in need of further schooling was appealing. I had just started to get over Gary when Jeff ended a study group by kissing me goodnight, so I decided to accept his invitation for dinner the following night. Dinner turned into a two-year relationship, which ended four months before I met Dan when Jeff moved to Washington to be a White House correspondent for CNN. Not only was I once again being left behind for bigger and better things, it was a job that I had also applied for. Soon afterward,

Courtney introduced me to Daniel McCafferty, and you know the rest.

"Fine," Courtney concedes, "you don't have to buy the condoms."

"Thank you," I say, hanging up the phone and looking to the next item. "Cocktail napkins," I say under my breath and make a U-turn with my cart.

It is 6:19 when I arrive in the produce section to procure the final item on my list, apples, and where I will pretend to be shocked to see Dan. Since he always begins his shopping in this department, my timing is perfect. I hang around the somewhat meager selection of apples and wonder why Courtney and Tiffany hadn't put a more seasonally appropriate fruit on my list. It's summertime . . . shouldn't I be buying peaches or watermelon? I look down at the items in my cart and remember that it is supposed to look like I'm shopping to entertain; the apples would go well with the bread and cheese. I put a few gala apples in a plastic bag and then, since there is no sign of Dan yet, I make an executive decision to also get strawberries. Not only would they go well with the pint of vanilla Häagen-Dazs that is melting in my basket, they are Dan's favorite.

I arrive in front of the strawberries and pretend to examine each little green plastic basket. In reality, I am relentlessly watching the door for Dan's arrival. I am so focused on the door that I don't notice a friendly-faced grocer approach, and I jump a mile when he says,

"Can I help you pick out a basket of berries?"

"Oh, uh, no . . . I'm just browsing," I say lamely, trying to recover from such a surprise.

"Okee-doke. Lemme know if you change your mind," he says with a smile and then steps away to hose off the romaine lettuce.

I smile and catch my breath while continuing to loiter in front of the strawberries. It's 6:25—where is Dan? My insides start to tense that he's not coming, that for some reason there has been a change to his schedule. "What if he has a date?" I ask myself in horror. Just as I start to build his fictional date up in my mind as a stunning blonde lawyer, I see him enter the market pushing a metal cart. I tense even more—this is it.

I focus on my breathing and remaining calm. I turn away from the door and wait until I think we will be almost face-to-face before turning around. Instead, I find myself face-to-face with the same grocer, giving me such a fright that I cry out.

"You sure you don't need a hand with those straws?" he asks.

"I said I'm fine!" I snap, pissed off that this man has frightened me twice and has now thrown me off my game.

Before the grocer can say another word, I see Dan approaching from my left side.

"Elizabeth, is that you?" he asks coolly from halfway down the aisle.

"Oh my God, Dan! What a surprise," I say, and I realize too late that I sound like a moronic sorority girl, not the sophisticated woman I was hoping to come across as. "Thanks again for your help," I say sweetly to the grocer, who gives me a look like I am crazy (which I probably am). "Dan, how are you?" I say turning back in his direction, but he's gone.

I quickly scan the entire produce department and he's nowhere to be seen. Panic creeps into my chest and I cut across the market looking down each aisle for Dan. How can someone have disappeared into thin air? I pick up my cell phone and dial his number. The phone goes directly to voice mail and I leave a message,

"Hey, it's Elizabeth. I thought I just saw you at Gelson's, but now you're nowhere to be found. Anyway, your phone probably doesn't get reception in here, but I'm going to be in the coffee bar area for a while, so when you finish your shopping if you want to grab a latte and catch up, I'd love to . . .

it's been too long." I hit the red "end" button and feel that my mouth has somehow turned into a runaway train. "It's been too long?" I replay in my mind . . . it's been like a week and a half.

Feeling slightly humiliated, but holding out hope, I pay for my groceries and sit down in the little area of the bakery where they make coffee drinks. I sit there for an hour before coming to terms with the fact that Dan won't be joining me. I pick up the brown paper bag with my groceries, and my now liquid ice cream runs through the bottom corner. I sigh and tell myself to prepare for Plan B.

~27~

When it got close to eight o'clock and Tiffany hadn't heard from Elizabeth, she started to assume things had gone well. She was wrong. Just as she'd started to relax and feel confidant that Elizabeth was with Dan, she heard the key turn in the door and her stomach turned into a knot. If things had gone well, would she be home? Wouldn't she be spending the night with him? Maybe not, Tiffany told herself . . . maybe there was a chance that they were happily reconciled, but because both had work early the next morning Elizabeth was returning home alone? Or maybe, her mind continued to race, Dan was with Elizabeth? Maybe, Tiffany thought excitedly, Lizzie had told him all about her and he was eager to meet her.

All the questions were answered without one word. As soon as the butterfly lock flipped to the side and the door opened, Tiffany knew from Elizabeth's face that the evening had not been a success. She came through the door silently, carrying a soggy-bottomed grocery bag in one arm and her workbag in the other. The lip gloss Tiffany had reminded Elizabeth to apply had worn off and was left in little globs along the inner edge of her lips. Tiffany sat on the couch in silence, not sure what to say, as Elizabeth set the bags down on the table.

"Did work call?" she asked, sounding genuinely concerned.

"Nope, you're in the clear," Tiffany said, trying to sound upbeat.

"Good. I'm going to bed," Elizabeth said, sounding truly exhausted.

"G'night," Tiffany replied sweetly. She was desperate to hear the details but didn't dare push Elizabeth to share them. A few minutes later, the phone rang and Tiffany jumped to grab it after the first ring. Courtney was on the other end.

"Oh my God, she's not home?!?" Courtney shrieked.

"No, she's home," Tiffany told her quietly.

"She is? How'd it go?"

"Not well," Tiffany answered almost in a whisper.

"What happened?" Courtney asked, confused, since she thought the plan was pretty foolproof. She herself had used the supermarket bump-in on several occasions and it had always been a success.

"I don't know. She went straight to bed," Tiffany informed her.

"Damn it," Courtney cursed. "She should have bought the condoms."

Tiffany had no idea what she was talking about. The two girls agreed that Plan B would be more successful and said good night. It was still very early, and Tiffany tended to be a night owl anyway. She curled up on the couch that she knew hadn't often been curled up on and turned to a movie she had seen TBS advertising during the day.

Early the next morning, a much brighter-eyed Elizabeth stood at the door of the the guest room that had become Tiffany's. Tiffany was still asleep—she had probably gone to bed only a few hours earlier.

"Tiffany," Elizabeth whispered louder and louder until the volume was her normal speaking voice and loud enough to wake the teenager.

"Lizzie?" Tiffany groaned, forgetting Elizabeth's preference for her full name.

"I'm ready for Plan B," she said determinedly.

Tiffany opened her eyes and saw Elizabeth dressed in a black tank top and khaki capri pants. She rolled on her side and saw it was not quite eight.

"Okay, Plan B," Tiffany agreed.

"I've got to get to work and get caught up. When I get home tonight, we'll work out the details. Make sure Courtney is here," she said. "I'm getting my life back on track," she added, and Tiffany felt as if Elizabeth were commanding herself as much as she was informing Tiffany.

As instructed, Tiffany made sure that she and Courtney were there waiting for Elizabeth when she returned from work that night. Courtney arrived an hour before Elizabeth was due home so that she and Tiffany could go over the instructions for Plan B, but instead Courtney spent the entire hour asking Tiffany questions about Buck Platner. It almost seemed as if she were researching him in preparation for his visit in a few days. Courtney seemed nice enough to Tiffany, and she thought that if Buck had a girlfriend in Los Angeles his visits would be more frequent, so she was happy to share everything she knew about Buck with Courtney. Secretly, she wished that Buck and Lizzie would end up together, but she considered Courtney to be the next best thing.

When Elizabeth got home, the three girls sat down to go over Plan B. Courtney and Tiffany knew she wasn't going to like it and had played several rounds of rock-paper-scissors to decide who would explain the plan. Tiffany was quite relieved that Courtney had lost in the final sudden death round by throwing scissors to Tiffany's rock.

"Okay, you're not going to like it . . . but it's going to work and it's less extreme than Plan C or D," Courtney began, and Tiffany noted it was the first time she'd seen Lizzie's friend proceed with caution. "It's called a reverse rear-end—"

"A reverse rear-end?" Lizzie repeated, already sounding skeptical.

"Here's what happens," Courtney began to explain. "You'll need to position yourself in front of Dan at a red light. When the light turns green, you quickly throw your car into reverse and back into him. As soon as there is impact, put your car back in drive. He'll assume he hit you and not the other way around."

Lizzie looked sickened by the plan but didn't say a word. In the short time Tiffany had known Lizzie, it was clear not only that she loved (cherished) her little old BMW but that she liked to keep everything around her as perfect and pristine as possible. Plan B was damaging to both of these desires.

"I saw it once on *Beverly Hills, 90210* and it works," Courtney said matter-of-factly, as if *Beverly Hills, 90210* was a source more impressive than an out-of-date primetime soap opera.

"Someone got back together with a man by doing this?" Lizzie asked, still looking extremely unconvinced.

"Well, no," Courtney admitted, "it wasn't exactly like this. A woman did the reverse rear-end to Brenda and then tried to sue for a lot of money, but Brenda felt so badly about hurting the woman she went to her house and found her working out. But it's the Brenda feeling so badly part that really applies here. Dan will feel horrible at the thought of hurting you, and in doing so, he'll realize how much he still cares about you."

Elizabeth's expression started to change from doubtful to hopeful. Tiffany thought she was going to agree to it, but instead she shook her head from side to side, "I dunno. What's Plan C?"

"It's way more extreme," Tiffany piped up, breaking her silence.

"Oh, and by the way," Courtney cut back in. "You should do a 'did you call me?' in a couple of days."

"A 'did you call me?' " Elizabeth looked confused.

"Yeah, you call Dan, and when he answers you say, 'Did you just call me, because I saw your number on my caller ID?' " Courtney explained.

"So he hears your voice and thinks about you, but without being stockerish and calling him for no reason," Tiffany adds, reciting verbatim the explanation Courtney had given her.

"Okay, I'll do that. Now, what is Plan C?" Lizzie pressed.

"It involves volunteering for jury duty in Dan's courtroom," Courtney said, hoping Elizabeth would reject the idea.

Instead, the hopeful expression returned to Lizzie's face. "Let's try that one next," she said definitively.

Tiffany and Courtney looked at each other before both shrugging and giving in.

"Okay," they all agreed and put their heads together to plot the new Plan C.

~28~

The night Tiffany and Courtney had explained their original Plan C, which I had bumped up to be the new Plan B, it had sounded genius and foolproof. Now it is Friday morning—a mere four days since the failed supermarket run into—and I'm dressing to go into the Beverly Hills courthouse and volunteer for jury duty. It sounds fairly insane. I mean, seriously, what kind of nut actually *volunteers* for jury duty? Most people try desperately to get out of it. Plus, on top of the very real risk of coming off like a crazy person, the "did you just call me?" call hadn't gone very well.

First, I got Dan's voice mail, panicked, and hung up. Then I realized that I should have left a message, so he could hear my voice and miss me, but when I called back he answered. When I said, "Did you just call me?" He said, "No, you just called me." Which I had, but for some reason I decided to lie (badly) about it. "No, my caller ID says I missed a call from you," I insisted. We went back and forth a few times in what I hoped he would consider adorable banter, but I'm quite certain Dan didn't because finally he said, "Well, I didn't call you. Good-bye," and hung up.

"Tiffany!" I roar from in front of my open closet. "What's a good jury duty outfit?" I ask as she walks into the room.

I have quickly gone from despising Tiffany's existence to

being grateful for her presence every single day. She is so much like her mom, except in the ways in which she was exactly like me.

"I need an outfit that is seductive enough to win Dan back but conservative enough that I can get on a jury," I explain, aware that nothing in my closet is at all seductive. "And how dressed up am I supposed to be?" I ask, thinking about the beautiful Brooks Brothers suits Dan always wore to work.

I had gone shopping with him once, about eight months ago, for suits. I felt like we were playing pretend as I sat in a brocade wingback chair and watched as he modeled gorgeous cashmere suits in front of a three-way mirror. The suits were ridiculously expensive, but Dan had explained that when you're an attorney you have to look a certain way to get a certain type of respect. I completely understood what he was talking about and helped him select one gray pinstriped and one navy blue suit. I wonder if he'll be wearing one today? I especially love him in the navy blue.

"I don't think people get very dressed up for jury duty," Tiffany says, raising her eyebrows and scrunching her nose. She is thinking what I know—what everyone knows: most people don't care how they look for jury duty because they'd rather be anywhere in the world but there. "Wear jeans," she instructs.

I end up wearing my Seven jeans with a black sleeveless top from Ann Taylor and black wedge sandals. It's casual without looking like I am dressed to clean out the garage, as my mother would say. The Queen of Keds and pedal pushers would frequently scowl at anyone dressed more casually than herself and hiss, "She looks like she's dressed to clean out her garage." I probably wouldn't even wear the type of stuff my mom does while cleaning out my garage, but I don't have a garage, so I guess I can't say for sure. Plus, Keds are coming back with the whole Mischa Barton campaign thing. I should probably stop bad-mouthing them.

I put some work papers and the copy of *Living History*, Hillary Clinton's autobiography, that Dan had given me but I had never even opened, in my bag and head out the door. I feel the kind of nervous excitement you feel on your first day of a new job. I know from a jury summons Courtney received and ignored that new jurors are supposed to arrive at the courthouse at 7:45 a.m., so that's what I'm doing. At such an early hour there isn't any traffic, and I arrive at the Beverly Hills courthouse at 7:35. I quickly apply a fresh coat from my Lancôme Juicy Tube and head toward the building. I figure the fewer people around to hear me explain that I haven't been summoned but that I am volunteering to serve on jury duty the better.

I enter the building and am immediately sorry that I am wearing a sleeveless top and haven't brought a sweater. The building is cooled to around the temperature of a refrigerator. I guess that's how Dan can wear wool suits all day and be comfortable. I find my way through security and upstairs to the door marked "Jury Room." There are a handful of people standing around in the long hallway. One man, in a shirt and tie, is yelling into his cell phone. People who yell into their cell phones are high on my list of pet peeves. A couple of other people are reading the newspaper, and one woman is just staring miserably out the window. I pause and wonder what they are here for. Are they criminals, attorneys, or have they been subpoenaed? Unfortunately, I don't have time to think about it. I stride past them, careful not to make eye contact in case they are killers—although none of them looks particularly threatening—and reach for the handle to the jury room door. I pull and it doesn't budge. It's locked. I juggle it a little to no avail, and then I knock. At this point, the girl staring out the window speaks.

"I don't know why they told us to get here at seven forty-five . . . nobody's even here."

Oh, she's a fellow juror. "Nobody's here?"

"Not a soul," she says, turning back toward the window.

"Crap," I think to myself as I lean against the wall and pull Hillary's memoir out of my bag. I had really hoped to get myself signed up. Oh well. I look up and down the hallway. Maybe I'll run into Dan, just standing here, and I won't have to go through with the whole jury service thing anyway. I open the book about a quarter of the way through and pretend to read as I peer over the top at the people moving up and down the hall and those gathering in front of the sealed "Jury Room."

Almost an hour later, a grouchy-looking woman opens the door to the jury room. She has a large, unattractive mole on her neck and I can't help wondering why she never bothered to have it removed. Not only is it ugly, it looks possibly cancerous as well. The wait had gotten so long and boring that I had resorted to actually reading the former first lady's life story and was legitimately a quarter of the way through when Neck Mole stood her squat frame on a chair and waved a flabby arm over her head.

"Attention, jurors! None of the following are acceptable reasons to be excused from jury service: work demands, transportation hardships, physical ailments—including hearing loss, vision loss, or overactive bladder—scheduled travel, or religious beliefs."

The statement is met by groans from the crowd, which I join in on in an effort to fit in. I will definitely have to keep my volunteer status on the down low.

"If anybody has any issues they need to discuss above and beyond those I just listed, please form a single file line in front of me."

This is my moment. I snap the page shut and hurry to the front of the line. Without looking down, Neck Mole says, "Last name?"

"Castle," I reply.

She scans the long list attached to her crummy brown

clipboard. It makes me think about my red clipboard at work and gives me a slight pang of guilt for missing yet another day on the job.

"With a C?" she asks.

"Yes, C-A-S-T-L-E," I spell.

"I don't have you here. Lemme see your summons," she says holding out her hand. She still stands on the chair, but isn't that much taller than I am.

"Oh, um, actually . . . I don't have a summons . . . I'm here to volunteer," I explain with a smile.

"VOLUNTEER?!?" she shouts loudly enough for everyone surrounding me to stop what they are doing and look in my direction.

"Yes, that's right. Specifically, in whichever courtroom Daniel McCafferty is in today," I add in a whisper.

"You seriously want to volunteer for jury duty?" she asks again, looking at me like I'm crazy. It is a look I have prepared myself for.

I swallow, take a breath and nod.

She shrugs and climbs off the chair, "Lemme go see if we have a form for that."

She waddles back into the jury room, and returns a short time later with a piece of paper.

"We don't actually have volunteer forms. Write your name and address down here and I'll get you in the system. I can't promise you'll be in your boyfriend's court though . . . and anyway, if you were you'd probably get dismissed. I think there's rules about that."

"Oh, actually, he's my ex-fiancé," I explain with a meaningful look.

For a split second, Neck Mole and I connect. She gives me a tiny crack of a smile before saying, "Write down that info and I'll get you in the system."

"Thanks," I say, heading back through the crowd to find something I can lean on.

I quickly jot down my information and turn to bring it back to Neck Mole, but I see that a long line has now formed in front of her. Not wanting to draw extra attention to myself, I go stand in the back of the line. It takes an eternity to make my way up to the front, but when I do, Neck Mole steps down off her chair to take my paper.

"Your boyfriend's court is in session today," she says with another tiny smile. "I don't know if the judge will let you stay, but I'll assign you to that room."

"Oh my gosh, you are a doll," I tell her gratefully and feel bad for having such nasty thoughts about her unfortunate growth.

"I was engaged once, too," she tells me, sounding slightly wistful.

I can't stop myself from wondering if the mole was what ended her relationship. I certainly wouldn't want to roll over in bed and see that thing staring back at me for the rest of my life. She takes my paper and with an *oof* sound climbs back up on the chair.

"Okay, the following people will report to courtroom six today." She starts calling names and each one is followed by a groan or a grunt. When she finally says "Elizabeth Castle," I make a groaning sound just to fit in but give her a small, grateful wink as I turn and head in the direction of the courtroom.

"Oh, Ms. Castle," Neck Mole calls after me. "Don't forget your badge." She hands me a small cardboard badge in a clear plastic holder with my newly appointed juror number handwritten with a black Sharpee.

"Thanks," I say as I take the badge. As I walk away I try to figure out where to clip the thing on my tank top. Again, I am quite sorry I didn't bring some sort of sweater. At last I decide to clip it to the bottom of my shirt at my hipbone. I follow my fellow jurors into the courtroom in a single-file line. As we enter, a bailiff directs us to fill a row of movie theater–style seats that make up the audience (is that what you call people watching a trial?) section of a courtroom.

I get a little wave of excitement because the room almost looks like a movie set. It's exactly how courtrooms look on television: there is a high-countered desk for the judge at the front of the room, and a little desk for the court reporter on the floor in front of it. There is a table on either side of the room for the prosecutor and defender and their clients, and a box of more movie theater–style seats for the jury. My excitement grows, because seated at the table on the right side of the room is Dan! His back is to me, and my heart flutters at the sight of his cleanly shaved neck. He is dressed in the navy blue suit—suddenly I'm glad I'm wearing the tank top because the temperature in the room has suddenly gone up! He's bent over a pile of papers and is furiously scribbling notes on a yellow legal pad. I can tell just by looking what a good attorney he is, and I hope the others jurors see it, too.

I follow the leader down a row of seats and sit without taking my eyes off Dan. No sooner are we seated than the bailiff holds up a list and starts calling names.

"The following people should take the seat I assign to them in the jury box. Understood?" We all nod. "Carl Woods, take seat one." We all watch as a middle-aged man stands up and makes his way to the jury box. The bailiff has the jury box about half full when he says, "Elizabeth Castle, take seat nine." I had been gazing at Dan so intently that I jump at the sound of my own name. Dan also jumps at the sound of my name and turns around. Our eyes meet and I give him a little wave. He stands up and walks toward me. We meet right at the little gate that separates the audience area from the rest of the room.

"Hi," I say quietly. I don't want to make the others jealous that I know the district attorney.

"She can't be on this case," Dan says to the bailiff without looking at me.

"Take it up with the judge," the bailiff replies without taking his eyes off his list of names. "Melissa Moonridge, take seat ten."

I pause awkwardly for a second, thinking Dan is going to talk to me, but without a word he turns and storms back to his desk. After a beat, I hurry to seat nine. I guess he's not allowed to talk to members of the jury.

Once all the seats in the jury box are full, and the remainder of our group stands in position to move in as people are dismissed during voir dire, the bailiff leaves the courtroom through a door at the opposite side of the room from the one we came in through. It really is like a set—and he's just gone backstage. Tiffany would love this place, since she's fascinated with anything at all "Hollywood." The girl has come to so many tapings of *The Renee Foster Show!* in the short time she's been here that I wonder how she doesn't lose her mind.

I glance around at the other people seated in the jury box. Naturally, they all look unhappy to be there. Next I look out across the courtroom. Dan has returned to his desk and the pile of files he has on it. The defense attorney, a woman around my age, talks quietly to her client, an almost teenage-looking boy. She has her long blonde hair pulled back in a low French braid, and I don't notice until she looks up to glance at the panel of jurors assembled how bright her green eyes are. She's wearing a smart black suit with a knee-length skirt that looks like it came from Ann Taylor. She takes in the jury for another beat before putting her head back down next to her client again. A few seconds later she gets up and crosses to Dan's side of the room. The defender leans against the side of Dan's desk and he leans back, arms folded across his chest, and smiles at her.

Panic grips me and my chest feels tight. Aren't the prosecutor and the defender supposed to be enemies? They're on opposite sides! Dan can't talk to a juror who is his fiancée (ex-fiancée), but he can mingle with the opposing counsel? A strange, sharp gasping noise escapes my throat when Dan laughs his full, open-mouthed laugh at something this attorney has said. I get a strange look from the juror to my left, and I try to mask my bizarre sound with a cough.

"Sorry, allergies," I explain lamely.

The fellow juror tries to scoot away from me, but the chairs are fused together with a single, shared armrest between them. I'm too focused on what is happening in front of me to notice her attempt. The slutty prosecutor is now leaning over toward Dan, and if I'm not mistaken (which I'm not), he can easily see down the light blue silk blouse she is wearing. Where on earth is the judge? Shouldn't he be in here to put an end to this fraternizing of enemies?

A higher power hears my pleas, and I am relieved to see the bailiff return through the door he exited. When the slut sees him, she puts her hand on Dan's shoulder and they both smile, causing another gurgling gasp from me and another dirty look from my neighbor.

"Sorry, I think these seats are wool," I whisper stupidly.

"All rise for the honorable Judge William Santos," the bailiff commands the room. I rise, eagerly anticipating a man who in my mind looks like Judge Wapner from the *People's Court* episodes of my youth. Instead, a much younger—probably in his '40s—much sterner man with hair almost as dark as his billowy black robe enters and takes his seat behind the bench.

"Be seated," he commands, and everyone obeys.

He opens a folder on his desk and quickly glances over the documents inside.

"Okay, we have the people versus Gabe North. Mr. North is accused of check fraud. We have a panel of jurors—let's get through voir dire before my tee time."

"Your honor, may I approach the bench?"

The question came from Dan. I feel a surge of pride and excitement watching him at work. He's so professional.

"Fine, Mr. McCafferty, let's make it brief, though," the judge says with a sigh of annoyance.

I am distracted by how rude Judge Santos was to Dan and don't hear him when he says, "Juror number nine, please stand."

The girl to my right, who had tried to get as far away from me as possible, pokes me in the elbow and hisses, "That's you, stand up," which snaps me back to reality.

"Number nine?" the judge repeats, obviously quickly losing his patience.

"Oh, uh, yes sir," I say quickly jumping to my feet.

"Were you involved in a personal relationship with counsel?" he asks, nodding slightly in Dan's direction.

"Yes, we're engaged," I answer, my cheeks suddenly flaming. "We were engaged," I correct myself, generously peppering my voice with sadness.

"And would this relationship cause you to be biased in any way in regard to the case he will be presenting?" the judge asks sternly.

"Absolutely not," I reply, suddenly feeling a little frightened by him.

"Then it's fine. You may sit down, number nine."

"Your Honor!" Dan protests as I take my seat. "She cannot stay on this jury. Let's bring in one of the alternates."

"She said she won't be biased, all jurors take an oath, and I want to finish this case before my vacation," Judge Santos says without even looking at Dan.

He sighs and returns to his seat. I silently cheer that I'll be staying on the case. I can picture Dan and me getting lunch in the courthouse cafeteria (I wonder if there is one), or going for a drink after court at a bar like the one the people on *Ally McBeal* went to. By the time this guy goes to jail, or wherever people who commit check fraud go, Dan and I will be back together forever.

I spend the rest of the afternoon daydreaming about the

reconciliation celebration that Dan and I will have—I don't need to pay attention to the case since obviously I'm on Dan's side. I'm thinking maybe dinner at Crustacean . . . or spending the night at the Hotel Bel Air and getting room service. And maybe the passion of makeup sex will give Dan a boost in the bedroom that will benefit us both.

I'll be honest—I've never had *great* sex. Of the select group I have been with, some (all) have been better than Dan, but nobody has been mind-blowing—or even bending. It's the one and only area of my relationship with Dan that doesn't exactly fit into my fantasy plan, since ideally my husband and soul mate would be able to give me an orgasm. It's okay, though, because I'm a good faker and Dan usually likes to go to sleep shortly after he comes—which doesn't take very long—and then I can sneak into the bathroom with my dildo and finish the job. I wonder where I'll hide my dildo once we are living together?

Before I have figured out an ideal hiding place, the judge is dismissing us for the weekend with strict instructions not to discuss any part of the case with anyone outside the courtroom involved in the case or not. I was going to use the excuse of having some questions about the case to invite Dan to have a drink with me and decide not to be dissuaded. It's probably one of those rules that is meant to be broken. The jury is led out of the courtroom in a single-file line and set free in the hallway outside the courtroom.

All the other jurors scatter as if the building is on fire, but I linger in the hallway. I mosey down to one end and take a drink from a water fountain, then saunter all the way to the other end to see if Neck Mole is still in the jury room so I can thank her one more time. I assume Dan with be exiting the courtroom quickly, but it takes almost forty-five minutes for him to enter the hallway where I have been mindlessly lingering for close to an hour.

"Oh, Dan, hi!" I say brightly when I see him.

Coldly he says, "Liz, what are you still doing here?"

I feel a shiver. Dan almost never calls me Liz and it feels strange. "Oh, I just thought I'd wait and see if maybe you wanted to go grab a drink." There is a second of awkward pause, and in a desperate attempt I add, "I have a couple of questions about the case."

"We are not allowed to discuss the case. Didn't you hear Judge Santos's instructions?" he asks in a know-it-all tone that I don't particularly appreciate.

I feel like a busted kid in the sandbox. "Oh, of course—"

I don't get to say another word—to plead my own case for a drink—because the blonde defense attorney walks out of the courtroom, unraveling her dorky braid by running her fingers through her beautiful hair. She looks much better (really good) with her hair down. Without acknowledging my presence she looks at Dan and says with a smile, "You ready to go?"

He returns her smile with one of his own and says, "Sure thing." Then, without so much as a glance in my direction, they take off down the hall together.

I stand frozen in shock and horror. The humiliation stings and the heartbreak aches as I watch Dan hold open the door to the stairwell for her to walk through. He's already replaced me? I'm not quite sure what to do next. I have gotten myself stuck on this case, which means I will have God-knows-how-many days of watching Dan and Defender Bitch together. Plan B for Bust . . . another failure, and given Dan's new relationship, I'm not sure that there is any point in continuing.

I lean against the wall and try to think of an alternative life plan that could make me as happy as the one I'd pictured sharing with Dan. It just doesn't exist, and somehow I've made a mess of the few things I actually did have going for me. I've taken off so much time from work in the last month that I'm probably at risk of being fired . . . and now I'm stuck on this stupid case that will keep me out of the office even longer. Plus, I ignored all the evidence presented today, certain that I would just side with Dan, but now I don't want to—although I don't want to side with Defender Bitch, either. Things were supposed to be getting better, but undoubtedly they are getting worse.

I take a deep breath and walk toward the elevator. At least tomorrow is Saturday. I have two days to recover from today before I have to watch Dan and his new love on display. I enter the slow old elevator and press the "L" button. The doors grind shut and with great effort the car delivers me down three floors. The doors reopen as if they are pulling taffy apart and I step out into the almost empty lobby. As I leave the building, a security guard calls out, "Have a nice weekend, miss." I try to muster a smile, but I'm pretty sure I fail. He probably thinks I'm some sort of criminal who just got convicted, but I don't have the energy to let him know that I am an innocent victim.

~29~

Buck had been counting the days, hours, minutes, and seconds until the weekend and his trip to Los Angeles. On Saturday morning, without the help of an alarm clock, he got up shortly after the sun, eager to get on the road. His stomach churned like a child's on Christmas morning as he quickly showered and dressed. He quickly gave Wildcat an extra bowl of water and a heaping dish of kibble before heading out the front door and climbing into the truck he had filled with gas the night before on his way home from work.

He had talked to Tiffany yesterday afternoon and she had promised that Lizzie would be happy to have him spend the night at her apartment, since he had let her stay over at his house, which only added to Buck's excitement (and anxiety). It did offer a tiny bit of relief that she didn't hate him after their run-in in the kitchen. He thought he'd felt a spark between them, but then feeling typically insecure, he'd spent a good part of the week worrying that she felt nothing but freaked out by him. He had read her wrong at his prom, so Buck knew that there was a good chance he was reading her wrong now as well.

The highway was mostly clear at this hour on a Saturday morning except for the big tanker trucks that transport goods up and down the state. Buck set his cruise control at 75 miles per hour and ran through scenarios in his head. The first was the one in which Lizzie was thrilled to see him and openly admitted that she had thought about him as much during the week as he had thought about her. This scenario was his favorite. The others were less desirable. There was one in which she was openly hostile with him for coming on to her when she was grieving the death of her long-lost friend, another in which she was completely indifferent to him, hardly noticing his presence in her apartment, and his least favorite: the one in which she had gotten back together with the ex-boyfriend, leaving no chance of the first scenario ever becoming reality.

As he cruised along, Buck spotted a Starbucks ahead. As much as he hated to admit it to Tiffany and encourage her obsession, it was good coffee, and he could go for some right now. It wasn't quite eight o'clock and Buck was a good part of the distance to Los Angeles, so he decided to make a quick pit stop, since arriving too early and waking Lizzie up probably would greatly diminish his chances of realizing scenario one.

Inside, the Starbucks was almost empty. There was a couple waiting at the far counter to receive their prepared drinks, and a single girl sitting at a small round table with an issue of *Cosmopolitan*. The couple were clearly on their way up to the mountain and were dressed in designer resort wear. The weekend in the mountains must have been a romantic getaway for them and they were already getting started on the romance. As they waited for their beverages, the guy, who looked a few years younger than Buck, kept his hands firmly planted on the girl's round behind. Their lips remained locked, except when he broke free to give the green-aproned employee a brief thank-you nod before removing his hands from his girlfriend's ass and picking up their drinks. As he did this, she moved her affection down to his neck, which she nibbled until he stepped back and handed her the white paper cup with the brown insulation band. Only when they finally broke apart did Buck get a look at the girl. She certainly wasn't what he would have expected. She was a great deal older than the man she had been making out with. Buck did a double take, because there was something familiar about them. Only after a second look did he recognize her to be the host of the show Lizzie worked on and a man he had seen operating a camera over the monitor in Elizabeth's office. Renee Foster looked much different standing in Starbucks without her hair or makeup done. Buck thought about going up and introducing himself, but then what would he say? "Hi, I'm secretly in love with one of your employees"? His connection to Elizabeth was too complicated to explain . . . plus Renee had taken one sip of her coffee and then returned to playing tonsil hockey with her young companion. Buck collected his own drink and climbed back into the truck.

As the caffeine pulsed through his veins, he steered the oversize truck down the crowded city streets toward Lizzie's apartment. After circling the block three times, he finally lucked out and found a spot big enough for the F150, when a couple in designer sweatsuits climbed into their Hummer H2 and drove away. Buck felt a little girly doing so, but nonetheless redirected the rearview mirror so he could see himself. He ran his hand over the short hairs covering his head and checked his teeth for any remnants of his blueberry muffin. He quickly popped a Tic Tac into his mouth and chewed it up as he walked across the street and up to Elizabeth's apartment. Once at the door, he knocked quietly and then stood waiting, his heart racing with anticipation, for Lizzie to open it.

Instead, it was Tiffany who threw open the door and greeted Buck with a warm hug. He returned the hug and stepped into the apartment, purposely diverting his eyes from the small hall closet Lizzie had locked Tiffany in the last time he had been at her apartment. She had absolutely changed since then, even though it had been only a couple weeks.

"Come in, come in," Tiffany encouraged him in a loud whisper.

"Why are we whispering?" Buck asked, copying her low tone.

"Elizabeth is still asleep," she informed him. "But I'm going to wake her up anyway and see if she wants to come get pancakes with us," she added in her normal speaking voice. "I read that a lot of celebrities go to Du-Pars at the Farmers Market for pancakes on the weekend, so we've got to go there," she told Buck as she walked down the hall towards Lizzie's closed bedroom door.

Buck couldn't help smiling and wondered how long Tiffany's celebrity infatuation would last. He stood in Lizzie's foyer and waited . . . and listened.

"Pssst . . . Lizzie . . . Elizabeth. Buck and I are going for pancakes. Wanna come?" Tiffany asked.

Buck strained to hear Lizzie's response. "Buck Platner is here? Oh my God . . . I forgot he was coming," followed by muffled sounds he couldn't make out.

His heart fell that she had forgotten altogether that he was coming. The "indifference" scenario wasn't the worst, but it certainly wasn't the best. His spirits lifted slightly when Tiffany exited the darkened room and said, "She's gonna throw on clothes and come with us."

Maybe it wasn't indifference. If she was indifferent or hostile she probably wouldn't get out of bed to come eat pancakes with him, right? He and Tiffany made small talk, chatting about the happenings in her week. It seemed mostly to consist of attending tapings of the show Lizzie worked at because, according to Tiffany, that was the most surefire way to see celebrities.

"There's, like, a Starbucks on every corner and it's impossible to predict which one a celebrity will go to and when they'll be there," she explained seriously, and Buck concentrated furiously on maintaining a straight face.

She continued on, naming each celebrity she'd seen and how he or she differed from how they look on television or in the movies. Apparently, some who appeared short on screen were really rather tall, which Tiffany found fascinating, since she thought people appeared bigger on TV than in real life. Not laughing was getting harder and harder, making Buck even happier to see Elizabeth coming out of her room.

"Morning," she said with a slightly sheepish grin.

Was the sheepishness for Buck or because she had been caught still sleeping?

"Hey, there," he greeted her warmly, hoping he didn't come off as too eager. Why could he never properly control his brain-to-mouth connection?

Then, to his surprise and delight, Lizzie sleepily crossed the room and put her head against his chest in a warm embrace.

"Good to see you," she said absentmindedly and then immediately crossed over and picked up her purse. "Where for pancakes?"

"I told you, Du-Pars" Tiffany replied eagerly, "unless you know of another place where more celebrities will be," she quickly added.

"Hmmm . . . Du-Pars or Jerry's, but Du-Pars sounds good. Let's go there." She opened the apartment door and Tiffany quickly stepped out. "Shall we?" Elizabeth said to Buck.

"Let's," he answered, following her out of the apartment.

"Why don't I drive so that you don't have to lose your spot?" Lizzie offered as they walked around the apartment's Spanish tiled pool in the Melrose Place-ish courtyard.

"That would be great," Buck said, thinking of the difficulty getting a parking spot to begin with. That was definitely something about Los Angeles that would get really old really fast. In Victory, there were always plenty of places to park, and since most of the town's residents had trucks, all the spots were big enough for them.

The three climbed into Lizzie's little white convertible. Thankfully, Tiffany cheerfully offered to take the backseat, since Buck was positive that he wouldn't be able to fit in the glorified storage area. Even the front seat was a bit cramped for his long legs, and his head was touching the roof. Elizabeth started the engine and then hit a button on the dashboard that caused the roof to roll back and fold itself into a storage area behind the one Tiffany was seated in.

"That'll give you a little more headroom," Lizzie said with a tired smile.

Buck was grateful for the headroom, but the wind and road noise once the top was down made it practically impossible to talk at all. That was probably a good thing, he told himself as Elizabeth expertly maneuvered the little car down the L.A. streets that were already crowded, even though it was still relatively early on a Saturday morning. Soon they were in the Farmers Market parking lot and searching for a space. Buck had visited the Farmers Market once as a kid when his parents took him and his older brother, Larry J, to Los Angeles for a vacation. They had attended a taping of *The Price is Right*, and then wandered around the open-air market that sold everything from Chinese food to rubber stamps. The market had changed a lot since then—an entire upscale, outdoor mall seemed to have grown out the side of the old attraction.

Eventually Elizabeth found a spot and the three piled out of the convertible. Lizzie pressed a button on her keychain, which caused the car to let out a robotic peep, but to Buck's amazement she left the top down. He thought crime was rampant in Los Angeles. Lizzie led the way into the old section of the market toward Du-Pars, which upon first glance seemed to fall somewhere between Mug's in Victory and

Denny's in Lone Oak (the next town over). The coffee shop was old-fashioned, boasting many different kinds of pies and a line of people waiting for breakfast. Elizabeth wove her way through the crowd to put their name on the list of people. She emerged a minute later and informed them the wait was only twenty minutes. Buck doubted he had ever waited twenty minutes just to sit down at a restaurant table in his entire life, but he responded to Elizabeth that the wait was not too bad.

Lizzie then led Tiffany and Buck through the market and into the newer section, which she explained was called The Grove, to a Coffee Bean and Tea Leaf.

"Isn't there a Starbucks?" Tiffany asked anxiously, clearly not wanting to waste coffee consumption at a place in which she didn't have a chance of spotting a celebrity and possibly not wanting to cheat on her steady venue.

"Everybody gets a latte here while they wait to get seated at Du-Pars," Lizzie explained, and Tiffany immediately played it cool.

Buck was certain Lizzie had her at "everybody," so they joined the line that extended out the door of the Coffee Bean. The three got their drinks in little paper cups and returned to Du-Pars just in time to hear their name being called. Buck felt completely out of place. Out of place in line at the Coffee Bean, where he was the only man not wearing a worn-out, backward baseball cap, and out of place at Du-Pars, where everyone held an L.A. Times in one hand and a BlackBerry in the other. He tried not to notice it and hoped that Lizzie wouldn't either.

They sat down in the beige vinyl booth and each picked up a menu. Almost immediately, Lizzie looked up,

"I don't know why I bother to look. I always get the same thing—a short stack," she informed them, setting the menu back on the table.

"That's what I'll get, too," Tiffany quickly said, and also closed her menu.

Buck studied his for a few more minutes before deciding on a combination breakfast that included eggs and sausage. He could not live on pancakes alone. They ordered, and in less time than it had taken to be seated, plates of food were delivered to their table. Along with the pancakes were little containers of melted butter, in which everyone gluttonously drenched their cakes. As they began stuffing their faces, Tiffany said to Elizabeth, "So, jury duty sucked?"

She sounded sympathetic, which made sense to Buck. Even in a town as small as Victory, folks hated jury duty. The town housed the courthouse for the entire county, and as a result, Victory residents seemed to get called more than those from the surrounding towns.

"You have no idea," Lizzie began, and then told a story about Dan (who Buck remembered as the fiancé who had dumped her so harshly just a couple weeks earlier) and the case's defender.

"What bad luck to get assigned to his courtroom," Buck sympathized, as if jury duty could get any worse.

"Oh, no," Lizzie corrected him. "I *volunteered* to serve there as a way to get back together with Dan," she said, sounding slightly ashamed.

The information stung Buck like a bee. She was trying to get back together with that jerk? What about him?? What about their moment in the kitchen last weekend?!? The blister on his foot where Lizzie had spilled coffee on him was still tender and he thought about it with every step he took— although he probably would have even if his foot were fine.

"I know it doesn't seem like it," Tiffany said in between bites, "but the new girlfriend is a good thing."

Buck agreed wholeheartedly. A new girlfriend meant that Lizzie and Dan would not be getting back together, but before he could figure out words to sound sympathetic and not thrilled about this, Tiffany had a thought.

"He has to rebound to realize what a good thing he had with you."

"You think?" Lizzie said, sounding vulnerable.

Anger swelled up through Buck. This Dan guy didn't realize how great he had had it.

"Absolutely," Tiffany confirmed. "Don't you think, Buck?"

Caught with half a sausage link in his mouth, Buck mumbled, "I guess," without taking his eyes off his plate. The breakfast was much better than Mug's or Denny's. The eggs were well cooked, the sausage not too greasy, and the pancakes some of the best Buck had tasted since he used to live at home. Unfortunately, he couldn't really enjoy it because the knowledge that Elizabeth was trying to get back together with her ex-boyfriend ruined it for him. He thought his luck with this girl had finally changed—that she was available— and through Tiffany he had a good excuse to see her. The news of her hopeful reunion with Dan added a whole new scenario to the options in Buck's head.

Another factor that Buck wasn't sure how to deal with came up when the three arrived back at Elizabeth's apartment, stomachs painfully full of pancakes. Elizabeth's lawyer, Courtney, was waiting outside for them. Seeing her sitting on the first step of the apartment with her tanned legs stretched out in the sun and a rhinestoned cell phone on her ear gave the huge breakfast sitting in Buck's stomach an unwelcome lurch. It was unclear how long Courtney had been there, but it had been long enough that she had removed her orange rubber flip-flops and pulled her wide-legged pants up around her knees. She had a clear plastic cup half full of a frozen coffee drink by her side. When she saw them walking toward her, she quickly flipped her phone shut and stood up.

"Where have you guys been?" she asked, sounding slightly annoyed but trying to cover it with cheerfulness.

"Du-Pars," Tiffany answered innocently, "but we didn't see a single celebrity," she added, voicing the disappointment she had been voicing during the entire drive home from the coffee shop.

Buck didn't say a word but surveyed the situation on edge. He had thought the "new Lizzie" was through trying to get out of her role as Tiffany's guardian. Was he foolish to believe that because she hadn't raised the issue last weekend in Victory she had accepted it?

"Buck," Courtney said stepping toward him, and he stiffened, "you should have called me when you got into town!"

Before he could answer, she was putting her arms around him and kissing him at the very top of his neck, almost at his jawbone. It was a very nice place to be kissed and only added to Buck's confusion, not to mention the stifled snort of laughter coming from Lizzie as she searched through her purse for the keys to the apartment.

"Uh, sorry," he mustered, desperately wanting to ask why he should have called her.

Buck glanced over at Tiffany, who seemed as relaxed with Courtney's appearance as Lizzie did, and he wondered what was going on. If Elizabeth and Courtney had been plotting to ditch Tiffany all week, wouldn't the teenager have caught on?

Without pausing to acknowledge or accept his half-assed apology, Courtney continued, "So, what's on the agenda today?"

"The beach!" Tiffany answered excitedly.

Buck knew just how excited she was because almost every time they had talked during the week (which had been almost every day) she had mentioned that they were going to the beach on Saturday. She was definitely picturing the day to be straight out of an episode of *The OC*.

Courtney soared right over Tiffany's response and continued her own dialogue. "Cause here's what I was thinking. I'll take Buck to do a little L.A. sightseeing." She turned to him and half whispered as though sharing a juicy secret, "I'm one of the few born and raised," then returned to her normal tone. "And then maybe we'll meet up with you guys for some dinner. We'll see how the day is going."

Buck wanted desperately to protest, but he actually found himself speechless. Before he could coordinate the words, Lizzie gave an amused-looking grin and said, "Sure, whatever." She then turned and looked at Tiffany, who also had an amused grin on her face. Buck felt duped—how could he have been so blind? Lizzie was trying to set him up with her friend. Another scenario he had not planned for.

"Well, I was kind of looking forward to the beach," Buck admitted. He had been . . . both spending time at the ocean *and* spending time with Tiffany, but *mostly* spending time with Lizzie.

"Well, maybe there'll be a little beach on our tour," Courtney said seductively, and Buck felt firmly wedged between a rock and a hard place. His whole life getting women had been ridiculously easy—except for the one woman he really wanted! He looked longingly at Lizzie. She caught his gaze and returned it with an adorable smile. Then Courtney took him by the arm, the same way she had when she took him out to "discuss" Lizzie's legal case, and led him out of the apartment.

~30~

The weekend went fast—ridiculously faster than usual—and before I know it, it is Monday morning and I am getting ready to report for the jury duty that I had volunteered for and now dreaded. The excited anticipation with which I went into the courthouse on Friday is gone. Instead, I feel hopeless and more than a little disappointed. Although Tiffany had insisted, and Courtney had agreed, that any relationship Dan might be having with Defender Bitch was inconsequential, I still feel let down and, if nothing else, that this speed bump on the road to my happiness will cause a delay.

I pull on a pair of black gaucho pants and (having learned from my mistake last week) a light pink cashmere sweater, despite the hot summer day the weather report is predicting, and sweep my hair into a high ponytail since I decide not to bother washing it. Armed with my copy of Hillary's autobiography, a book which I now feel a great and inexplicable animosity toward—combined with an unstoppable compulsion to read every last page—I head to the courthouse.

As I sit in bumper-to-bumper traffic on Wilshire I look down at Hillary, smiling up boldly, almost smugly, at me. Her husband cheated on her with a fat intern and her marriage survived! Hillary certainly didn't let anything stand in her way of achieving her life goals . . . look at her today, a senator from New York and *still married*. If the Clintons could work through such a humiliating scandal, Dan and I could certainly work out our little spat—and his potential affair with Defender Bitch. I just hope it's an affair without "sexual relations" like the one the president had . . . the thought drives me to snort with sarcastic laughter. In my limited encounters, Dan is definitely the least adventurous person in the bedroom. I definitely (probably) don't have a problem with that, but the thought of his venturing to insert anything into a woman besides his own well-covered penis is a laugh.

As soon as I arrive at the courthouse I notice a problem. Gone are the subzero temperatures of my previous visit . . . inside, the building is swelteringly hot. I sweat through the lobby, up the elevator, and into the courtroom, where all of my fellow jurors are loosening collars and fanning themselves with any loose pieces of paper they can find. My cashmere sweater is sticking to my skin and starting to itch horribly. All I have under it is an extremely thin camisole, and perhaps the only thing that could drive me to remove the sweater and bare so much of my bony body is if the garment were actually on fire—and I'd probably try to extinguish the flames before I resorted to removing the sweater. Miserable, I sit down, careful to avoid eye contact with either Dan or Defender Bitch.

Minutes that feel like hours later, the bailiff makes his Rusty Burrell announcement and we all rise for Judge Santos. The Judge, still in his black robe but looking even grouchier than before, with sweat glistening at his temples and above his lip, quickly takes his seat and orders the rest of the room to do the same.

"Well, I'm sure you've all noticed that our air-conditioning seems to have gone on the fritz," he announces to the room. His statement is met with groans of agreement. "Luckily for all of you," he says motioning to the fourteen of us crammed together in the jury box, "over the weekend, the parties in this case were able to reach a settlement and therefore your services are not needed."

There is a moment of confusion during which we all look around at each other, unsure of what to do. Is it like being dismissed early from high school math? Do you just grab your stuff and run like hell in fear that the teacher will remember another equation that needs solving?

"You are all free to go," Judge Santos says, answering our question.

Elated to be released from the burning inferno of hell that is the courtroom, I quickly rise and am one of the first jurors out of the room and the building. It is only as I step outside into the summer heat that feels cool in comparison with the courthouse that I realize what the judge said—a settlement was reached over the weekend. Dan and Defender Bitch spent the weekend together. Not only that, but they must have broken the judge's rule about not discussing the case. I have a flashing drive to return to Judge Santos's courtroom and rat Dan and DB out, but I stop. Not only does the mere thought of returning to the courthouse induce the beginning of a heatstroke, but it is still my intention to get back together with Dan, and getting him fired could make that trickier than it already is.

I shake the image of Dan and DB entangled in the navy blue sheets that I selected for him and focus on Tiffany and Courtney's insistence that this rebound fling is a good thing. I slide into my car and quickly remove the sweater. Being almost naked in my own car is embarrassing, but it's something I can deal with given the current temperature. As I speed away from the courthouse toward my office, I turn on my phone and command, "Work," into the voice-activated speed dial that immediately connects me to Hope.

"Hope, it's me. My case settled and I was excused. I'm on

my way in," I tell her, feeling relief that I'll be able to put some more time and effort into my career while I still have one.

"Elizabeth, we've been trying to reach you all morning. Renee had a hiking accident over the weekend and is stuck in bed with her leg in traction. The studio wants you to anchor the show," she says, trying to deliver the information impartially but letting her own excitement be heard.

"Oh my God, me . . . really?" I ask, feeling sick to my stomach and glancing in the rearview mirror and my unwashed and now extremely sweaty ponytail.

"They want you," Hope replies, and I can tell from her voice that she is smiling.

This is the moment I have waited for my entire life . . . I desperately wish I could smile as well.

~31~

I fight the traffic across town, hitting every possible light. My heart is racing, and playing over and over in my head are Hope's words, "The studio wants you to anchor the show." In my mind I have continually justified my demeaned existence on *The Renee Foster Show!* by telling myself that the limited on-air time I was receiving would be my springboard for bigger and better things. I don't think I ever really believed it until this very second. After all that I have put in, it is finally happening. I look over at Hillary's autobiography and suddenly feel a sense of camaraderie with the former first lady. We were both screwed over by the men we loved and both went on to achieve great things in our careers. I smile at her before once again commanding my cell phone to dial Hope.

"Traffic is horrible, as always," I inform her as soon as she answers the phone.

"How far away are you?" she asks, urgency in her voice.

"I think probably fifteen minutes," I answer hopefully. It'll take fifteen minutes if I could possibly make one green light between my current location and my office driveway.

"That's okay," she says exhaling audibly. "Taping is set to begin in an hour. As soon as you get here you'll go straight into hair and makeup. I'll have all the show notes waiting for you down there. I'm also going to put you on a call with

Renee to go over her segment—you are going to do a live-via-satellite interview with Renee from her hospital bed."

That bitch . . . she can't just lie back and die quietly, can she? I have to roll my eyes at the thought that she thinks people actually care about her and her stupid leg. They watch the show to see the celebrities. I can see that, why can't she? It's hard to believe that Renee was ever any sort of legitimate journalist. I shake it off . . . it doesn't matter. How much of the show could she possibly demand be devoted to her? It will still be considerably more air time than I have ever had. I disconnect my call with Hope and focus on relaxing my racing heart before getting to work.

It's hard to relax, though—this is the most exciting thing that has ever happened to me. I have to share it with someone. I pick up the phone and think about whom to call first. Dan? (Probably not a good idea.) Courtney? Tiffany? My mother? I scroll through the short list of numbers in my phone's address book and immediately know whom to call. I press the button and then listen to three rings before I hear a gruff "Hello?"

"Buck, you'll never guess what's happening to me." I tell him, and for some inexplicable reason I feel a second, separate surge of excitement to be talking to Buck Platner. It must just be the excitement of telling another person about the show, I reason, but I'm really happy to be talking to him even though it's been less than twenty-four hours since we've seen each other. Courtney held him captive most of the weekend, but Tiffany and I did get to spend little bits of time with him here and there.

"What?" he asks and the gruffness is completely gone from his deep voice.

"Renee broke her leg hiking and I'm going to host the show!" I say, hardly able to believe it's the truth.

Something about his response—a totally generic, "That's phenomenal"—melts my heart. Why is Buck Platner's opinion melting my heart? Why did I even call him? By the time I pull up to the studio, though, I'm still talking to him, and I'm feeling completely relaxed and even confident. Something about talking to Buck makes me feel like the best version of myself. I'm not usually confident with men, but for some reason, with him, none of my normal insecurities come up.

"Maybe I'll bring Tiffany up to Victory this weekend. I think she's missing her friends. Maybe I'll see you?" I say, without even meaning to. I have never in my entire life volunteered a return to Victory.

"That would be great," he says, and my heart does the weird melting thing again.

We hang up and I quickly park in my assigned spot, which is about halfway across the parking lot. I hurry into the building and go straight to the hair and makeup room, which is really just a station in the hallway behind the set.

As soon as Marcela sees me she says, "Let's get to work," and I sit in the seat. "She's here!" Marcela calls over her shoulder, and Carly, the hairdresser, comes rushing up with her tool belt of brushes, sprays, and curling irons around her waist.

"What the hell happened to your hair?" she asks with disgust before even laying a hand on me.

"I didn't know this was happening today," I explain.

She removes the thin elastic band that held my greasy hair up and makes a disappointed sound as my locks fall limply to my shoulders. "It's actually not as bad as Renee's," she says quietly and gets right to work.

Before I have the chance or the ability, since it seems there has been a mascara wand in my eye since the second I sat down, to let Hope know I've arrived, she appears next to me. Apparently Marcela's announcement made its way all the way upstairs.

"Okay, Elizabeth." She gives me an entire rundown on

what Renee's situation is and what I'm going to be doing. Before she can finish, the show's executive producer comes up to me. I can't actually see him approach since my eyes are still closed, but I hear his voice and jump slightly.

"Remember to be still," Marcela scolds.

"Elizabeth," Ryan, the executive producer begins, "the studio is determined to have you anchor, so try not to fuck up too much."

"Thanks," I reply sarcastically, careful not to move any part of my face as I speak. Ryan's not a bad guy; he's just extremely focused on sucking up to Renee as much as is humanly possible. He actually has quite a talent for it. I'm positive that, like Renee, he doesn't think there is any way on earth that I am anywhere near capable enough to fill her shoes. The quandary that he must be finding himself in is that while Renee treats him like her personal bitch, he actually works for the studio and therefore has to put the show before his own feelings. I've never been positive if Ryan is straight and wants to be *with* Renee or gay and wants to *be* Renee. I don't know if Ryan himself is even sure.

Personal annoyances aside, he does do a thorough job of preparing me to host the show. He goes over every second of air time—the opening monologue, which has been written on large cue cards that I simply have to read; the first satellite interview with Renee; the celebrity interviews (both followed by satellite interviews with Renee); and the closing monologue. He actually makes it sound simple. He will be in the producers' booth the entire time, connected to me via a tiny piece of equipment that will be in my ear, and the director will be onstage with me to make sure things go okay.

The voice from above booms, "FIVE MINUTES," just as Marcela says, "Okay, I think we're done."

I open my eyes and do a double take at my reflection. In the short time I've been seated in front of them, the women have performed a miracle transformation. Gone are the greasy hair and baggy eyes. I look like a different person. My face is flawless and my hair is perfect. I move to stand up, just as one of the members of the wardrobe department dives underneath me with a pair of black Gucci sandals.

"Just put these on," she instructs. "Everything else is adorable—totally Jessica Simpson."

I look down and gasp in sudden horror that I am still wearing my almost transparent camisole with my gaucho pants.

"I'm practically naked," I plead.

The wardrobe people are beyond fashionable and I often hear them bitching about the boring restrictions Renee puts on them. I don't want them to feel the same way about me, but I also don't want my debut hosting experience to be in the buff.

"Fine," she says stifling an eye roll. "Put this on," she instructs handing me a white crocheted poncho almost as sheer as the item I am already wearing.

I slip it over my head, careful of my hair and makeup, hoping that the two sheer fabrics together give me some sort of coverage. I glance in the mirror and see that the result is good enough. Actually, it looks great. I almost can't believe it's me. Something in the back of my head hopes that Buck will be watching, but I quickly scold myself and correct my emotion so that I hope Dan is watching. Then I quickly dial Tiffany to *make sure* that she is tuned in.

I practically have to hang up on the teenager screaming with excitement as I hear, "ONE MINUTE!" and then Ryan's voice in my right ear. I hadn't realized the piece had been implanted and I jump.

"Ryan, can you hear me?" I whisper.

"Of course I can hear you . . . but I can't see you. Get your ass in your seat," he commands, and I quickly slip onto the stage and seat myself on the cream couch Renee always does her opening monologue from. It feels weird . . . beyond weird.

I feel like I shouldn't be there, like any second now Renee is going to walk up behind me and bitch me out for sitting in her spot. Before I can adjust, Ryan is in my ear counting down, the director is making hand gestures in my direction, and then a red light is blinking on all four cameras, which are all pointed in my direction.

Without missing a beat I say, "Hello everyone, and welcome to *The Renee Foster Show!*" just as Renee always does. "As you can see, I'm not Renee Foster, I'm your favorite fact girl, Elizabeth Castle, filling in for Renee, who suffered a painful hiking accident this weekend. We have a great show for you today. Nicole Kidman is here to chat with us about her newest film, as well as Sarah Jessica Parker, who has transitioned from playing a writer on television to authoring her first book, *Looking Sexy in Any City*. But first, let's check in on Renee and see how she's feeling."

"Great job," Ryan buzzes in my ear as the satellite feed of Renee, propped up on pink satin pillows, fills a huge screen behind me. I beam from his words, but before he says it, I already know it. As soon as that red light went on, something inside me clicked and every second felt so right. I am positively soaring as I act concerned and ask Renee about her horrible accident and painful recovery. This is the greatest day of my life.

Tiffany couldn't deny the fact that living in Los Angeles was far more boring than she had anticipated. She had thought it was going to be as glamorous and star-studded as it appeared on television and in the magazines she used to spend hours poring over. Unfortunately, in a lot of ways it was even more boring than life in Victory. At least in Victory she had friends and a boyfriend to help pass the empty days. Here she had nothing. The celebrity sightings turned out to be few and far between, and without a car (or a license) she couldn't really get to the right places at the right times even if she could figure out exactly where or when they were. Instead, her options were to sit in Lizzie's apartment—which in fairness was far less cataloglike than it had been when Tiffany first arrived and felt like she couldn't even sit on the couch—watching television, or go to work with Lizzie and watch Renee Foster tape her talk show.

For the first few weeks, Tiffany had gone to the show almost every day. It did place her just a few feet away from some of the biggest celebrities in Hollywood. Lizzie had even managed to briefly introduce her to a few of her favorites, like Mischa Barton and Jared Padalecki. Although these quick hellos were majorly beefed up when relayed to her friends back in Victory during the long phone calls and even longer e-mails she focused on during the days she stayed home, they really weren't thrilling enough to keep Tiffany getting up early and sitting in the freezing-cold studio the show taped in. In reality, these tapings were a lot like watching the show at home, except without the freedom to get up to pee when you had to, and having to cheer wildly when you really didn't give a damn.

Tiffany had sat through way more than her share of *The Renee Foster Show!* tapings and was glad to be sitting at home doing nothing while Lizzie completed the jury duty stint that was the failed Plan B. Little did she know as she sat at Lizzie's once immaculate desk that the day wouldn't turn out to be so boring. Tiffany logged onto her e-mail and was pleased to find seven new messages waiting for her. Three of them were from her boyfriend, Red; two of them from her best friend, Laci; one from her friend Katie; and the seventh from her grandmother, who was pretty new to e-mail and did annoying things like write in ALL CAPS and put explanations in parenthesis following symbols—like after colon, dash, end parenthesis she wrote (smiling face), as if Tiffany hadn't been reading e-mail slang her entire life. Nonetheless, seven e-mails was enough to keep her busy through the morning and remind her how loved and missed she was back home . . . and was probably more fun than another taping of *The Renee Foster Show!*

Halfway through reading Red's first (and overly emotional) e-mail, the little message counter beeped and an eighth new message appeared. Tiffany clicked over, halfway through Red's sentence about how every day without her felt like more than twenty-four hours, to see what the newcomer was. It was a funny forward from Buck, who entertained her a few times a week with silly images like fat kids dancing around with light sabers or cats turning on television sets. This forward was a page full of pictures of cats in sunglasses being compared to celebrities. As she studied side-by-side portraits of a tabby in

Ray-Bans and a Material Girl–era shot of Madonna, the phone on the desk rang. Eyes still glued to the computer screen, Tiffany answered. The sad fact was that she got far more calls than Lizzie did.

It actually was Lizzie calling, and Tiffany braced herself. She had expected a miserable Elizabeth to call as soon as she was given a break from jury duty and permission to use the phone. Instead of the despondent person she was expecting, an overly joyous caller greeted Tiffany. Lizzie quickly explained that Renee had taken a fall down a mountain and that she would be hosting the show in her place.

"She really wants the network to play repeats, but they want *me* to do it," Elizabeth reported.

Tiffany was thrilled for Elizabeth, and more than a little upset that the one day she stayed home something of interest was actually going to happen on the talk show. Tiffany could hear the warning signs in the background that the show was about to start, so they hung up. She quickly went into the living room and turned the television on, forgetting about the half-read e-love letter from Red still sitting on the computer's desktop.

Moments later, there was Elizabeth sitting in the chair normally occupied by Renee Foster. Her hair and makeup looked incredible and something inside her seemed to glow while she was on-camera. She welcomed the audience to the show and then cut to an image of Renee, larger than life, on a screen behind Elizabeth. Renee sat propped up, looked into the camera, and told "her" viewers that the studio and network wanted to run encore episodes of some of her best shows, but she insisted that "her" viewers deserved first-run television and that the "fact girl" could fill in for a few days.

Tiffany couldn't help but roll her eyes at how obnoxious the show's host was, but she didn't waste long dwelling on it because soon the camera was back on Elizabeth. Suddenly Tiffany realized that she needed to spread the word—she needed to call everyone and make sure they were watching *The Renee Foster Show!* right this very second. She pulled the cord of the old-fashioned phone in the hallway as far toward the television as it could possibly reach and started dialing. First, she dialed Courtney, whose number went straight to voice mail. Second, she called her grandmother, who she knew wouldn't be far from Elizabeth's mother and able to spread the word. Sure enough, the two women were together and both were excited to watch the show. She called a few of her girlfriends in Victory who she had done immense amounts of bragging to—this would only give her more bragging ammunition. Tiffany decided to try Courtney's number once more, and this time she picked up. Tiffany gave her the news and promised to share Courtney's congratulations with Lizzie. Courtney was getting on a plane at LAX to go to a gift show convention in Las Vegas for SparkleCourt.

"Who next?" she thought. "Buck!" She decided the attorney-turned-friend would want to know.

She dialed Buck's number and he answered distractedly.

"Buck," Tiffany told him, "the normal host of the show Lizzie works on is sick and she's filling in."

As soon as she said it, she doubted if she should have made the phone call. Did Buck actually like or care about Lizzie? Was she interrupting his busy day with information he couldn't care less about? The weekend of the funeral, Tiffany thought she had sensed something between them besides the discomfort and disdain that had previously been at the forefront of their communications; but then the weekend Buck came down to Los Angeles he had spent the entire time with Courtney. Was Lizzie nothing more than a friend of his new girlfriend?

"I know, she already called me. I'm watching right now," he said.

She already called him? Tiffany replayed his response in her head. Lizzie hadn't called her best friend or her mother, but she'd called Buck Platner? This was interesting to Tiffany, as was Buck's next comment, "She looks amazing."

"Yeah, definitely," Tiffany agreed.

They watched together, over the phone, in silence for a few seconds before another person popped into Tiffany's head.

"Do you think I should try to let Dan know that she's on TV?" Tiffany asked Buck.

He paused for a split second before answering, "No, I don't think so," in an odd and forced tone.

Tiffany let it go and said good-bye to Buck so that she could focus on watching Elizabeth. She was sitting across from Nicole Kidman, and they were chatting like old friends.

"Lizzie mentioned a visit up to Victory, so hopefully I'll be seeing you soon," Buck told Tiffany as he hung up his phone.

Tiffany set the phone back on its cradle and tried to un-tangle the cord as best she could while a commercial for Tampax filled the screen. A tangled phone cord was definitely the kind of thing that the old Elizabeth would have freaked out about, but which the new Lizzie tried hard to ignore. She had not only called Buck to tell him about her television debut, she had also talked to him about visiting Victory?!? Tiffany couldn't help wondering what was going on, but she didn't have much time to ponder it because the Tampax was gone and there again were Elizabeth and Nicole, their heads huddled together in an adorable fit of giggles.

~33~

My week has been amazing. I can't deny the fact that Renee's unfortunate (extremely fortunate) accident has been a priceless gift to me. Much to Renee's and a little to Ryan's horror, the show's ratings have been as good as or better with me as the host than Renee and—get this—I've been getting almost twice the fan mail she does. As I said, it's been amazing. Unfortunately, I cannot completely sit back and bask in the glory of my dreams coming true since thus far all attempts to reunite with Dan have failed miserably. Besides the failed supermarket bump-into and the horrific jury duty volunteering, we can't forget the bungled "Did you call me?" stunt as well as the radio station song dedication plot suggested by Tiffany and accepted after half a bottle of celebratory Veuve Clicquot (sent over as a gift from the studio!).

Now I sit in the passenger seat of Courtney's Range Rover in Friday night traffic as the three of us—Courtney, Tiffany, and I—drive to Victory for the promised-under-the-influence-of-exciting-news visit. I had mentioned a visit when I called Buck . . . a call I still can't completely explain why I placed, (especially to Courtney), and then Tiffany got extremely excited about seeing her friends. So I was stuck. Then, when I made the mistake of complaining about the trip to Courtney, she eagerly attached herself to the journey, and that is how the three of us ended up on this excursion together. The truth is that I really, *really* didn't want Courtney accompanying us to Victory—especially to Buck's house, which is our planned destination—but I couldn't figure out a good reason to leave her behind, so again I found myself stuck.

The upside is that we are able to use the drive to work out the details of Plan C to get Dan back. At first Tiffany and Courtney urged me to resort to the original Plan B—the reverse-rear-end-bump, but once again I shot the idea down in favor of something (anything) else. The something else involves a Los Angeles Harvard Alumni event and a charity date auction. The plan is actually quite simple: 1. Attend the charity date auction; 2. Bid on Dan. 3; Win the date with Dan; 4. Go on date, where Dan sees how much he misses me and realizes how badly he wants to be with me. The tricky things are: 1. There isn't currently a charity date auction planned by the Los Angeles Harvard Alumni; 2. I didn't go to Harvard, and besides Dan, I don't know anyone who did. These are the points that most of our discussion is focusing around.

"Okay, it's really not as difficult as you're making it, Elizabeth," Courtney says as she cuts off an extremely large gasoline tanker on the narrow highway. "You need to call the Los Angeles Harvard Alumni Association president and explain that you've recently moved here from—wherever—and you were really active in your old chapter and you're eager to dive right in and you want to start by planning this charity event."

It is clear that Courtney thinks dealing with the Harvard alums is going to be as simple as planning a sorority social.

"But Dan is a member of the association," I protest. "He'll find out what I'm doing and rat me out for not being a member."

"So you'll use a fake name," Tiffany pipes up from the backseat, where she is belted into the center seat.

"Exactly," Courtney agrees.

"What name?" I ask, hoping that at some point I'll stump them and they'll come up with a different (and easier) plan.

"What was it they called you back in Victory?" Courtney asks, more to herself than to me. "Betsy? Say your name is Betsy Platner. Buck won't mind," she adds, with an authority that I wonder how she got.

"Lizzie," I correct, not that it matters. "Lizzie Platner sounds like a total hick name, though."

For some reason, saying "Lizzie Platner" makes my cheeks flush hot and red, and I turn my head to look out the Range Rover's window even though it is unlikely anyone could see into the dark car.

"Actually, I think it sounds pretty cute," Tiffany pipes up again.

Her compliment causes another wave of prickles in my cheeks and adds one in my stomach. For the moment I give in, mostly because I fear that any more discussion of what my alias will be might cause an uncontrollable and unexplainable giggle to escape me.

"Okay, so let's say I can get membership to the association and they are willing to let me plan the event. Then what?" I ask, trying to get my eyes back on the prize.

"You're home free!" Courtney explains as she veers off the road. "Oh shit, this is the town, huh? I think I saw a sign."

I look up. I'd hardly been paying attention as we cruised along in the dark. It's only around nine o'clock, but my new role on the show is much more exhausting that my usual "fact girl" duties. From the backseat Tiffany gives Courtney the limited directions to take us from the highway/Main Street to Buck's house.

"My God, it's good to be home!" Tiffany exclaims as we cruise past Mug's and turn onto Buck's street.

I hate to admit it, but it does feel a little good. Plus, the arrival at Buck's means a break from the Plan C scheming that is starting to cause a shooting pain behind my left eye. We cruise down the street, and even though it isn't even ten o'clock—early by L.A. standards— the street is as quiet as if it were three in the morning. The car's large tires crunch over the gravel that mysteriously finds its way onto Victory's streets and rolls to a stop outside Buck's house, one of the few that still has lights on.

We park and climb out of the car, each of us toting a weekend bag—Tiffany's old duffel, my outlet Coach bag, and Courtney's pink-and green Juicy bag. Before we reach the porch, Buck opens the front door and steps into the jamb. My heart does a flip at the sight of him, dressed in mesh basketball shorts and a well-worn U of A shirt that clings to his defined pectorals and biceps. He looks straight at me and gives me a dimpled smile as he runs his hand over his freshly shorn hair. I can't help wondering if he's always had such a cute smile. His expression quickly changes, though, as Courtney grabs the back of his head and kisses him on the lips.

"Surprise, sweetie!" she exclaims.

Buck looks surprised . . . actually, shocked. My eyes widen for a second and I look at Tiffany, who is looking back at me with the same expression. Neither of us realized that Buck did not know Courtney was joining us. She had made it sound as though she had been invited, that he had insisted that she join us in Victory for the weekend.

"Oh, uh, Courtney . . . what a surprise," he fumbles for words. His face registers the kind of surprise you don't like . . . like: surprise, you thought your car needed a new battery, but actually we have to rebuild the whole engine and it'll cost you two paychecks. (That actually happened to me, so I know the face it causes.) "I didn't realize you were joining the girls. Gosh . . . we're a little tight on space," he says, looking back at the couch where his big golden dog is clearly settled in for the night.

"We'll be fine," Courtney says, clearly not picking up on

any of Buck's misgivings. "The girls can stay where they stayed last time," she says, adopting a woman-of-the-house tone. "Obviously I'll be in your bed," she adds in a suggestive whisper.

"Oh, right, well . . . I actually never, *never* sleep in my bed. I'm much more comfortable out here with Wildcat, so you make yourself comfortable in the bedroom."

Courtney's face finally shows a slight understanding of what's going on here, but she quickly laughs it off. "So, Buck, we need your opinion on something, don't we, girls?" she says to Tiffany and me. Neither of us has any idea what she's talking about.

"Oh, sure," Buck says hesitantly, "why don't you all sit down and get comfortable. Anybody want anything?"

We all gather around the living room's cluttered coffee table. Buck has clearly cleaned up for our visit, but the table is still littered by newspapers and issues of *Sports Illustrated*. I pleasantly note that the swimsuit issue is absent from the collection. Tiffany climbs into the small space on the couch where the dozing dog isn't, and I curl up in a large chair. Across from me, Courtney sits on the loveseat, her arm lying across the back. Poor Buck takes a glance around the room and then takes a seat on the floor in front of Wildcat. As if the dog could protect him from the predatory Courtney—ha!

"So, what's the needed opinion?" Buck says quickly, obviously wanting to engage everyone in a topic that will distract Courtney from insisting he sit with her. Normally in these situations, which are sadly common, when Courtney sets her sights on a man who is far from interested, I pity my friend; but for some strange reason, in this particular case it is Buck that I am feeling protective of.

"Don't you think buying Dan in a charity date auction is a brilliant way for Elizabeth to win him back?" she says, beaming with pride over her idea.

I am horrified and humiliated. For some reason, I do not

want Buck to know anything about Plan C . . . or any of the plans. My face flushes with red-hot embarrassment.

"I hardly think Buck is interested in this," I say quickly. "Should we see what's on TV?" I reach for the remote.

"Wait, no . . . she's going to *buy* him back?" Buck asks, his expression a complicated combination of amusement and horror.

I'm noticing for the first time how much he looks like Josh Lucas (whom I actually met and interviewed this week . . . he was so hot that I was actually sweating from being near him). I wish he didn't look so much like Josh, and I'm wishing he didn't look so intrigued by the details of Plan C.

"It's Plan C," Tiffany says, nonchalantly thumbing through the pile of magazines, ""Don't you have anything besides *Sports Illustrated*?" she whines.

"*Plan C?*" Buck repeats, and I cringe.

"Yeah, Plan A was the supermarket thing and Plan B was the jury duty thing. We want her to do the reverse-rear-end thing, but she refuses," Tiffany continues, without taking any notice of my silent cues, commands, and pleas to stop talking.

"You're kidding, right?" he asks me.

"Well, it's kind of just for fun," I say, pathetically trying to cover. Obviously, no one in her right mind would have fun humiliating herself repeatedly in front of her ex-fiancé.

"So, what is this charity date auction where you're going to buy him?" Buck asks skeptically.

"Oh, it's complicated," I say. "Is *The Apprentice* on tonight?"

"She actually has to organize the auction," Courtney pipes up. She has draped herself across the loveseat and has removed her Juicy hoody to reveal a revealing SparkleCourt bedazzled wife beater. "She has to join the Los Angeles Harvard Alumni Association and then volunteer to plan the event. It's not really that complicated," she continues, gazing at Buck. Then she turns to me. "Elizabeth, didn't you say you were exhausted?"

It's not a very subtle hint—Courtney wants to be alone with Buck. Although there is part of me that doesn't want this to happen (the same part that didn't like seeing Courtney and Buck walk down the hall together the first night he came to L.A.), there is another part that will do anything to escape continuing this conversation with Buck.

"Right, I am exhausted. Tiff, didn't you say you were, too?" I carefully avoid looking at Buck and stare directly at Tiffany, who begins to shake her head, then sees my look and catches on.

"I really am exhausted. I'm going to turn in, too," she says, without sounding at all convincing.

We get up to leave and Buck quickly stands. "Are you sure you're tired? You look okay."

"We're exhausted," I confirm, "goodnight," and with that, Tiffany and I retreat to our guest room, where the inflatable bed is already set up on the floor.

Buck is left alone with Courtney, and Tiffany and I have nothing to do but go to sleep. I actually am exhausted, although I have a hard time falling asleep because I can't stop thinking about Buck and Courtney alone together. I don't know why it eats away at me, but it does. I'm restless the entire night because I am preoccupied with the hope that they didn't have sex. I don't know why I care so much, but I do.

I wake up early—or rather, I stop trying and failing to sleep early and pad out into the hallway. I am desperate to see if Buck is asleep on the small couch or if he has spent the night in his bed with Courtney. I tiptoe down the hall and into the living room. I hold my breath and say silent prayers that Buck will be on the couch. I hear soft snoring and relief fills me until I peer over the back of the couch and find Wildcat stretched out comfortably. I am crushed and angered. How could he sleep with Courtney? He hardly knows her!

I stomp into the kitchen and bang through the cupboards

looking for coffee. I'm about halfway through the kitchen when I hear "Shhh" behind me. I turn around and find Buck, shirtless in the same workout shorts as the night before, his eyes not completely open yet. His chest is perfectly sculpted, with just a small amount of golden hair between his hard pecs. I want to put my hands on his hard body and press my own against it. I'm incredibly jealous that Courtney got to do just that. Why can't Dan's body be like Buck's? "It's early," he says sleepily.

"Sorry," I say coldly, "I couldn't sleep and I'd like some coffee."

"Whoa, wake up on the wrong side of the air mattress?" he says with an adorable smile. The smile pisses me off.

"I can't believe you slept with Courtney," I say and as soon as the words are out of my mouth I can't believe I've let them go.

The truth is that I have absolutely no right or legitimate reason to be upset. Aside from his being a high school dance date that I blew off, I have absolutely no claim to Buck Platner. I have to spin this.

"She really likes you, and if you're going to treat her like just another conquest you should be ashamed of yourself," I say, and immediately feel ashamed of myself. I cannot believe I have gotten myself into this conversation and I can't believe that I keep digging in deeper.

Buck looks right at me and his normally warm eyes turn icy. Immediately I know I've gone too far.

"Your friend Courtney is extremely aggressive," he says.

"She's extremely passionate," I counter. I don't know why . . . somehow my brain and my mouth are no longer connected and I can't stop myself.

He looks at me like I'm crazy, but before he can say anything, Courtney saunters out of the bedroom and toward the kitchen. She is dressed in the T-shirt Buck greeted us in the night before. Her blonde curls are cascading down her shoulders in a sexy mess. I feel pathetic, with my thin ponytail and Old Navy pajama pants.

"Good morning, lover," she calls to Buck, who flushes slightly.

Just before Courtney reaches us he turns to me and intensely looks me in the eye. "I did not have sex with her," he says.

I feel catapulted to the moon. I want to grab him and kiss him and tell him how relieved I am . . . but I can't. Courtney steps up behind him and puts her arms around his bare chest. He noticeably flinches, but she doesn't notice. What she does notice, apparently for the first time, is me.

"Oh, hey, Elizabeth," she says with a grin.

Buck turns away from me and toward Courtney. "Did you sleep alright?" he asks her.

The rest of the weekend is a sucky blur. Courtney dominates most of Buck's time . . . not that it matters, since I clearly offended him and he isn't letting it go. Sunday night, as Courtney and Tiffany are packing up the car, I find myself alone in the living room with Buck. I open my mouth to talk to him, and my tongue feels thick and clumsy.

"Buck, I'm so sorry," I start.

The tension that has surrounded him like a shell all weekend immediately melts away. "No, don't be. I was just in a bad mood. Courtney is a handful."

"Yeah, I know she is," I admit.

"It was good to see you and Tiffany, though," he says.

"Thanks, it was good to see you, too," and I lean forward to hug him good-bye.

I turn my head to kiss him on the cheek, but something strange happens. Buck also moves his head in a way that puts us on a direct path to an unavoidable lip collision. Before I know it, the kiss has come and gone. It was just a tiny peck. "Friendly," is probably too generous a description, but it leaves my lips tingling and my cheeks warm. I look up at Buck, but his face doesn't register that anything out of the ordinary has occurred.

"Good luck with Plan C," he says gently, and my cheeks flame to a scarlet red.

Before I can say a word, Courtney dramatically comes through the front door exclaiming, "I can't believe it's already Sunday!"

Me neither, I think at the exact same time Buck says it out loud. I glance up at him; he is looking over Courtney's shoulder—she's embracing him now as if they are long-lost sweethearts—directly at me.

~34~

Much too quickly for my taste, Renee recovers from her accident and is back in the anchor chair (couch) and I am demoted back to my "Fact Girl" desk for less than a minute a day. All I have left of my moment in the spotlight are e-mails of praise from the studio and network and a small pile of fan mail. Yes, I actually received fan mail and it's some of the most simultaneously gratifying and terrifying letters I have ever seen. The only fortunate thing about Renee's return to work is that not hosting the show lightens my schedule significantly and gives me much more time to work on Plan C.

For reasons I still cannot figure out, I have become a member of the Los Angeles Harvard Alumni Association under the name Lizzie Platner. Not only that, I have struck up a friendship with the association's president, Suzanne McNally, who thinks she remembers me from her freshman dorm. This supposed Ivy Leaguer *insists* that we lived down the hall from each other for an entire year. I really have no choice but to agree with her. After countless trips down a memory lane I have never even visited, I finally work up the guts to suggest the charity date auction.

I think part of me is hoping she will reject the idea and save me from the possible (probable) humiliation that Plan C is sure to bring. Unfortunately, Suzanne's love life doesn't have much life in it and any opportunity to land a man is one that she jumps at. She loves the idea, and before I have a moment to catch my breath, we're planning away. I had intended to work on this project alone, but Suzanne is so excited about it that we end up as cochairs. The best thing about this is that Suzanne, ever eager for any exposure to the opposite sex, is happy to call all the Los Angeles alumni between twenty-five and forty years old listed as "single" in their membership profile. This means that I don't have to worry about Dan's recognizing my voice and putting an end to Plan C before it even begins. (And I don't have to worry about his *not* recognizing my voice and driving me to suicide.) The only concern now is that Dan's relationship with Defender Bitch has taken him from "single" to "double."

Within weeks, Suzanne has a list of twenty-seven eligible Harvard male grads for the single (desperate) alumnae in the Los Angeles area to bid on. Ironically, what started as an extremely selfish act has turned rather unselfish, since the auction will be raising money to help a local homeless shelter. I sit across from her in her mostly pink West Los Angeles apartment—anything west of the 405 and north of Pico is considered prime "Westside" property—eyeing the neatly typed-up spreadsheet of bachelors. Today's project is to set a starting price for each man . . . it's actually a pretty entertaining way to spend a Saturday afternoon. We study each man's picture, along with his résumé, and set prices ranging from twenty-five to one hundred dollars. Mind you, these are only starting prices . . . hopefully, there will be lots of bidding on everyone except Dan. I actually still don't know for a fact that Dan is a participant, but at this point I'm not sure I'll be able to drop out of the event even if I don't come across his name on the list.

I'm starting to lose hope by the time we get to the second

page, and I'm also growing really bored with setting fifty- to seventy-five-dollar starting prices for Century City corporate attorneys who enjoy golfing and wine tasting. Finally, the third name on the second page is Dan's.

"Daniel McCafferty," Suzanne says, "Beverly Hills assistant D.A. Oooh, lives in Beverly Hills, and it says he just got out of a relationship." Suzanne had each man fill out a detailed questionnaire about himself after his acceptance to be auctioned off. "He's pretty cute," she says, handing me a small picture of Dan.

An arrow pierces my heart as I take the picture . . . it was once a picture of the two of us standing side-by-side at his friend Lee's wedding. Dan is dressed in a tuxedo and looking extremely handsome. You can still see part of my hand dangling next to his, but the rest of me has been cut off.

"You think?" I ask, trying to play it cool.

"Definitely. I bet we could make him a hundred-dollar bachelor," she says and starts to mark it on his profile page.

"No!" I almost shout. "He's only an A.D.A.," I point out, trying to regain my composure, "and I actually think I kind of remember him being a jerk."

"Really?" Suzanne asks and then tilts her head to one side. "Oh my gosh—Danny McCafferty . . . I totally remember him now, he *was* a jerk. Remember, he lived downstairs from us? He was the one who had sex with that really fat girl, Marly Something . . . Marty Something, and then never called her. Fifty dollars," she says with a look of distaste on her face.

I also have a look of distaste on my face, and a sick feeling in my stomach. Dan and I had supposedly shared all of our previous sexual encounters with each other. He had *never* mentioned a one-night stand in his college dorm. Suzanne obviously doesn't have a good memory, I try to console myself. She remembers me living down the hall from her and I didn't even *attend* Harvard. She could easily have Dan confused with some other chubby chaser. And at least now Dan's starting bid is fifty dollars, so hopefully I won't lose my rent buying back my fiancé.

~35~

Things go smoothly right up until the week before the date auction. Really, things were going too smoothly and I should have realized that it wasn't realistic that they would remain that way. One week—actually six days—before the auction, Suzanne calls me.

"So, Lizzie," she says. I used to cringe, almost convulse, when I was called Lizzie, but neither Tiffany nor Buck seem able to break the habit so I'm growing accustomed to it. "I don't think either of us should bid at the auction."

"What?!?" I ask in confusion and alarm. Not only is this *entire* thing a waste for me if I'm not "allowed" to bid on Dan, I'm completely confused that Suzanne, the biggest manhunter I've ever met (aside from Courtney), doesn't want to bid.

"I think it might look weird if we were bidding. Like we rigged it or something. Although Alex Turner, class of '93, is a hottie . . ." she trails off.

"He is a total hottie!" I encourage. "You should totally bid on him. No one will think we rigged a charity date auction. He could be the one for you," I add, dangling the happily ever after that I know she desperately seeks.

"No," she states, quickly collecting her resolve. "It's inappropriate. In fact, I think we should bring dates," she adds.

"Dates?" I ask. "I thought the whole point of the auction was to get a date."

It turns out that Suzanne met someone at her speed-dating session earlier in the week. In a breathlessly dreamy voice, she explains that she had been doing speed dating every week for almost a year and a half and certainly didn't expect to meet someone now, but she has, and although it's only been four days, they are very much in love. So she's invited him to the "charity event" she is hosting and doesn't want him to know that she ever considered bidding on a date because that would make her look like she was totally desperate. I use every ounce of my energy to avoid saying that the mere fact that she has done speed dating for eighteen months proves just how very desperate she was, and I find myself agreeing that we will bring dates and not bid on any of the bachelors.

"Fuck, fuck, fuck," I say as I hang up the phone, although I rarely curse.

"Everything alright?" Renee's shrill voice asks from the door to my office. She stands there dressed in yet another Juicy warm-up suit, this one a pale pink terry cloth, leaning on a cane with her right foot wrapped in a bright pink plaster cast.

Fuck, fuck, fuck, I silently repeat in my head. See . . . I save it for *really* bad things.

"Elizabeth, I need to go over a couple of facts for items on next week's shows," she says. Then she leans against the doorway and says, "Ow, I really need to sit." I motion to the couch against the glass wall opposite my desk. She looks at it for a second before saying, "A chair would be better," looking at the chair behind my desk.

"Here, Renee," I say graciously, "sit in my desk chair," and I roll it over to where she stands.

"Oh, aren't you sweet. That would be perfect," she says, sitting down as if she hadn't even thought of sitting in MY chair. I lean against the edge of the desk.

"Don't you want to sit?" she asks in her saccharine-sweet voice, and she motions toward the couch.

No way. If the couch isn't good enough for her, it isn't good enough for me. "I'm fine, thanks. This way I'm closer to all my info," I say, motioning to the color-coded file folders neatly arranged on my desk.

I am only able to give half my attention to Renee as she asks question after detailed question about what I consider to be extremely trivial matters because most of my brain is focusing on Suzanne's instruction that I bring a date to the date auction. Now that I have had experience hosting the show, I honestly consider my daily (often twice-daily) fact sessions with Renee almost completely useless. She wants to know the answer to every single question she is going to ask before she asks it. It's a complete waste of my time, especially given the more important things I need to address. Not to mention how stale it makes her interviews feel.

What on earth am I going to do about a date? I don't feel comfortable going against Suzanne or rocking the boat too much, since pissing her off might spark her to do thirty seconds or so of research on Lizzie Platner and realize that she didn't actually attend Harvard—or really exist at all! I mean, really, it is only a stroke of luck that she hasn't even turned on *The Renee Foster Show!* and seen me giving my daily facts . . . although I guess few Harvard grads watch daytime TV. Almost immediately my mind goes to Buck, probably because it's his name I'm using or because he's basically the only guy I know—yes, it definitely must be one of those reasons. The truth is that he really is my only option. But if I'm there with Buck, how am I going to get Dan? I think about Tiffany and having her come along as well to bid on Dan, but I quickly realize that a fifteen-year-old is going to stand out as a non-Harvard grad even more than I do. That leaves Courtney as my only option.

I groan a little and Renee stops in mid-sentence. "Are you

alright?" she asks, clearly annoyed that she has been interrupted.

"Oh, yes, sorry . . . toothache," I lie and put my hand to my jaw.

"I understand pain," she says melodramatically and motions to her leg. "Call my assistant, Mary, and have her give you the name of my dentist. Dr. Kelson is the absolute best in Los Angeles."

"I will, thanks," I say, sneaking a peek at the small clock on my desk. Renee has been in my office for almost twenty minutes. I look back up at her hoping that she leaves soon, but she is staring back at me expectantly.

"Have her bring me a Diet Coke from the soda fountain while you have her on the line," Renee demands.

This woman is unbelievable. I don't even have a toothache, and even if I did, I don't need Dr. Kelson's phone number because I already go to him, since long ago, before I realized how much I hate Renee, she mentioned him and it turns out he really is the best dentist in Los Angeles. Rather than explain all this, I simply pick up the phone and dial Mary's extension. The fact that Renee is asking for a Diet Coke is actually a good sign . . . it means she is getting tired and needs caffeine. What she doesn't know is that Mary is a genius, and whenever Renee requests a soda fountain drink, Mary gives her *Caffeine-Free* Diet Coke, which has no effect on her exhaustion and encourages her to go home earlier.

As we wait for Mary to deliver Renee's beverage, she continues asking me crazy questions. "Do we have a sign worked out with Kate Winslet to let us know if she's thirsty?

"I think if she's thirsty she'll probably just ask you for a glass of water during the break," I answer.

"Does she prefer flat or bubbly?"

"I'm not sure. We'll find that out," I answer, writing it down and focusing huge amounts of energy on not rolling my eyes.

"We really should have that kind of information," Renee hisses.

"I agree," I answer. She is sucking my soul out.

Just when I think I can't take another second and am contemplating taking her cane and beating her to death with it, Mary shows up with the Diet Coke.

She hands the glass to Renee, who looks at it as if she's never seen such a drink in her life.

"Actually, I think I'm too exhausted for caffeine to even have an effect on me. I'm so addicted that I'm practically immune," she informs us. "I think I'm just going to head home to my beautiful family. Mary, get my things together," she commands, and she slowly lifts herself out of my chair. "Elizabeth, figure out the water thing and we'll continue this tomorrow."

"Sounds good, Renee. Have a good night," I say sweetly.

I often wonder how Renee's family can love her. Her husband, Steve, is one of the nicest guys I've ever met. He actually writes children's books, so he can work at home and take care of their sons. I have visions of him cringing when she walks in the door at night the same way I do when she walks in the door of my office. I've seen them together, though, and he is clearly crazy about her. She must be nicer at home than she is here.

Once she has hobbled her bony ass out of my sight I breathe a sigh of relief. I think I have all the answers worked out in my head. I'll take Buck as my date to the auction and bring Courtney along as well. She will bid on Dan for me, and once he is purchased, she'll simply give the prize to me. It seems simple enough.

~36~

Buck feels as if he is in quicksand. Here he is, as crazy about Lizzie as ever and seeing more of her than he has since the twelfth grade, but Courtney is on him like Velcro. Every time he thinks he's going to have a chance for five minutes alone with Lizzie, there Courtney is, grabbing him around the waist and whispering "Hello, lover," in his ear . . . and they are not even lovers! They have not slept together, which took a lot of strength on Buck's part. On top of this, Lizzie doesn't believe him. She thinks he is taking horrible advantage of her vulnerable friend. The truth is the complete opposite. He is desperate for Lizzie to know that he doesn't want Courtney. He wants Lizzie, but it's proving beyond difficult to get that point across . . . until he gets a surprise phone call from her.

Every once in a while, out of the blue, Buck gets a call from Lizzie. It sounds pathetic, but the calls brighten his day. Buck is preparing to spend another Sunday night watching television with Wildcat when his phone rings. On the other end, Lizzie greets him with a desperate-sounding, "I need your help." "Anything," he answers, hoping he doesn't sound too desperate himself. Her phone call alone lifts his spirits up from what has been a difficult week. It was one of those weeks when nothing went right. He had been late to work, forgot a court date, and as always found his tongue in knots when trying to explain his absence to both his father and the judge (who was an old friend of his father's). In truth, his mind wasn't on his work lately because it was unavoidably on Lizzie. Buck just couldn't stop thinking about her, which is why he was thrilled when she invited him to the charity event she was hosting. A real date!

It takes less than a minute for his joy to crash and burn. It's not just a charity event, it's the stupid "Plan C" that the girls told him about when they visited Victory. It gets worse and worse. Not only does she want him to come with her as her date, Courtney will be there, bidding on Dan, whom she will then give to Lizzie so that they can get back together. Buck's too nice, though, and he finds himself agreeing to help her out. At least if he's there with Lizzie he'll get to spend a bit of time with her before she gets back together with her obnoxious fiancé, and Courtney won't be able to maul him too much since he'll be posing as Elizabeth's date.

"Oh, one more thing," she adds, sounding uncomfortable. "I had to use your name—well it didn't have to be *yours*, but it's just what popped into my head, so that Dan wouldn't see my name as a host and catch on to what I am doing . . . so you're going to have to use another name."

Buck's attention stalls on one tiny detail: "I had to use your name . . . it just popped into my head." A small amount of joy returns to him . . . she must think about him at least a little bit if his name is floating around in her head. "What name should I use?" he asks with a smile so adorable that Elizabeth can hear it through the phone.

"I dunno . . . Castle?" she suggests.

"You want me to use your name?" he asks, almost teasingly. "Buck Castle?"

There is a second of awkward pause. "Maybe not Buck—since Dan met you once before and there aren't many Bucks floating around . . . I dunno," she says, sounding really uncomfortable. It is a stupid nickname, even Buck thought so, but it's so stuck on him that he's just grown used to it.

"How about Benjamin Castle?" he asks.

"Benjamin . . . that's nice, where'd that come from?" she asks.

"It's my name," Buck answers. "You thought my birth name was Buck?"

"I guess I never thought about it. You never know in Victory. Benjamin's a nice name," she says, sounding a little dreamy. "So you'll be Benjamin Castle and I'll be Lizzie Platner," she tells him.

"You can call me Ben," he says coolly. "But I thought you hated 'Lizzie'?" For some reason he has had a horrible time getting his brain to remember. He'll be completely prepared to say "Elizabeth," and then "Lizzie" just comes out.

"I guess it's kind of growing on me," she says.

They are silent for a second while they both smile.

"Good night, Elizabeth," Buck says in a way that is completely innocent and yet totally meaningful (and seductive) at the same time.

Elizabeth is silent for a split second—her apartment just got much hotter and it takes a beat to adjust.

"Goodnight," she answers in a small voice.

They hang up and Buck smiles. He's going to be Lizzie's date. True, her plan might be to get back together with her ex, but Buck's got a different plan for the evening. He cracks open a can of Budweiser with one hand and takes a big sip. He swallows and leans back with a satiated sigh.

~37~

On the night of the auction, the plan no longer seems simple. It seems like a disaster waiting to happen . . . what was I thinking inviting Buck to be my date? He is sitting in the living room, looking amazing in a tuxedo, joking around with Tiffany while I pace back and forth across the bedroom in a black lace bra and panty set purchased especially for the occasion. I bought the lingerie for my reunion with Dan but found myself wondering what Buck would like as I uncomfortably tried on different ensembles in the dressing room of Victoria's Secret during my lunch break. Most of the choices accentuated my nearly flat chest and butt, but this one, with its push-up bra and boy-short bottoms, almost (*almost*) makes me look curvaceous.

I slip into a simple black dress and slide my feet into black satin heels. The shoes, too, are a splurge for the evening and I'll probably never be able to wear them again. Since I'm only two inches shorter than Dan, he always prefers me in flats; since Buck is a good six inches taller, I felt like taking advantage of being able to wear heels without towering over my date like Nancy Archer, the fifty-foot woman. I think I wouldn't be feeling so uncomfortable about the whole thing if Buck didn't look so incredibly hot in the tuxedo he informed me he bought since he doesn't think rentals look as

good. I hate how rented tuxedos look, but Dan always refused to spend the money on something he would wear so in-
frequently.

I take a final look in the mirror and add a dab of lip gloss.
I look like I'm going to throw up, probably because I feel like
I'm going to throw up. I felt sick most of the day, but the
nausea really hit when I opened the apartment door, still
wrapped in my robe, to find Buck standing there looking
ready to walk the red carpet. Now I make my way toward the
living room, hoping that he has miraculously uglied up while
I dressed, leaving me able to function. No such luck. I take
two steps into the room and he cuts off whatever he's saying
to Tiffany in mid-sentence. He stands up and says, "You look
amazing," with the kind of passion and intensity that Tom
Cruise talked about Katie Holmes before he jumped on
Oprah's couch.

"Not at all," I say bashfully, but for some reason inside I
am soaring. (He likes how I look!) "We should get going," I
say, deciding that changing the subject is a good idea.

"Okay," Buck says, straightening the black satin tie around
his neck. I hate bow ties—this looks so much better.

"Courtney is meeting us there," I explain, and secretly I
am pleased to have Buck to myself. Even though I am still
100 percent, completely in love with Dan, there is something
about watching Buck with Courtney and the way she constantly has to touch him that bothers me to no end.

He smiles at me and I think I catch a glimpse of something mischievous in his eye, but when I turn around to look
again it's gone. One after the other we cross to the front door,
and when we get there, Buck reaches around me and with
one arm opens the door; the other hand he places on the
small of my back and guides me out of the apartment. Tiny
shivers run up and down my spine and I have to work hard to
get my mind back on the evening's goal.

We make comfortable small talk between my apartment

and the restaurant where the auction is being held. We talk about the weather—we both love the cold of winter the best. We talk about movies—we both think Monty Python is hilarious. We talk about food—we both love yellow cake made from a mix with canned chocolate frosting. It's insane how much we have in common and how relaxed I feel sharing my true emotions with him. It might sound silly, but I couldn't admit any of those facts to another soul. Everyone in L.A. hates the cold, and when it drops below 70, people have a hard time functioning; Monty Python is considered idiotic and unsophisticated; and my favorite food would have to be something far more gourmet and interesting.

We pull up to the valet at the restaurant—a place I have been a handful of times with Dan and selected for the event, and yet have never felt comfortable in because it is painfully trendy; the kind of place where the staff is rude to you and you gratefully accept it. As the valet opens Buck's door, a flash of insecurity and embarrassment strikes me to be arriving at such a place in a Ford pickup truck. My insecurity quickly melts away when the valet greets Buck with a humble smile, and Buck himself hurries around to open my door and help me down. Unfortunately, we haven't made it halfway to the front door before Courtney comes rushing up looking breathtaking in a gold minidress. She looks so beyond sexy that I feel like a sandcastle at the beach getting unceremoniously washed away by a breaking wave.

"Oh my God, you guys, I'm so glad you're here," she says, sounding truly grateful to see familiar faces, and I feel bad for being unhappy in return. Courtney is amazing. I would never (never, ever) have the guts to show up alone at a party to which I'm not technically invited, and at a place like this. Courtney has done just this, though, and she's done it for me.

"Let's go," I tell her with a grateful smile. I step in front of her and lead the way into the restaurant. Behind me, I hear Courtney quietly say to Buck, "It's going to be so hard for me to keep my hands off you tonight. You look so hot." My good feelings toward her quickly tank, but I am pettily happy to hear Buck reply, "Thanks. You look great." Amazing is better than great, and Buck said I look amazing. Even though my dress is plain black and about a mile longer than Courtney's gold frock, I look "amazing."

With a small surge of confidence, I open the door and hold it for Courtney to enter. As she steps through, I can't help but admire the way she walks into the place as if she owns it . . . although I guess there is a decent chance that she does own it, since her father owns real estate all over Los Angeles. Buck reaches behind me and takes the door from me.

"After you," he says as I step past.

Inside, the maître d' shows us to the private room where the event is being held. Since I am a hostess, we have arrived on the early side, so it is easy to spot Suzanne on the other side of the room. As soon as she sees me, she grabs her date by the hand and drags him toward us.

"Lizzie, you're here! It's our big night," she almost squeals with excitement. "I want you to meet Elliott," she says, turning to beam at the man standing to her left.

Elliott looks almost identical to the guy in *Sideways*—not the guy who used to be on *Wings*, the other guy.

"Nice to meet you," he says, extending a slightly limp and sweaty palm.

I smile, return the sentiment, and introduce my companions. "Ben Castle and Courtney Cambridge."

"Courtney, what year are you?" Suzanne asks with a slightly skeptical eye. Of course I had to lie and say Courtney is a Harvard graduate since explaining who she really is would have been a bit of a mess.

"Courtney and I were freshman year roommates," I jump in.

"Of course! Duh . . . that's why you look so familiar," Suzanne giggles. Thankfully for a Harvard graduate she is remarkably bubble-headed. "Cambridge?" she repeats, then adds almost in a whisper, "Are you—"

"That's right," Courtney says with a twinkle in her eye, "main line."

Suzanne takes a deep, sharp breath and her face glows. People from the East Coast are so impressed with this main line nonsense—people who had family members on the *May-flower*. Courtney and I both know that Suzanne had come close to placing her as the daughter of Bennett and Alana Cambridge, but Courtney knows how to throw people off.

"So, we're all set and ready to go?" I jump in.

"We're ready. I think everything is handled and we can just relax and enjoy the fruits of our labor," Suzanne answers.

With that, she sees someone she knows—someone who presumably actually attended Harvard—and drags poor sweaty Elliott across the room again.

Courtney, Buck, and I head toward the bar and stake out a private spot on the short side along the wall. From there, we watch as the room fills up. It's about three-quarters full and Dan hasn't arrived yet. I glance at the clock and start to feel worried. He had agreed to be auctioned off, but if he doesn't show, the whole evening will have been for nothing. What if he is sick? Or what if he and Defender Bitch decided to elope or something? The thought panics me, but thankfully, just as I start to feel as if I might hyperventilate, the door opens and Dan walks in—alone (thank God).

Instead of his arrival helping the panic subside, it only adds fuel to the fire, and I am suddenly overcome with fear that he will see me, expose me, and end Plan C on the spot. So, instead of the calm, cool, and collected future wife of a future district attorney that I intended to come off as, I spend the entire evening huddled in the corner drinking Sauvignon Blanc. By the time the Sotheby's auctioneer that Suzanne managed to convince to man our auction goes to the lectern my face is tingling.

"Oh my God, this is it," I slur to Courtney and Buck. "Take your paddle," I hiss at Courtney, shoving the Ping-Pong paddle that Suzanne and I personally prepared.

Courtney bursts into giggles but takes the paddle as instructed and moves toward the center of the room.

"Please let this work," I say as the auction starts.

The first bachelor up for bid is one of the many lawyers in the group. He is slightly balding but otherwise fairly good-looking. The bidding starts slowly but quickly heats up as two girls, both early thirties and dressed in borderline doughty business suits, fight for the man. In the end, the slightly (*slightly*) more attractive girl takes the prize for $250 and the bachelor beams with pride. As he heads through the crowd to meet his date amid enthusiastic applause, I scan the room for Dan.

I finally see him leaning on a tall pedestal table chatting with a slightly chubby girl with dark curly hair. The girl isn't at all Dan's type, so I know I don't have to feel insecure. If anything, she makes me feel more certain that tonight is the night Dan and I will reunite. Unlike Defender Bitch, who was a more attractive version of my tall, light-haired self, this girl isn't any sort of competition. They are both laughing, and seeing his big, open-mouthed grin makes me smile. Dan has an adorable laugh; it's more of a guffaw, an almost goofy-sounding spasm that comes from his belly. It's completely infectious, though, and I can never hear him laugh without giggling a little myself.

"Can I get you anything?" Buck asks, breaking my stare.

Most of my face is numb, but I'm still feeling pretty nervous, so I decide that one more glass of wine would be a good idea. Buck quickly returns carrying two glasses and hands one to me.

"Cheers," he says, looking (really, what can only be described as gazing) into my eyes as our glasses clink. "I hope the night turns out the way you want it to," he adds in a tone that confuses me. My eyes follow his glass as it travels to his lips. His face is covered with the beginnings of blond stubble. I have secretly always thought a five o'clock shadow extremely sexy and often begged Dan to skip his razor on the weekends. He always refused. In the end, it's probably better, because a smooth face is so nice to snuggle against and you don't have to worry about getting one of those unattractive face rashes à la Katie Holmes from too much kissing. I take a sip from my own glass and then turn my attention back to the auction.

The Harvard alumnae are apparently both wealthy and desperate because each bachelor is raking in more dough than the one before. In fact, the bidding is getting pretty cutthroat. I am halfway through my third (fifth) glass when the auctioneer announces in his speedy monosyllabic voice that the next bachelor up for bid is "Daniel McCafferty. Ladies, this former midwesterner both lives and works as an assistant district attorney right here in beautiful Beverly Hills, 90210."

Lives in 90212, I silently say to myself. I don't know why, but it's probably the only thing that bugs me about Dan . . . the fact that he is constantly trying to pass off his south-of-Wilshire apartment—which is a beautiful apartment—as 90210.

"Let's start the bidding at two hundred dollars," the auctioneer concludes, and I snap to attention. Dan was supposed to be a fifty-dollar bachelor. There weren't any two-hundred-dollar bachelors!

Almost on cue, Suzanne comes up to me, her speed date still tagging along like a lost puppy. "Lizzie," she says with a smile, "we are making so much! These girls are so desperate that I upped everyone's opening bids, starting with this guy," she says.

"But this guy was so mean to Fatty What's-her-name in our dorm!" I say with a pout before realizing how bad I sound.

Suzanne looks taken aback for a second. "Martha Wheeler, but she's been chatting with him all night, so I figure if she can forgive him he must not be that bad," she explains, motioning at the round, curly-haired brunette that had Dan laughing up a storm. I look at her in shock and horror—my fiancé had sex with her and never told me about it . . . and clearly she *is* my competition tonight because not only were she and Dan chatting like old friends (which I guess they technically are), her red Ping-Pong paddle is proudly held high. My eyes widen in horror.

"That's my Lizzie, she's so defensive of her girlfriends," Buck says adoringly, slipping one strong arm around my waist. "One of the many qualities I can't help but love," he adds.

He smells so incredibly good that I am completely distracted and don't even notice Courtney holding up her paddle when the auctioneer asks, "Do I hear five hundred?"

"I wish I could auction you off," Suzanne says without taking her eyes off Buck. "We'd get enough to house all the homeless."

"I'm incredibly taken," Buck answers gently and leans down to give me a peck. His lips land in the little space behind my jawbone and under my ear. It's such an innocent gesture, but I tingle between my legs and my panties feel moist. His arm is still around my waist as I turn and look up into his blue eyes. Suddenly we are the only two people in the room and I desperately want to kiss him. I have to feel the warmth of his lips and taste his tongue. I have been wondering—my mouth has been watering for it since the day in his kitchen so long ago. The expensive white wine pulsing through my veins gives me courage and I grab his lower lip between my own. I kiss him and he softly kisses me back. I hear Suzanne say, "Aaah," to my side, but I have no shame. I slip my tongue into Buck's mouth and his kissing intensifies. Dan would never kiss me like this in public (or private), I think with delight, but then much too quickly I come screeching back to reality.

I hear Dan's voice yelling about the buzz of the crowd, but it takes me a second to realize what he is saying.

"That girl is NOT a Harvard graduate!" he hollers, motioning at Courtney, who is standing like a deer in headlights with her auction paddle still raised half way. "Who is in charge here?" Dan summons.

"We are!" Suzanne retorts from beside me, motioning at me as she speaks. "Courtney Cambridge is a Harvard grad . . . and she's *main line* . . . she was Lizzie Platner's freshman year roommate. Right, Lizzie?" she asks me to confirm.

"Oh, um, well . . . I thought she was. It's hard to remember," I fumble, my mind too cloudy from alcohol and my legs still wobbly from Buck's kiss.

"Elizabeth?" Dan demands from the stage.

"Hi," I greet him brightly. All I can do now is hope he's happy to see me. It takes about a split second to see that he is not happy. I sense that everyone in the room is staring at me. I am vaguely aware of a flash of gold rushing in front of me hissing, "Let's get out of here!" and then Buck's hand is grabbing my own and pulling me through the crowd and out the door into the cool night air. Once outside, I gulp a breath of air and look back at the restaurant door, unsure of what will happen next.

"You seriously had to flee the party while everyone there chanted, 'Crashers go home!'?!?" Tiffany asked for probably the fourth time. Each time she asked, she sounded a little less horrified and a little more delighted. There was part of her that couldn't believe that her completely average and boring small-town existence had turned into this. Spending her summer vacation trying to help her resistant godmother reunite with her unwilling ex-fiancé definitely wasn't how Tiffany had imagined her break would be.

The morning after the third failed attempt to get Dan to take Elizabeth back, Tiffany wondered how long this was going to go on. The first two were kind of fun, and this third one ended up being entertaining, but even a teenager could see that this man didn't want Lizzie back. How long until she would figure it out? Plus, it was extremely clear that there was a man who *did* want Lizzie—Buck Platner. Buck seemed to spend most of their visits trying to dodge Courtney and be with Lizzie, who seemed completely unaware. It seemed that the only time she gave him a second glance was when Courtney was dragging him away.

Tiffany had to physically restrain herself when Elizabeth said with a sigh over her morning coffee, "Oh well, I guess Plan C didn't work ... what's Plan D?" Tiffany, Elizabeth,

Buck, and Courtney were all crowded around a table at Du-Pars. Although Tiffany had yet to see a celebrity, the coffee shop had become her favorite breakfast place, so she convinced everyone to go there almost every weekend. Tiffany looked up from her bite of pancake, melted butter dripping back down onto her plate. Elizabeth was looking around the table waiting for a response. Courtney shrugged slightly as she picked at a veggie egg-white omelet, and Buck visibly cringed. Tiffany also shrugged, but her shrug was directed at Buck. She honestly couldn't figure out why Elizabeth couldn't figure this one out.

"I think all we have left is the reverse rear-end bump," Tiffany offered, hoping that Elizabeth would continue to reject the plan that would damage her beloved car.

As she said it, she watched Lizzie's face. Much to Tiffany's horror, her expression changed from a scowling, head-shaking look to one of resignation and acceptance.

"Well, if that's what we've got, then I guess we have no choice," she said solemnly.

Tiffany almost choked on the large mouthful she had just shoveled in . . . she couldn't believe it had come to this.

Back at the apartment, she cornered Elizabeth in the narrow hallway between their bedrooms. Buck was in the living room trying to avoid Courtney. It seemed that there wasn't a seat he could sit in where she wouldn't find a way to practically climb on top of him. He had taken to standing six inches in front of the television set as if he couldn't get a good enough view of the large screen from the sofa a few feet away.

"You really want to go through with Plan D?" Tiffany asked Elizabeth, blocking her path to the bathroom.

"What choice do I have?" she asked. Her voice sounded as if she had been worn down.

"There are other guys in the world," Tiffany said pointedly. She then raised her eyebrows and tilted her head down the hall where a few steps away Buck was avoiding Courtney by feigning great interest in the remote control.

Elizabeth wrinkled her brow with confusion before gasping, "Buck?!?" Her cheeks flushed such a bright shade of red that she looked sunburned. "Oh my God . . . no," she finished.

"Why not?" Tiffany pressured. "He's totally hot."

Tiffany felt hopeful for a moment. Elizabeth's face continued to glow like a sunset, and she seemed to be thinking it over.

Finally she said, "No. He's just not what I'm looking for. He's a great guy, a great friend . . . but he's . . . he's not . . . and besides, he's with Courtney." Elizabeth didn't seem to have a real reason, just a lame answer.

Tiffany let out a disappointed sigh and shrugged. "He's not interested in Courtney," she said quietly as she turned and sulked down the hall. At fifteen years old, she could see the mistake Elizabeth was making, but her thirty-two-year-old godmother didn't seem to get it.

~39~

Twenty-four hours later, the conversation with Tiffany is still running through my head on a never-ending replay. She came right out and said what I have been secretly asking myself for months. Why not? Why not Buck? As Tiffany put it, "He's totally hot," not to mention polite, sincere, thoughtful, kind, fun . . . I could go on and on. Why can I go on and on?!? It's just because he's a great friend. I could go on and on about Courtney as well—also a good friend, who happens to be totally in love with Buck. Tiffany is right, though; he's not interested in Courtney. Ugh! I cannot think like that. I have important things to concentrate on . . . like Plan D . . . and my job.

At this moment, I am stuck in the middle of an intersection on Santa Monica Boulevard breaking strict gridlock laws. The light was green when I entered the intersection, but halfway through, the traffic suddenly stopped and I got caught as the light turned yellow and then red. Now I'm blocking the cross-traffic and having to endure honking, cursing, and gesturing. Not to mention the bright flash from the odd-looking box on the corner—I'll be getting my ticket in the mail. Lots of intersections have been outfitted with cameras that take your picture if you run a red light and then mail you indisputable proof of the infraction. Should I have smiled for the camera? I'm kind of (just slightly) a minor celebrity now. If nothing else is happening in the world, my moving violation could get noticed. I start to daydream about seeing myself in *Us Weekly*'s "Stars: They're Just Like Us" section.

Finally, my lane begins to move and I am able to escape the crossfire of angry drivers traveling north and south for their morning commute. I suffer through the stop and go all the way to my office, and it feels good to stretch my legs when I finally get out of the car. My apartment is about six miles from where the show tapes, but it takes almost thirty minutes in the morning. I make my way up to my office, as always taking the back steps to avoid any Renee run-ins that aren't absolutely necessary. I am almost at my door when Hope runs up from behind.

"Elizabeth," she hisses, and I stop in my tracks. Hope and I have an agreement that she will always warn me when Renee is up to something. I can tell by her voice that a warning is coming. "Kevin and Max are in your office," she says.

Fuck. Kevin and Max are the heads of the studio that produces the show. It's never a good sign when they come to the stage or production offices. Most of their communication with anyone on our staff is through the lower-level executives who report to them. The fact that they are waiting for me is a really bad sign. I peek at my watch. It's 9:07 a.m. I am on time 99 percent of the time—why did traffic have to be so exceptionally bad today of all days?

"Kevin, Max," I say, trying to sound both competent and confident as I walk into my office, where the suited men are sitting on the couch that wasn't good enough for Renee. "I'm so sorry, I didn't realize you would be here this morning."

"That's alright, Elizabeth," Max says, "Why don't you close the door."

My heart sinks into my stomach, creating an uncomfortable digestion issue on contact.

"Do you need a moment to get settled?" Kevin asks.

They are known for playing "good cop/bad cop," but nobody ever knows which will be which on any given day—apparently today Kevin is the good cop.

"No, I'm always ready to go," I answer, shoving my belongings under my desk as I take a seat behind it. "What's going on?"

I brace myself for what they are about to say. I have never been fired from a job in my entire life. I have never failed at anything . . . there isn't room for failure in the plan. (Do not think that I have failed to get back together with Dan, because it's not a failure until I give up and I have absolutely no intention of giving up.) What should I do? Should I fight for my job? My eyes dart to the other side of the room, where I still have my respectably sized pile of fan mail. I should show it to them.

"We want to make some changes on the show," Max says coldly.

Before he says it, I know that they are cutting out the "fact girl" segment. I know it's a stupid segment, but it's those sixty seconds of air time each day that keep me here. Without that, this is a pathetic job as a fact checker.

"The fact girl segment is out," he continues.

Just like that. I knew he was going to say it, but the weight of actually hearing the words hits me hard.

"People really like me," I manage to get out. "I have a pile of fan mail from when I filled in for Renee," I add weakly. In my head it sounded like an argument on my behalf, but coming out of my mouth it sounds more like a plea for my life.

"We agree," Kevin says, pushing his small metal-framed glasses up his nose. "That's why we want you to cohost the show with Renee," he says.

"Excuse me?" I couldn't possibly have heard him right.

"No more 'fact girl.' You're on the couch with Renee—it's

like *The View* but cut in half, like Regis and Kelly," Max barks. He is keeping up his bad cop persona, but it's really not as powerful when delivering good news.

"What does Renee think?" I ask timidly.

"Do I look like I care?" Max asks.

I can't help smiling. "Sounds fantastic," I tell him. It's hard to stay in my chair, I'm so excited. It's actually happening—at long last my career is taking off.

"Figure out who on your staff can assume your role as the head of this department and prep them. As of Monday, you're in your new post."

"Thank you, I will," is all I can muster. I am beaming from ear to ear, and then it gets better. I watch as Renee walks past my glass wall and sees Kevin and Max sitting on my couch. Without bothering to knock, she opens the door to my office.

"Gentlemen!" she gushes. "Were you looking for me?"

"Why would we be in here with the door closed if we were looking for you?" Max asks totally deadpan. Renee just stares at him, completely at a loss for words. Gone are the days when the studio sucked up to her.

"We would like to have a word, though," Kevin adds.

"Of course. Is there some sort of a problem with Elizabeth's department?" she asks.

Inside I seethe that she would assume such a thing, but secretly I rejoice at the train they are about to run her over with.

"Not at all," Kevin reassures her. "Why don't we step into your office," he suggests.

Renee looks confused but leads the executives out my door and down the hall to her posh corner office that is decorated more like a living room than a place of business.

As soon as they are out of earshot, I let out a squeal of joy. This is a sign . . . it's a sign that all my hard work is finally paying off. I'm finally on the road to having the life I've dreamed of. I think it's a sign that Plan D is going to work and things will once and for all be perfect.

I pick up the phone to spread my news, and once again the first person I think of to dial is Buck. I hang up the phone . . . I can't call him. I need to get him out of my head—permanently. Instead, I call out my door, "Hope! It's promotion time!" and as I wait for her to come in, the fantasy of being in *Us Weekly* fills my head again.

~40~

A few nights later, I am sitting in my apartment with Tiffany and Courtney finalizing the brilliant (horrific) plan that is Plan D.

"Okay." Courtney leads the group. "So we know that every morning Dan leaves his apartment at eight thirty-five," she says, pointing to a large white page on which she has drawn a clock with the small hand on the eight and the big hand on the seven. She's being extremely dramatic, but it's pretty entertaining so Tiffany and I are going along with it. "Now," she continues, "it is my recommendation that you be parked down the street from his apartment no later than eight twenty-five on the designated morning (which happens to be tomorrow) to ensure that you are ready to go."

I nod my head in agreement. This isn't the first time that she has laid this all out for me. The first time, she admitted that while she has never actually performed the reverse rear-end bump, she has followed people many times and has a lot of light to shed on that topic. The plan isn't complicated, and this repeat run-through isn't necessary except to make me laugh at Courtney acting like she's preparing troops to go into battle.

She's getting to my least favorite part—the part where there is metal-to-metal contact between my adorable BMW and Dan's perfect Audi—when the doorbell rings. I jump up to answer, confused, since I'm not expecting anyone (my only two friends are already inside). On the other side of the door stands a man, his entire face and most of his torso covered by an arrangement of yellow roses with red tips, and hot-pink roses. They are just starting to bloom, and the swirls of pink, yellow, and red makes the bouquet look like a perfect California sunset.

"Elizabeth Castle?" he asks, his voice muffled through the sea of blooms.

"Yes," I say, astounded and excited that the roses are for me and he didn't say something like, 'Your neighbor's not home, can I leave these here?' "Sign here," he says, shifting the entire arrangement to one side and holding out a small clipboard.

I quickly sign and take the flowers, which turn out to be in a basket filled with moss and ivy. It's a signature arrangement from Mark's Garden, one of the best florists in Los Angeles. If there are flowers from a celebrity wedding in a magazine, chances are that Mark's Garden was responsible, and Renee insists that a fresh bouquet from the florist fill her dressing room every three days. As I struggle to close the door and balance the heavy arrangement, my mind races trying to figure out the sender's identity.

Could it be Renee? Seems unlikely, since at this point in time her sending me dead flowers feels more realistic. Besides Courtney though, she's the only one I can think of who could afford them.

"I wonder who they're from!" Tiffany asks in awe. I am quite certain that she's never seen anything like this in Victory, since the town's little florist shop is mostly filled with carnations wrapped in cellophane.

"Maybe we won't need Plan D after all," Courtney suggests, and my heart soars at the thought . . . on all fronts it would be a dream come true.

I struggle over to the small bistro table, which is completely covered by the arrangement, and search around the mass of roses for the small card I know must be tucked somewhere. At last I find it, tied subtly to an especially large pink rose. Excitedly, I rip the miniature envelope open and read the note.

Elizabeth—
You've already mastered breaking hearts and burning feet . . .
now break a leg.
Yours,
Buck

I'm speechless. Simultaneously, I am devastated and thrilled. I knew before I opened it that the flowers weren't from Dan. Never in his life has he ordered from Mark's Garden, but it would have been so easy if they had been. Receiving these flowers (and this note) from Buck is a bad thing—it only feeds the feelings I am desperately trying to quell . . . but it feels so good. I silently stare at the little white card and read his message over and over. *"Breaking hearts . . ."* What does he mean by that?

"Well?!?" Tiffany almost screams, bursting with anticipation.

I look down at Tiff and Courtney, their faces portraying their eagerness to know the sender's identity. How will Courtney take this? I subtly palm the tiny note. "They are a congratulations bouquet from Buck," I say trying to sound nonchalant. "I don't even know how he knew I got promoted," I add.

"I told him," Tiffany booms proudly, and gives me a look that clearly goes along with the talk she gave me regarding Buck's great worth.

I glance at Courtney, who looks a little confused. "That's

weird," she says, "he never sends me flowers. I wonder what's going on?"

Even though it's against my better judgment and I hate doing it in front of Tiffany for fear that I will add fuel to her fire to get me together with Buck, I can't pass up the opportunity.

"What *is* going on with you guys?" I probe, careful to avoid eye contact with either of them.

"Uh, I dunno," she groans. I'm nervous she's going to stop there, but it's not Courtney's style. "To be honest, it's not really going anywhere. I mean, he's totally hot . . . but he's kind of a prude . . . and he's sort of boring," she explains, twisting a blonde ringlet around her finger as she talks.

I try to be reserved, but I can't hide my smile. I am completely relieved that she considers him a prude. I still can't stand the thought of anything happening between them.

"Buck's not boring!" Tiffany defends him.

I'm glad to hear he's boring—just another reason why he isn't right for me. If he bores Courtney, it means that despite the sexy tuxedo and the beautiful flowers, he is the small-town meathead I thought he was.

"All he ever wants to talk about is Elizabeth," Courtney complains to Tiffany, and my cheeks flush. She doesn't dwell on it though. "Anyway," she continues, "we should probably finish going over this stuff so you're ready for tomorrow." She flips to another page of diagrams. On this page, she has drawn two cars colliding and hearts floating up from the wreckage.

Tiffany gives me another look, her eyebrows raised. I know that if she could speak freely she would repeat, "All he ever wants to talk about is Elizabeth." She wouldn't need to repeat it because it's playing nonstop in my head.

I glance back at the flowers. They are more than just a friendly "Congratulations" bouquet . . . aren't they? Red roses mean love, but what does yellow with red rims mean and what does hot pink signify? And the note . . . the note is extremely suggestive, isn't it? Or is it just meant to be funny? The only thing I know for sure is that it's the time of year that roses smell the best, and this many in my apartment is creating an overwhelming scent that I find completely intoxicating.

~41~

Buck knows that Lizzie thinks of the auction as a complete disaster, but he actually considers it to have been a pretty successful weekend—at least the first half. He was finally able to get time alone with Lizzie and was positive that he felt the connection between them that he had sensed lingering all this time—she was the one who had kissed him after all, and the kiss was amazing. It was everything Buck had hoped it would be—and it definitely wasn't a surprise to him that their lips ended up locked. He had pulled out all the stops.

The only unfortunate thing was that Dan the Asshole picked that moment to expose Courtney and Elizabeth as imposters and party crashers. Buck could only imagine where the night might have gone if he'd had just a few more seconds. In his mind, their kiss would have happened in time to leave the event before the bidding on Daniel McCafferty even began. The upside was that Buck felt certain that after seeing how nasty Dan was, Lizzie would once and for all be over the jerk. Unfortunately, the next morning, her behavior toward Buck had returned to being mysteriously vague and she was talking about other ideas to get back together with Dan.

Sunday morning as their group left Du-Pars, Elizabeth and

Courtney were deep in conversation about the particulars of yet another moronic plan, this one dubbed "Plan D." Tiffany fell behind and walked alongside Buck.

"I don't know what her deal is," the teenager explained, a hint of sorrow in her voice.

"Me neither," Buck agreed.

"I wish the two of you would end up together," Tiffany admitted somewhat wistfully, and when she did, a light went on in Buck's head. Tiffany could be his man on the inside. She knew every detail about Lizzie's life because she lived right in the middle of it.

"Me too," Buck answered quietly, on high alert to gauge her response.

"You do?!?" Tiffany gasped. "Maybe I could help you!" she offered, enthusiastically taking his bait.

"Maybe you could," Buck told her. Even in front of Tiffany he didn't want to appear desperate.

From that moment on, Buck had Tiffany in his corner and the playing field suddenly sloped drastically in his favor. That very night Tiffany asked Lizzie about Buck and reported back that there was a lot of blushing, and that concern over Courtney's feelings was the only hang-up about getting together with Buck that she could verbalize. Every day Buck and Tiffany would talk and she would give him updates on the progress of Plan D and what was going on in Lizzie's life, including the big promotion at work that propelled her to become the cohost of the show. As soon as Buck hung up with Tiffany, he called the florist in Los Angeles (actually Sherman Oaks) that he had heard Lizzie talk about at the date auction and spent a ridiculous amount on flowers.

Buck knew what time the flowers would be delivered and waited patiently by the phone for Elizabeth's thank-you call. He knew it would come, he just had to wait a couple of hours. A little after ten o'clock, his phone rang.

"Buck, I don't know what to say," Lizzie said, truly sounding like her breath was taken away. "They are the most beautiful flowers ever."

"I'm glad you like them. Congratulations," Buck replied.

The call lasted over two hours. They talked about almost everything that had happened in their lives since the night of Buck's senior prom. He told her about playing Wildcat football and attending law school, she told him about her days at UCLA and how she ended up in her current position at *The Renee Foster Show!*. By the end of the call, Buck could hardly keep his eyes open, but even after they said good night and hung up, he had trouble falling asleep. He was completely crazy about Lizzie and had a feeling she might be feeling the same way about him.

~42~

I think the reason I put off calling to thank Buck for the beautiful flowers until after ten o'clock is because I have a feeling I know how it will end. I wait until Courtney has gone home and Tiffany has gone to sleep before getting in my own bed and dialing Buck's number on my cordless phone. The moment he says, "Hello??" little shivers begin to travel my spine. The conversation is so easy and natural—two hours and twenty minutes fly by, and even after that long I want to talk more. After exchanging sleepy "goodnights," I click off my phone and hold it tightly to my chest. My mind can't help but wander back to the night of the charity auction and my kiss with Buck. I wonder where it would have gone if Dan hadn't snapped me back to reality? Ugh . . . Dan . . . I really don't want to think about him tonight—tomorrow morning, in a few short hours, I'm supposed to attempt the reverse rear-end that will hopefully reunite me with Dan once and for all.

I go back to thinking about Buck, and I picture him sitting in his comfortably messy (I have no idea how I have changed so much as to recognize that there could be comfort among mess) living room talking to me on the phone. In my version, he is wearing the long mesh gym shorts he often wears around his house, but his perfectly toned chest is bare. I let my imagination take me away and I find myself in the house with him, summoning him to his bedroom. I am wearing the lingerie purchased for the charity auction, and when he sees me, a noticeable bulge rises in his gym shorts and his blue eyes twinkle mischievously. He reaches out and pulls me into his body with one strong arm and kisses me the way he did at the auction. Quickly though, his kissing becomes more passionate and moves down my body. He gently removes the black lace bra and softly kisses my erect nipples. In my fantasy I groan quietly with pleasure, but I also let out a small moan in the silence of my bedroom, startling myself. I close my eyes again and allow Buck to lay me down on his bed and climb on top of me, his skin smooth and warm. I desperately want him inside me, but all I can do is reach into the small drawer of my nightstand and take out my pink plastic vibrator. As I insert it, another small groan of pleasure escapes me and I scold myself that this will be the last time I fantasize about Buck Platner.

~43~

The next morning, when my alarm goes off early, it takes me a minute to remember why I am waking up at such an ungodly hour. When it dawns on me that the day of the reverse rear-end has arrived, I contemplate turning off the alarm and going back to sleep. I remind myself that I can't—getting back together with Dan is the best thing for me, and if Plan D can make it happen, then it's worth a shot.

I carefully apply my makeup so that it looks like I'm not wearing any—the way Dan likes it—and get dressed. I'm a ball of nerves both about hurting my precious car and facing Dan again. Let's be honest: all the previous encounters have gone quite poorly and I'm anxious that this one will be the same. I step out of my room, ready to go, in hopes that Tiffany will be waiting to wish me good luck. She's not, the door to her room is shut and she must still be asleep. I bypass the kitchen, too nervous to eat, and leave the apartment. When I arrive at my car, I am overcome with guilt . . . there it sits, innocently waiting for me to come and drive to work. "I'm sorry," I tell it as I get inside and put my workbag on the passenger seat.

There is only a small amount of traffic and I'm parked down the street from Dan's apartment at twenty minutes after eight. Now I just have to sit and wait for Dan to leave. I feel completely self-conscious, as if all the neighbors are looking out their windows and talking about how incredibly pathetic I have become. I feel completely ashamed—I *have* become pathetic. As I sit there, I try to look as if I have a purpose and I'm not just waiting to stalk my ex-boyfriend. I pull out some paperwork regarding next week's show. I look like someone who's waiting to pick up a coworker, I decide, and hope that the people who have walked by either with their dogs or to their own cars think that's my purpose as well. I hold the stack of papers in front of my face, high enough so that I have some coverage, but low enough so that I can see the driveway of Dan's apartment. His building has underground parking and I keep my eye on the gate for signs of movement. As I sit there, I can't help thinking about Buck and our conversation. We talked about everything going on in our lives—except Plan D (or A, B and C)—and the feeling that I kept it from him adds to my growing shame.

At 8:36, I see the wrought iron gate in front of Dan's driveway start to move and his blue Audi emerges. The butterflies in my stomach begin to swarm and I start the engine and pull away from the curb. I follow Dan for a few blocks, staying a couple of cars behind him to avoid being seen. About a mile into it, my confidence emerges and I know it's time to go past him. It's important not to look at Dan while I'm doing this. Just in case he notices me, it's best to look like I don't notice him—like it's just a coincidence that we're on the same road at the same time. I move into the left lane, which is moving slightly faster than the right, and I apply pressure to the gas. The car obediently charges forward and a few seconds later, I am past Dan. I realize once I am ahead of him that I had been holding my breath, and I let out a huge rush of air . . . it's time to get into position for the reverse rear-end. I watch in my rearview mirror for the moment to pull in front of Dan. This is the moment when getting caught is the greatest risk, but about a million people in L.A. have white BMW convertibles, so I just have to hope that the car doesn't attract Dan's attention too much.

Suddenly, there it is . . . the opening in the traffic and the spot that I need to pull into. I quickly turn on my signal and start to move over. Before my car is safely in the right lane, I hear a huge crashing sound and feel a bang from behind and to the right. I've been hit! I don't know what to do—I am absolutely paralyzed by shock. I stop the car and take inventory of my body . . . I'm in one piece and nothing seems injured. I can't believe this is happening to me. Not only is my precious car damaged, but I didn't even get to do the reverse rear-end that was going to reunite me with Dan. I slump over the steering wheel and break into tears.

The sound of someone tapping on my window gets my attention, and through tear-filled eyes I look to my left.

"Are you okay?" the person is yelling through the glass. "Can you move to the side?"

Suddenly I remember that in an accident you're not supposed to completely block Wilshire Boulevard while you bawl your eyes out. I nod and collect myself enough to maneuver the car two lanes over and into a vacant parking spot. I am so upset by the accident that my body is actually shaking and my head is spinning. Trying hard to remember the protocol, I reach into the glove compartment for my registration and insurance information. I finally find it and open the door to find the other person involved—I'm really not even sure if I am at fault or not. I stand up and my legs feel as wobbly as noodles. I look around me, but everything is a blur behind the watery tears that still fill my eyes. In an instant, someone— a man—rushes up and grabs me.

"Oh my God, Elizabeth. Are you okay?"

The voice belongs to Daniel McCafferty.

"Dan?" I ask, needing confirmation.

Squished in his tight embrace, I look around, actually

wondering for a split second if I survived the accident. Could I be in heaven?

"Elizabeth, I didn't see you. What are you even doing in this part of town? I can't believe of all the cars on the road, yours is the one I hit," Dan says, his voice overflowing with guilt.

"You're the one who hit me?" I ask, still completely confused. "Was it my fault?"

"I don't know whose fault it was," Dan says, still holding me (which is adding to my confusion), his voice softening, "but I feel like there is a reason you keep popping up in my life," he continues. "Maybe we really are meant to be together."

Did Dan just say that he and I are meant to be together? "You and me?" I ask, my tears turning to tears of joy.

"I think so," Dan says and kisses me.

My head spins like a top. Here I am, standing on the curb, rush-hour traffic passing me by (and giving nasty gestures as they go), and Dan is holding me tightly.

I did it. Plan D might not have gone exactly according to plan, but it is a success. I have Dan back—I have my dream life back. I kiss him back. With all the adrenaline and emotion of the morning, I fail to notice that the kiss lacks any of the chemistry that my liplock with Buck had.

~44~

A week later, it's as if the breakup never happened. Dan and I are back in our routine of red-rose bouquets, date nights, and sleeping apart for convenience. I have put the diamond ring back on my left hand, but aside from the decision that I should do that, we have completely avoided talking about the future. Dan has been politely cold to Tiffany and she has been (barely) civil in return. I am trying to bask in the happiness that my life is falling back into place, but for some odd reason I am completely miserable.

I don't know why I can't work myself out of this rut. Every morning when I go outside and see the navy blue dent on the right side of my car I feel like I want to throw up. At work, things couldn't be better—aside from the fact that every chance she gets Renee glares at me as if I somehow influenced the studio to turn against her. Please . . . if I had that kind of power, I would have wielded it ages ago! Things at work are so good that when I leave the building, I am actually feeling good and happy, but then I see my car and the nausea returns. If only it wasn't Daylight Saving Time and it was dark out when I left the building . . . I could hang on to the euphoria that comes from finally being a full-time on-air host (and torturing Renee at the same time).

Once I get home, I have to deal with the nonstop sulking that Tiffany has taken to.

"You know, you have become the kind of teenager who gives teenagers a bad name," I tell her while waiting for Dan to pick me up for dinner.

"Hmmm," she snips at me before turning the volume up on the TV.

"I was never going to be with him," I add.

The truth is that I'm having a hard enough time not thinking about Buck without Tiffany throwing a fit that the relationship that was never going to happen to begin with didn't happen. She ignores me when I say this and all I can do is sigh. Dan rings the bell and I head to the door. I open it, hoping that when I see him I'll have some sort of a reaction that confirms my life choices. There he stands in creased chinos and a dark green Lacoste shirt. His hair is a little messed up from pulling the collared shirt over his head, and he greets me with his adorable grin.

"Hungry?" he asks

"Definitely," I answer, heading out the door without inviting Dan to step inside. The farther I can keep him from Tiffany, the happier everyone will be.

I feel angry with myself for not feeling differently. I got my wish—my dream came true, so I can't understand why I am not elated.

"How was work?" I ask Dan, trying to fill my mind. Unfortunately he has parked across the street, making the white dent on the front left corner of his car the first thing I see when I exit my building. My appetite disappears.

"Work was work, Elizabeth," he answers. I used to find this type of answer, "work was work/golf was golf/traffic was traffic," adorable, but now I find it annoying and bordering on obnoxious.

"Things are fantastic for me," I tell him, excited to share all the changes that have happened. Suddenly I have my own dressing room, wardrobe consultant, and hair and makeup person . . . plus the studio has given me enormous praise for my first full week as cohost.

"Great," he says. "Where do you want to eat? Anywhere you want . . . just not sushi because I had that for lunch."

I'm more than a little let down that "great" is all I get in response to my exciting news, but I realize that Dan is probably hungry and tired after a long day at work. "How about Italian," I suggest.

He moves his head from side to side, a gesture he makes that signals he is thinking about the information. Like the spinning dial the mouse arrow turns into when a computer is processing, Dan's head always moves shoulder-to-shoulder. Finally it stops bobbing, "Nah, let's get Chinese," he says.

"Okay," I concede. (I had Chinese for lunch.)

After dinner, Dan looks at me with one eyebrow up . . . I know what is coming. "Why don't we go back to my place for a little while." Translation: I want sex, but I don't want you spending the night.

He doesn't even wait for me to respond (my answer is yes) before steering the car toward his small apartment. I follow him upstairs and take a glance around. I haven't been in the apartment since we reunited. Things look exactly the same, but I can't help wondering if someone else—Defender Bitch or chubby Martha Wheeler—was here in my absence. I desperately want to ask Dan, but I feel the relationship is too delicate right now to risk upsetting the balance. Dan closes the door behind me and starts to kiss my neck.

He leads me over to the couch and gently pushes me down. He pulls his shirt over his head, turning it inside out, before climbing on top of me. It's all very spontaneous for Dan, who normally insists we be in the bedroom where he can neatly fold his shirt and drape it on the chair next to his bed before we do anything. He kisses me on the mouth and neck while unfastening his khaki pants and my jeans.

"Don't you want to go to the bedroom?" I ask.

"No," is his only response as he grabs at my black lace panties without bothering to notice them.

I should be incredibly turned on—it's like he's lost all self control and just can't wait to have me—but I'm not. Instead, I'm annoyed that he isn't even bothering with the uncomfortable foreplay he used to take great pride in, and I'm completely curious about why he doesn't want me in his bedroom.

I'm hardly even wet when Dan starts fumbling a condom onto his penis and pushes himself inside me. The latex skidding into my body hurts, but Dan takes my gasping sound to mean I am having as good a time as he is. Thankfully, he is finished in about eight minutes. He pulls out and rolls next to me on the couch, huffing and puffing like he's just completed a scene for a porno. I didn't bother to fake an orgasm—there really wasn't time. In fact, I'm pretty sore, but Dan doesn't inquire how my experience was, anyway.

I stand up and retrieve my underwear from the spot on the floor where Dan dropped it. It's so unlike him to leave clothes crumpled on the floor. I wonder if the new sex style is the preference of one of the women who was here in my absence? Does Defender Bitch like it like this? I pull on my panties and my jeans; Dan looks up at me.

"Ready to go home?" he asks.

"Yeah, I think so," I tell him. "I have an early morning," I explain, pulling a page from his playbook. Before our split, that was his most common reason for being unable to spend the night with me.

He stands up and gets dressed, then escorts me out of the room. I feel even worse than before . . . I've really got to snap out of this. I look over at Dan as he drives, the window down and the wind ruffling his dark hair. He is adorable. He is wonderful. He really is.

~45~

"Things are not good here," Tiffany pouted into the phone. She sat in the hallway with her back against the wall and her knees bent up against her chest. As she complained, she twisted the old-fashioned spiral cord of the phone.

"What's wrong?" Buck asked, genuinely concerned.

"Plan D worked and she's back with Dan," the teenager explained.

Buck let out a disappointed sigh. He really hadn't thought this would happen, and now he's not quite sure how to proceed. "Oh, well," he answered sadly.

"No, not 'oh, well,' " Tiffany snapped. "You have to fight for her."

"What can I do? She wanted to be with him all along . . . she was clear about that."

"She belongs with you," Tiffany answered sternly. "Oh shit, she's at the door . . . gotta go!" she quickly hung up the phone, lunged down the hall into her bedroom, and closed the door behind her. Avoiding Elizabeth, especially when she was with Dan, had become Tiffany's plan of action.

She was grateful that the guest room/office that had become her bedroom also housed Elizabeth's iMac, since e-mail was her primary connection with the outside world. Tiffany booted up the machine and immediately went to hotmail.com to check her e-mail. Six new messages were waiting for her. At first, the thought of having six new e-mails since she checked her account a few hours ago was pleasing, but as soon as Tiffany saw that five of the half dozen were from Red, her attitude changed. As if she didn't have enough drama dealing with Elizabeth's love life, Red had become an almost constant annoyance. True, he was her boyfriend, since she hadn't bothered to do anything to change that, but really Tiffany wished he could take a hint a bit better.

Tiffany knew from the beginning that Red was more interested in her than she was in him, but he wasn't a total idiot . . . he knew how recently her relationship with Scott had ended and he should have been able to figure out he was nothing but a rebound. Mind you, he was a total sweetheart. He always paid whenever they went out and did nice things like open car doors and offer her his sweatshirt in the cold. Plus, he never pressured Tiffany for so much as a goodnight kiss, let alone going all the way like Scott had. But still, Tiffany felt about him more like you feel about a friend . . . and maybe not even that strongly, since she'd missed her girlfriends quite a bit since leaving Victory but almost never thought about Red unless she was reading one of his many e-mails. Maybe she didn't miss him because he never gave her a chance to do so. He sent so many e-mails per day that Tiffany almost felt she needed a break from him.

The first of the five e-mails sent that afternoon was one of his generic "I miss you" ones. They were annoying, but Tiffany had grown pretty used to ignoring and rebuffing them, since he usually sent about five per day. The second was the same thing. Things got worse with Red's third e-mail. In this note, he laid out a "plan" to get Tiffany back to Victory, which involved the two of them getting engaged and living with his parents. The thought made Tiffany feel sick. Besides not being in love with the guy, and only fifteen years old, the truth is that Tiffany wasn't in any sort of hurry to return to her hometown. Obviously, she missed her life there and living in L.A. wasn't anything close to perfect, but getting out of Victory made Tiffany feel she finally had space to take deep breaths.

Tiffany reread Red's e-mail . . . she didn't have a clue how she was going to get out of this without specifically breaking up with him. It was something she knew she had to do, she just hadn't had the heart to do it yet. She couldn't help wondering why everybody had to have a plan—Elizabeth's plan to get back together with Dan, Buck's plan to win over Elizabeth, and now Red's plan to bring her back to Victory. Couldn't anybody just live their life? Red's fourth e-mail was a follow-up to his third. He wanted to know if she'd read his e-mail and if she wanted him (driven by his father) to come get her that weekend. Ugh . . . the fifth e-mail was a repeat of the third. At least Tiffany didn't have to deal with Red calling her all the time, since she had lied and told him Elizabeth only had a cell phone that she could use just in emergencies.

The sixth e-mail was from her best friend, Laci, and Tiffany was excited to read it both as a distraction from the Red problem and to catch up on the hometown gossip. Instead, it was just a complaint about how Red had started calling her in a frenzy because Tiffany wasn't returning his messages. *Ugh.* Tiffany clicked the mouse at the top of the screen and a blank e-mail popped up in front of her. She began to compose a breakup message but then stopped. This was something she had to do in person, and as much as she didn't want to deal with Lizzie, she needed a ride.

Tiffany tentatively stepped out of her room and tiptoed a few steps down the hall toward the dimly lit living room, where she could hear the television on low. She found Elizabeth sitting on the couch watching a *Friends* repeat. She didn't look happy.

"Hi," Tiffany said quietly.

"Oh, hey," a surprised Lizzie answered.

"I need to go to Victory this weekend," the teenager told her. "I need to break up with my boyfriend."

"Okay," Lizzie agreed. "Why are you breaking up?" she asked.

"He's just not the one," Tiffany told her, not wanting to get into the details.

Elizabeth nodded her head in understanding. Tiffany toyed with asking her if everything was okay, but she really didn't want to get into the details of Lizzie's love life either. Instead, she just said, "thanks," and returned to her room, where she sent an e-mail to Red telling him that she would be in town soon so they could talk and another to Laci promising to take care of things with Red. Then Tiffany opened a new e-mail and addressed it to Buck. She simply wrote: *She's not happy. We'll be in Victory this weekend. Figure something out! –T.*

~46~

"Hi, sweetie, how about a road trip this weekend?" I perkily ask Dan.

"Where?" he asks, sounding skeptical.

"To Eagle Lake. Tiffany needs to go to Victory this weekend, and I thought we could drop her off and then drive up to the mountain," I explain. I have the whole trip planned out (in my head).

"Isn't Eagle Lake a ski resort?" Dan asks.

"Yes, yes it is . . . but it's open all year long. They have fantastic hiking and fishing," I tell him, sounding like a page from a travel brochure.

"We don't hike or fish," he points out.

"Right," I agree, "they also have some beautiful spas."

"Look, this weekend really isn't good for me," he says almost sounding annoyed. "I have to golf on Saturday."

"Oh, there is fantastic golfing around Eagle Lake," I say, and I sound a bit more desperate than I'd planned.

I really need Dan to agree to go along on this trip with me. I have to take Tiffany to Victory, but if I stay I'll see Buck and I just don't think that's a good idea.

"Elizabeth," he says shifting from annoyed to exasperated, "I am trying to get invited to become a member at Hillcrest. That means that I need to golf there anytime a member invites me. I have been invited by a member to golf there on Saturday and it is important that I attend."

"Who is the member?" I ask.

There is an awkward pause before Dan says, "Chris Cupper." Chris Cupper is an old friend of Dan's from law school . . . this invitation is definitely not a one-time thing.

"Do you think you could get Chris to invite you next weekend?" I ask sweetly. "This weekend is so important to me . . . and for us. To celebrate our reunion," I explain.

Dan lets out a long sigh before saying, "Okay, if it's that important to you, I'll reschedule with Chris."

"Oh thank you! You won't be sorry. We're going to have the best time." I am overcome with relief.

As soon as we hang up, I turn on my computer, open Safari, and start actually planning the trip. Fortunately, the mountain town really isn't very busy during the summer months and I am able to secure a nice condo for a good price. I think about booking massages for us but decide to wait until we are up there so we can decide together how to fill our days. I have visions of us walking hand in hand, gazing at the beautiful scenery, lying on side-by-side tables while we enjoy massages, and looking into each other's eyes while we sip wine under the stars. This weekend is the perfect thing to renew our relationship (and keep my mind off Buck).

On Friday afternoon we all pile into Dan's Audi. The long drive with Dan and Tiffany together in the small car is the only downside to my plan. The good news is that I managed to load my belongings and myself into the car without making eye contact with the front left bumper, so I am nausea free. Luckily, the car has an appointment at the body shop Monday morning so I won't have to worry about seeing the dent much longer. My car, unfortunately, is another story. Dan doesn't want to report the accident to his insurance company because it will make his rates go up, so I'm going to have to wait a while to get my own car fixed. He thought it made the most sense to get his fixed ASAP and then take care of mine in a few months.

All three of us are silent almost the entire way to Victory . . . not a good, comfortable silence, but at least it's better than bickering. A few times I try to break the quiet by talking about work or even just the scenery, but each time, I am met with an unenthusiastic response. At least Dan and Tiffany have found something in common: they both like to ride along without saying a word. It's a start. Since Dan is a pretty fast driver, we pull into town before dusk and for a moment I feel embarrassed by my hometown.

I have spent most (all) of my relationship with Dan avoiding any and all discussion about Victory. He's only met my parents over the phone and I have been completely vague on details. Since Charla's funeral, however, my stance on the small town has softened and I decided that letting Dan see where I grew up wouldn't be the worst thing ever. Of course, I intend only to let him see it as we drive through town and drop Tiffany off . . . it's not like we're going to my mother's house or anything!

We pull up to Buck's house just as he's getting home from work and catch him climbing out of his big, black truck. He's dressed in wrinkled chinos, an untucked button-front shirt with the sleeves rolled up, and Nike running shoes . . . he's dressed the way Dan dresses on the weekend, but never for work. Buck looks incredibly good, but I command myself to ignore it (which is really hard to do).

"Oh, hey," he says warmly, walking up to the car. His smile melts my heart. "How are you, Tiff?" he asks, opening the rear passenger door. I feel silly that the smile that wasn't even directed my way had an effect on me.

Tiffany gets out of the car, slams the door, and says "Bye" over her shoulder before walking directly onto the porch and into Buck's house. Even Buck seems a little stunned by her behavior, because he is left standing in the driveway holding the Audi door in his hand.

"Okay, then. Did you two want to come in for a drink before heading up the mountain?" he asks courteously.

For some uncontrollable reason I do want to go in, but before I can answer, Dan coldly says, "No, thanks. We'll be back Sunday to pick her up," and puts the car in reverse.

Buck responds with another smile, this one not as warm as the first, and a nod. I feel embarrassed that Buck was being so gracious and Dan was so cold. I give a little wave at Buck, who stands in the driveway watching as Dan quickly backs out.

"Jesus," Dan says once we are back on the highway, "is everyone from the town like that?"

"Like what?" I ask, genuinely confused. I am the first one to be hypercritical of anyone or anything from Victory, but I couldn't find fault with Buck's behavior.

"It was totally rude of him to try and stall our romantic getaway any more that it already had been," Dan says, sounding annoyed.

On the one hand I feel a surge of joy that Dan considers this weekend a romantic getaway, but on the other I feel fiercely protective of Buck. "I think he was just trying to be nice since we'd had a long drive," I say, hoping that I don't come off as protective of him as I feel.

"Whatever," is Dan's only answer, and I have no idea how to read it.

He doesn't say much else for the rest of the drive. Once we are in the town of Eagle Lake, Dan asks me for directions to the hotel.

"Actually, it's a condo," I tell him and fish out the map I printed from the Internet.

"So no maid service?" Dan asks as he follows my navigation.

"I don't think so," I answer, suddenly feeling anxious that the place I thought was so perfect isn't good enough.

He doesn't say another word about it until we find the condominium complex and make our way to the rental office. We check in, and Dan inquires of the person behind the desk about local golf. He then schedules himself a tee time for the next morning. I hide my disappointment. Sitting alone in a condo while Dan is golfing isn't exactly how I pictured us spending our weekend together. I don't say anything, though, since it's more important that he has fun this weekend than that he spends every second of it with me.

~47~

The next morning I awake to Dan planting a minty kiss on my lips. Unfortunately, it's not the kind of good-morning kiss that leads to a *really* good morning. He's standing above me in khaki shorts and a powder-blue visor on his way out the door to golf.

"I'll be back in a few hours," he says sweetly, "go back to sleep.

I smile at him, my eyes only half open, and then close them again. I lie in bed, unable to go back to sleep, until I hear the front door shut. I look at the small digital clock beside the bed—it's seven thirty the first morning of our romantic vacation and I am left here alone. Somehow I had pictured breakfast (and maybe some other things) in bed to start the day. I get out of bed and pad into the condo's little kitchen. I am relieved to see a coffee maker sitting on the counter. I start opening cupboards looking for coffee, but after searching the entire kitchen top to bottom I find that there isn't any. My day is getting worse . . . not only am I stuck here alone, there isn't even any coffee!

I'm trying to calculate how far the walk into town would be when my cell phone rings. I jump at it, hoping it is Buck. I quickly amend my wish that the caller be Dan telling me he is on his way back. Neither wish comes true—it's Courtney.

"Hey," I answer trying to sound upbeat. Accepting defeat is not something I am programmed for, which means that not another soul on earth will ever know that this little road trip was anything but blissful.

"I met someone!" she squeals in delight on the other end.

The "I met someone" call is one I receive from Courtney about once a month. Usually, I haven't even had a chance to meet the previous month's Romeo before he is replaced. Obviously, this month it's different.

"What about Buck?" I ask defensively.

Courtney quickly blows me off. "I told you . . . boring and a prude. Alexander is amazing. He's a Greek shipping heir. I don't even know what that is. I know Paris Hilton was engaged to one, though, which means they are loaded, because that girl is the most materialistic person I've ever met. Plus, he went down on me the night we met!"

I have to catch my breath . . . while I'm a little jealous that she's getting some good action, I would never let someone I had just met go down on me. It would be so stressful I wouldn't even get to enjoy it . . . not that I've ever really gotten to enjoy it, since Dan isn't into it. My college boyfriend was the only one ever interested in visiting those areas with anything but his penis. I remember it being quite nice though.

"So," she continues, "I'm on my way to get a Brazilian because we're going to spend the weekend on his family's yacht. What are you up to?"

"My weekend away with Dan, remember?" I had talked to Courtney just a couple days earlier—had actually gotten romantic weekend tips from her. Breakfast (and other things) in bed was one of her suggestions.

"Oh, right. I won't keep you," she said. "Oh, but, how did Buck seem?" she asked, sounding only superficially concerned. "You saw him when you dropped Tiffany off, right?"

I'm taken aback for a second. "Did you tell him about

Alexander?" I ask, trying to search my brain for any aspect of Buck's behavior that seemed at all different.

"Well, no," she responds, as if I am a lunatic. "But I haven't called him in two days, so he probably realizes something is up. Do me a favor and tell him about Alex when you pick Tiffany up."

"You want *me* to tell him?" I ask. Even though I have dealt with Courtney for almost a dozen years, her behavior still manages to shock me.

"That would be great," she answers happily. "Oh my God, and Elizabeth, *totally* feel free to go for him now. I'm completely okay with it."

"I'm with Dan!" I blurt out—it's almost as much of a reminder to myself as it is to her. I wait for her response, but there isn't one. "Courtney! I'm happy with Dan!!" I holler, but it's no use, her cell phone (or mine) has dropped the call and we're no longer connected.

Her words, "totally feel free to go for him now," run through my head . . . why would she say that? She and Tiffany both know how hard I (we) worked to reunite with Dan—my dream man—and they are both encouraging me to get together with Buck?

I let out a long sigh and head for the shower. In the bathroom I find that Dan has used the only two towels provided by the rental company and left them both in a heap on the floor. I pick up a cold wet towel and hang it on the hook next to the shower, then turn on the water. I want to look good when Dan returns from golf—I'm sure there will be some romance then.

~48~

Five hours later I am still sitting alone in the stupid condo and am on the verge of dying of starvation. I am looking adorable in a Juicy terry lounge set that still cost over a hundred dollars at Marshall's, but Dan hasn't seen how cute I look because he hasn't come back from golf. Finally, at two forty-five my cell phone rings. I am so starved that I don't even have the energy to hope it's anybody in particular.

"Hey, hon," Dan says nonchalantly when I answer.

"Hi, sweetie!" I cheerfully exclaim, working hard to squash my desire to tell him off for being so inconsiderate. "On your way back?"

"Actually, I'm going to grab a beer with my fellow golfers and then I'll be back. I'm beat—I need a nap."

I am silent. I think I am too upset to actually form words. Finally I regain my composure.

"Actually, I thought we were going to try to go to the spa today," I say sweetly.

"I'm not really up for it. Why don't you go ahead and go now?" he tells me.

"I don't have a car," I snap.

"There's a tram that goes into town. Take that. Don't worry about being back by the time I get home," he says in his usual "I'm such a nice guy" voice.

"Okay," I tell him, too let down to argue and too annoyed at myself for not knowing about the tram five hours earlier when I needed coffee.

We hang up and I call the spa. They are booked all afternoon. I fight the urge to give up and collapse in a heap of tears. I put on my shoes, grab my purse, and take off in search of the tram into town.

The tram is really more of a bus for people to get up and down the mountain, which makes me the only person on board who isn't dressed for extreme sporting. People have loaded their mountain bikes onto a special bike rack on the front of the bus and most of them are wearing those Camel-back backpacks to remain hydrated through their active day. I feel completely out of place. I'm starting to feel this whole weekend was a mistake.

At last the bus stops in the little town and I climb off. The town is adorable and it would have been so much fun to stroll through hand in hand with Dan. I find a Starbucksesque coffee shop called Chiller Beans and get in line. I absentmindedly gaze at the pastry counter for a few minutes before my attention is snapped back to reality.

"Elizabeth?" the man in front of me asks.

My face flushes—it's my boss, Kevin.

"Kevin, hi!" I say. "What a coincidence . . . what are you doing up here?" I ask. Probably a stupid question, since his wife is standing right next to him—he's doing the same thing I'm doing . . . having a romantic weekend. I feel so stupid standing alone in the coffee shop.

"Actually, the studio owns a house up here, but Renee's been using it like her private property."

"Really?" I gasp. "I thought she did own a house up here."

"She let a lot of people think that," Kevin says with a slightly disgusted expression. "Apparently she'd been entertaining a lot of people in the house."

I give him a confused look so he adds, "Basically you and I

are the only ones she hasn't slept with here. Oh, and her husband."

I gasp again, utterly shocked. Here I thought Renee had the perfect life—wonderful husband, adorable children, perfect job—and all the time she was living a lie.

"Needless to say, the studio—and the network—aren't too thrilled about this," Kevin says.

He seems about to say more, but his turn to order coffee comes up and his wife gently tugs at his arm.

"Enjoy the rest of your weekend," he says as he turns around and starts ordering a soy latte.

I wish him the same and then order my own coffee, but my mind is racing. First the shocking news that Renee is not only a bitch at the office, but a totally slimy slut of a bitch in her personal life as well. Then add to that Kevin's words about the studio and network not being happy with her. What could that mean for me? Will the show be canceled altogether and will my big break collapse in my lap so quickly? Or will I get to fill her shoes completely and for good? *The Elizabeth Castle Show!* It has a nice ring to it. For so long Renee had been my idol. My whole life plan was practically modeled after her life . . . and I felt I was almost there. Now suddenly being like Renee Foster is the last thing I want. Almost in a blur I step outside the coffee shop and take a seat on an empty bench with my cappuccino. I suddenly feel that I have a lot to think about.

~49~

It was true that Tiffany needed to break up with Red Richley . . . and she knew that doing it in person was the right thing to do, but getting Lizzie away from Dan (and with Buck) for a weekend was almost more of a reason for a weekend in Victory than ending things with Red. Unfortunately, Elizabeth totally screwed things up by planning a weekend at Eagle Lake with Dan instead of staying at Buck's house as Tiffany had planned. In her head, it would have worked perfectly. It was clear that Elizabeth wasn't blissfully happy with Dan, and Tiffany knew that forty-eight hours away from him and around Buck would open her eyes. Of course, eyes that aren't present can't be opened.

On Saturday morning, Tiffany awoke to the sound of a doorbell. She blinked furiously as the bright light flooded into the room. The clock on the desk across from the bed showed it to be just before nine. She was annoyed to be awakened so early on a Saturday—although when you're on summer vacation, every day is like Saturday; plus, Buck was kind enough to let her stay with him—he couldn't also be expected to put his life on hold so she could sleep in. A few seconds later there was a soft knock at her door.

"Yeah?" she asked.

Buck stuck his head in. "Tiff," he said cautiously, "Red is here."

Tiffany let out an annoyed breath. "Oh, for Christ's sake. Let's get this over with," she said and swung her long legs over the side of the bed. Without so much as running her fingers through her hair, Tiffany walked out of the room, past Buck, and into the living room, where an overly eager Red stood waiting.

There was a different time (with a different boyfriend) when Tiffany would never have been seen in an old Victory High T-shirt and paisley boxer shorts. With Scott, she always made sure to look her best . . . hair brushed, makeup on, clothes form-fitting. She never cared as much with Red, and never cared as little as she did today.

"Hey, Tiffany." He greeted her with a big smile. So big and heartfelt that she felt a pang of guilt.

"Hey, Red," she answered. "Let's go sit on the porch."

He followed her like an eager puppy out the front door and onto the porch. Even though it was early, the day was already hot. Tiffany sat down on the top step and motioned for Red to sit beside her. She avoided looking at him and instead studied the light brown stubble on her shins. Inside, Buck headed to the kitchen to make a pot of coffee . . . the early morning visitor had also awakened him. Even inside with the air-conditioning on, Buck was already getting warm and instead decided to get his caffeine from a cold Coke. He cracked the red can open and let Wildcat out the kitchen door into the sun-filled yard.

"Red," Tiffany began slowly. "These last few months have been crazy for me," she started.

"I know," he answered quickly. "You didn't reply to my e-mail. I wish I could call you when you're in L.A. I have something for you," and before Tiffany could say a word, Red was fishing a small box out of his pocket.

Tiffany felt that she would either vomit or burst out laughing. She pinched her lips tightly together, since either response would be wrong. Red opened the box and Tiffany had to bite down on her tongue. Inside was a simple silver ring with a small pink heart-shaped stone. It was cute—extremely cheesy but sweet.

"It's a promise ring," Red said seriously. "I will marry you someday," he vowed, thrusting the box at Tiffany.

She gently took it from him and snapped it shut. "Red, I can't marry you," she told him without looking at him. She handed the box back. "You are wonderful, but my life is just too complicated right now." Tiffany had broken up with enough people to know how to word things. She knew she sounded like she was reciting lines from a movie, but she also knew what worked and what didn't. Letting Red down gently was the best thing to do. Victory was a small town and you had to think about public relations.

"I don't understand," Red said, bewildered. "I thought we were in love."

"Sometimes that's not enough," Tiffany said with a sigh. At this point it was much easier than having to explain that she had never, ever been in love with him. Red took the box and stuffed it back in his pocket.

"I'll always be here waiting for you, Tiffany," he said as he turned and walked down the gravel driveway to his mother's Ford Taurus station wagon.

"Thanks," Tiffany said with a gentle smile. "And congrats on getting your license." Then, without waiting for any sort of response, she turned and walked back into the house, letting the screen door slam behind her.

"How'd that go?" Buck asked from the couch.

Tiffany shrugged but smiled as she headed into the kitchen. A second later she returned with a Coke can in hand. She sat down beside Buck on the couch and cracked the soda open. Then she held it up for Buck, who clinked his own can against it. Half of her plans for the weekend had been completed successfully. Now Tiffany needed to figure out how to complete the rest of her mission. Elizabeth would be back in Victory tomorrow afternoon to pick her up. She had to figure out a way to get her and Buck together then.

~50~

By the time I got myself back to the condo via the town shuttle it was almost dark. I sat on the bench for hours trying to figure things out . . . unfortunately, I wasn't able to. My life plan has been such an integral part of my existence for so long that I cannot just shake everything I have been hoping and working for. I just wish for some sort of sign to confirm I am making all the right choices.

The short walk from the tram stop to our unit leaves me exhausted. I open the door and call to Dan that I am back.

"Sweetheart!" he says rushing up to me and grabbing me in his arms. The gesture rejuvenates me.

"Hi," I say enthusiastically.

"I've been worried about you," he says. "You left your cell phone here and I called the spa and they didn't have an appointment for you."

As he says it I realize that I left my phone charging on the kitchen counter.

"I'm sorry," I tell him. "I just went to get coffee—there isn't any here—and then I ran into Kevin and he told me—" I start to get excited about relaying the information I have learned.

"It doesn't matter," Dan says. "Let's not talk about work. Let's have our romantic evening."

I'm a little let down that Dan doesn't want to hear about my career. God knows I've spent enough hours listening to all his stupid legal stuff, but I'm able to put it aside, since he is finally interested in spending time with me.

We go to a nice dinner at a gourmet restaurant where we linger over candlelight and enjoy a bottle of wine. The alcohol certainly doesn't hurt, but I think it's the romance of the whole night that has me beaming and glowing. Dan talks about his golf game for most of the meal, but I decide to take this as a good thing—he's opening up about something that matters to him instead of saying, "Golf was golf." After dinner we take a stroll under the star-filled sky.

As we stroll hand in hand I say, "I think you should move into my place since yours doesn't have a room for Tiffany."

It's as if the whole evening was perched on top of a house of cards that suddenly comes crashing down. Dan pulls his hand out of mine and stops dead in his tracks.

"What are you talking about?"

"Moving in together . . . that's still the plan, right?" I ask sweetly. Although in my fantasy our reunion would come with a more normal engagement (aka *getting married*), I am willing to settle for simply picking up where we left off.

"Okay, first of all, I think it's completely premature to even talk about living together," he spits, "and second of all, we're not even going to think about living together until you have the Tiffany situation resolved. Figure it out, Elizabeth. Maybe she can live in Hicksville with Buck or whatever his name is."

His words sting me. "Victory," I mumble quietly.

"What?" he asks.

"It's called Victory, not Hicksville," I answer.

"Whatever," he responds. "Do you want ice cream?" he asks, stopping in front of a local parlor.

"No, I'm okay," I answer. My stomach has turned completely sour.

I stand outside, alone, while Dan goes in to get some ice cream. I can't help wondering why Dan even wanted to get back together . . . and why he agreed that I should put the engagement ring back on, since it seems that being engaged to me really isn't something he wants. Plus, the way he referred to "The Tiffany Situation," sticks with me . . . that's how I used to refer to becoming Tiffany's guardian; but now, just a few months later, I can imagine how empty my life would be without her. She's an amazing combination of a link to my past and a huge part of my future. Knowing Buck, he would let her come and live with him permanently—he's that generous and kind—but I wouldn't want her to live with Buck. I love having her with me.

Dan walks out of the ice cream shop with a cone stacked high with Rocky Road—his favorite and I've been eating it as long as I've been with him, but the truth is that I hate it.

"You sure you don't want some, hon?" he asks, as if nothing is wrong.

"Dan," I ask, "why did you agree that I should put my engagement ring back on?"

"I spent a boatload of money on it for starters, and I thought it was easier than having to explain why you weren't wearing it," he answers as he licks his cone.

"Oh," I nod. "That makes sense."

I look down at the ring . . . I find it hard to believe he spent a "boatload." I stare at the diamond for a second. The ring is beautiful and I love it—well, I really like it. It's not at all what I would have picked. I always wanted an emerald-cut diamond and this one is a princess-cut—a rectangle and a square are very similar. Plus, I'd only mentioned what kind of ring I wanted a few times, and really those were just in passing. Maybe this is the sign I was looking for?

Buck leaned back against the sofa in his living room and took a sip of beer. The sip was too big and the fizzy carbonation burned as it went down his throat, causing him to choke a little and spill the amber liquid down the front of his U of A T-shirt—not that it mattered. It was Saturday night, but Buck wasn't leaving the house. Par for the course, he thought. It felt like the story of his life—he tried for something and he failed. Of course, this was an extremely dramatic assessment. He was actually extraordinarily successful but never felt that way.

True, he graduated at the top of his class at Victory High and was hailed as a football hero. Yes, he did well at the University of Arizona and was again hailed as a football hero. Okay, he was also at the top of his law school class at Tulane and passed the bar immediately. Buck never focused on these things, though. What he focused on was his inability to get his point across when he needed to. He needed Lizzie to know how he felt about her, yet somehow he wasn't able to impart this information. Now it was too late.

There had never been a shortage of women in Buck's life, but few ever took him seriously. Elizabeth became his ideal woman because the night of his senior prom—the only date they ever went on—she didn't say one word about football.

Buck was thrilled to finally find someone who wanted to talk about other things. She had goals and dreams of her own, which he found fascinating, and was much more interested in Buck's nonsports plans. It was like a gift not to be asked if he was "going pro" after graduation.

His senior year at U of A he thought he had found someone and they dated throughout law school. Buck and Heather met at a football team party, which probably should have tipped him off, but she seemed different from most of the girls there. The majority of girls at these parties were looking to sleep with a team member . . . and Buck would admit that these types of parties and these types of girls made his college experience a lot more fun. Heather was an education major and seemed passionate about teaching elementary school. She and Buck lived together in New Orleans while he went to law school, and she taught second grade. Upon his graduation, though, a misunderstanding came up between them. Heather had quietly been under the assumption that after law school Buck would be playing for the NFL. Apparently she thought the Saints were somehow connected to his legal education, like some sort of ROTC-type program to educate players. With the force of a speeding train, Buck was hit with the fact that, like all the others, Heather was looking for an athlete (and that she herself wasn't very bright). They broke up, Buck returned home to Victory, and he'd pined for Lizzie Castle ever since.

Now he felt he had gotten so close to making it happen with her, but at the last minute things hadn't gone his way. He closed his eyes and rolled the cold glass bottle across his forehead. What could he have done differently? He thought he'd pulled out all the stops—every one except coming right out and telling her how he felt. He couldn't help wondering if that would have made a difference.

As he sat there feeling sorry for himself, the phone rang, and somewhere in the back of his head Buck hoped it was

Lizzie calling. Instead, it was Courtney. Courtney had called Buck every single day since his first trip to Los Angeles but had thankfully skipped the last two days. Buck had foolishly thought that perhaps the calls had ended permanently. The truth was that he actually liked Courtney. He just wasn't interested in dating her, which was a problem because she was very interested in dating him. Maybe in another time and place he would have been, but with Lizzie an arm's reach away, and Courtney being her best friend, it just wasn't meant to be.

"Hey, Courtney," he said somewhat reluctantly.

"Buck," she said dramatically. "First, I have to tell you that I've met someone else, sweetheart."

Buck's eyes brightened and his mouth formed itself into an uncontrollable grin. "I'm happy for you," he said, trying to feign humility.

"I'm actually calling you for professional reasons . . . and I apologize for doing this on a Saturday night. I just got a call from the head of the legal department at SparkleCourt. She had a baby three months ago and was supposed to be back at work next week, but apparently she's so damn attached to the little one that she can't bear to leave his side and she's resigned. I want you to come work for me."

Buck couldn't believe his ears. Was Courtney offering him a job? Normally, he would expect a job offer to come in the form of a question, but coming from Courtney it was more of a statement.

"You want me to come to Los Angeles and head your company's legal department?" Buck asked, needing clarification.

"Exactly," Courtney confirmed.

"But you don't even know my qualifications," Buck said, still slightly in shock.

"Here's the thing, and don't take this the wrong way because I'm sure you're a great lawyer . . . but all I really want is someone who *is* a lawyer that I get along with. It's all about personality clicks at my company," she said.

Buck took a deep breath and looked around his living room. Maybe it was time for a change.

"Can I think about it and let you know?" he asked.

"Call me tomorrow," she instructed. "And whatever your salary requirements are, I'll meet them, so don't make the decision about money."

"Courtney, thank you," Buck said, really meaning it. She really was a special person. "And congratulations on your new 'someone,' " he added.

"He's a sex god," Courtney gushed, and then stopped. "Is that hard or weird for you to hear?"

Buck smiled again. "No, I'm okay with it. I'll call you tomorrow."

They said goodnight and hung up. The call had come so out of nowhere for Buck that he wasn't even sure what to think about to make the decision. Victory was his home, and working for his father had always been what was expected of him. On the other hand, it was never what he wanted to do and he didn't have much (anything) tying him to the sleepy town. Los Angeles would be much more fun, plus he would be close to Tiffany . . . and to Lizzie. If only things had worked out differently with him and Elizabeth, this decision would be a no-brainer.

~52~

I spend most of the rest of the weekend inside my own head. It all kind of goes by in a blur. Dan is attentive for the remaining twenty-four hours—no more golf—but I suddenly feel a distance between us. I wonder if it's always been there and I'm just now noticing it. For so long Dan was my ideal, but maybe not because of who he is as a person. I feel I might just have been looking for what he represented and the life he would provide—or that I thought he would provide.

It also feels as if Dan and I have run out of things to talk about. Well, actually that we've run out of things that Dan wants to talk about. I have tons going on in my life since Tiffany showed up and my career has finally started to take off, but Dan doesn't seem interested in any of those things. So we chat about stupid things like the weather and the air quality, and when we're finished talking about those we are silent.

We are silent most of the ride back to Victory to pick Tiffany up. We arrive at Buck's house late in the afternoon on Sunday to find Tiffany sitting on the porch with him; they're both holding huge Popsicles. Their mouths are stained bright red and they are laughing. As soon as I see them, I feel an overwhelming urge to join them on the porch. I get out of the car and glance over at Dan. He doesn't make a move to turn the engine off. Instead, he leans forward to turn the radio on.

"Don't be too long," he says. "I don't want to get caught in too much traffic."

I walk up to the porch and Tiffany, between spurts of giggles, tells me that the ice cream truck came down the street and they just couldn't resist getting Cherry Bomb Pops. I smile and my mouth waters for one. I remember getting them as a little girl and I can still taste the sweet, tart cherry on my tongue. A bomb pop is almost as big as a child's arm and invariably extremely messy. My mother would only let me get one if I agreed to eat it outside, undressed. I would joyfully dance around our backyard in my panties while sticky red juice stained my mouth and dripped down my arm.

"So, how was the weekend?" I ask.

"Good," Buck says politely and then stands up and heads toward the house.

I am disappointed to see him go in.

"It was good," Tiffany confirms. "Thank God I'm single!" she sings.

"That went well?" I ask, referring to the planned breakup.

"As well as can be expected," she says, and nods with the Popsicle still in her mouth. I'm impressed by her maturity. "Should we go?" she asks.

"Probably," I answer, glancing back at the Audi purring in the driveway.

She turns and heads inside without a word. I'm unsure if I should follow her or not. I want to. I want to talk to Buck—to tell him what's going on at work and what I learned from Kevin over the weekend—but I don't know if I should. Before I can make a decision (or muster up the courage) Tiffany's back out on the porch holding her duffel bag.

"Bye, Buck!" she calls over her shoulder.

"Later, kiddo," he replies, and that's it.

Tiffany skips down the steps and opens the rear passenger

door of Dan's car. She gets in without a word and is silent (as am I) the rest of the ride back to Los Angeles. We arrive in front of my apartment shortly before nine and, as I expected, Dan has an early morning and can't come up. He waits in the driver's seat with the engine running while Tiffany and I unload our bags, and we carry them up the building's short staircase. At the top of the stairs, I turn around to wave one last good-bye, but Dan has already driven down the street and all I see are his red brake lights as he pauses at the stop sign at the end of the block.

~53~

A week later it's more of the same and I'm getting more miserable about it every day. I'm realizing that Dan hasn't changed. He's not a bad guy, but he might not be the guy for me. Somehow in the months we spent apart—really, the time since Charla died—I seem to have changed. On Monday morning, Dan sent me a dozen red roses at the office with a card that said, "For the great weekend." The flowers were a nice gesture—a signature Dan move—but I had to snort at the card. I certainly wouldn't call the weekend at Eagle Lake "great."

Even though my day is swamped with preparing for a musical guest show that includes Kanye West *and* Gwen Stefani (who arrives with the insanely adorable Kingston in tow), I find a minute to sit down at my desk and call Dan to thank him for the flowers.

"I love them," I gush, feeling completely fake.

"I knew you would," he replies, confidently. "I know they're your favorite."

I think for a second . . . I actually don't think red roses are my favorites. I think I like the yellow ones with the red rims the best.

"So," he continues, "I'm free Tuesday, Thursday, and Saturday this week. Are we set for those nights?"

He's scheduling me in every other day like I'm a workout routine or a plant that needs watering.

"Sure," I reply, then my other line beeps and I end the call with Dan.

I plan a girls' night with Courtney and Tiffany for Friday and find myself looking forward to that much more than any of the nights with Dan. Tuesday's and Thursday's "dates" run together. Everything is so expected and mundane. He picks me up, he takes me to dinner, he takes me back to his place . . . boring. We're back to have missionary sex in the bedroom and I wonder what he was hiding our first time back together when we did it on the couch. While Dan pumps back and forth on top of me moaning, "Oh God," I lie there wondering: had there been another girl? Had he not changed the sheets yet? Did she leave something behind? Or was he so happy to be back together that he couldn't wait the extra seconds it would take to get to the bed? (Yeah, right.)

Friday night is way more exciting. Courtney arrives with bags full of our favorite Chinese take-out and I agree to let everyone eat in the living room (as long as we sit on the floor). I really can't believe how much more relaxed I've become!

"So," Courtney says. "Midweek, Alexander totally cooled off."

Here we go again. Poor Courtney has an incredible knack for giving her whole heart to any guy she goes out with once, and it's constantly getting stomped on.

"But then I gave him one of my famous blow jobs, and last night he said he loves me," she continues, happily shoveling chow mein into her mouth.

Courtney's blow jobs probably are famous because she has given them to so many men.

"But then, this morning, I realized that I'm not into him. So I broke it off."

Courtney could probably be as famous for doing this as

she is for the blow jobs. It's her patented move. A guy dumps her, she gets him back, and then *she* dumps *him*. It all feels like a lot of work, but I guess it's important to her not to be the dumpee . . . or maybe she just doesn't realize something isn't what she wants until the second time around.

I think about this for a second as I chomp on an egg roll. In the background I hear Courtney telling all the annoying things Alexander was doing.

Suddenly I blurt out, "I want to break up with Dan."

They both freeze and without a sound turn and look at me. Tiffany's mouth is slightly agape. Courtney breaks the silence. "That's *my* move! You go girl!!" she says and raises her glass of wine in the air. Tiffany lets out a whoop and sends her Coke up to meet Courtney's glass. I just sit there, frozen. I cannot believe the words just came out of my mouth . . . and there's more coming.

"I think I want to be with Buck," I say quietly. I'm not sure either of them heard me.

"I told you so," Tiffany sneers at me. I look up at Courtney. Even though in her mind she broke up with Buck (in Buck's mind—and probably in reality—they were never together), I'm not sure how she'll feel about this.

"I think you're perfect for each other," she says matter-of-factly.

"I think it might be too late," I confess. His greeting when Dan and I picked Tiffany up five days earlier had been much different than usual.

"You don't think we can get you two together?" Courtney asks, referring to herself and Tiffany.

My face breaks into a big smile and I start to get that excited feeling in the middle of my chest that only happens when you realize you like someone new.

"What's Plan A?" Tiffany asks Courtney with a giggle. Here we go again.

"No, you guys," I interrupt. "I can do this myself," I tell them.

"Okay," Courtney nods. "But we're here if you need us." Then she raises her almost empty glass (again). "To Elizabeth and Buck!" she cheers. "And to me being single!" she adds.

"Me too!" Tiffany echoes.

We all clink glasses.

~54~

It's one thing to make the decision to break up with Dan . . . actually doing it is a whole other ordeal. I made my decision Friday night and thought I would implement it Saturday before our scheduled date, but Dan showed up with flowers (granted, they were boring red roses, but still a nice gesture) and I didn't have the heart. Then basically for the rest of the week I've been a chicken, but today I am going to do it. I am going over to Dan's apartment after work and I am going to give him back the engagement ring and tell him it's over.

It's a slow day at work, since we're having our two-week summer hiatus. That means that for ten days audiences get to see "best of" episodes—aka repeats. I suppose it sucks for viewers, but it's a great break for all of us who work on the show, especially because Renee hasn't even been bothering to come into the office. A little after five o'clock I come out of my office and tell Hope that I'm cutting out early and she should do the same. I know that the courts adjourn at five on the dot and that Dan will be home soon. I've got to get this over with sooner rather than later, and before I lose my nerve (again).

During the entire drive to Dan's apartment, I rehearse what I am going to say to him. It's been running through my mind nonstop all week, and weighing me down with worry and guilt. As nervous as I am, I am also relieved that today will finally be the day. I'm also excited to have it done with, because once I'm officially broken up with Dan, I can tell Buck exactly how I feel about him. That conversation has also been running through my head endlessly.

I pull up to Dan's apartment, park, and get out of the car. The butterflies in my stomach are going crazy—I'm almost dizzy with anxiety as I walk up to the apartment. I peek into the building's gated parking area and confirm that Dan's car is parked in his assigned spot. Then I take a deep breath and walk up to his door. I start to reach for his key on my key ring, but knock on the door instead. While I wait for him to answer, I slip the key off the ring. I stand there, key in hand, for a few seconds and Dan doesn't answer, so I knock again, a bit harder.

Finally, Dan opens the door looking a bit disheveled. He's dressed in Adidas shorts and a plain white T-shirt. He's a little sweaty—clearly he's been working out. Seeing him, I suddenly get cold feet. He looks so cute and I think it's adorable that he comes home from a hard day at work and exercises. I suddenly feel like I'm making a huge mistake. Am I crazy to throw away a man like Daniel McCafferty? He's perfect. All these months I've been obsessing over Buck, but what if it's just that . . . an obsession? An infatuation. What if in real life, Buck isn't what I want and need. I don't think I can break up with Dan.

"Elizabeth?" he asks, almost seeming panicked.

No, I tell myself. I have to do it. I think back to the miserable weekend at Eagle Lake. Dan is not the one . . . it might not be Buck (please, God, let it be Buck) but it's definitely not Dan. I take a deep breath and prepare to deliver my breakup speech.

"Dan," I say sadly, shaking my head slowly from side-to-side.

"Who is it?" I hear a voice call from inside the apartment.

"What?" I ask, confused about where the voice came from.

"What?" Dan asks quickly.

I shake it off and get back on track. "Dan," I repeat, "I can't marry you." I speak softly, and as I talk, I gently slide the diamond ring off my left hand. As I hold the diamond out to him to take, I have another moment of panic. I look up at Dan, and instead of the heartbroken or even confused expression I was expecting, I see a look of guilty shame.

"I'm sorry," Dan begins, and I'm about to tell him that he has nothing to be sorry for, but before I can say anything he continues, "I was with Kimberly once while we were apart and I didn't think this would happen . . ." his voice trails off.

I stand there in a confused stupor. I have no idea what he is talking about, but my breakup speech definitely doesn't include anything about a Kimberly.

"What?" I ask.

Dan looks like a deer in headlights. "You found out about Kimberly, right?" he asks.

I'm about to say "no," because I have no idea what he's talking about, when Defender Bitch walks out of Dan's room dressed only in the blue button-front shirt that I'm certain Dan wore all day at work. When she sees me she gasps, and I gasp, too.

"I'm sorry," Dan pleads, his eyes brimming with tears as he looks at me. "I do love you."

"What?!?" Defender Bitch/Kimberly screeches. "You said you love *me*!"

"I do," Dan says miserably. "I don't know what to do," he almost whimpers.

I look at him and realize that he hadn't been working out . . . he'd been fucking Defender Bitch! I am completely disgusted. Suddenly I am positive that the night Dan did me on the couch had everything to do with this other woman having been in his bed. I stare for a minute at Dan, tears in his eyes, and at Kimberly, hands on her hips again, and again screaming, "You said you love *me*," and I honestly don't know if I want to laugh or cry.

"Here," I say, again holding the engagement ring out to him.

He reaches out and takes it, opening his mouth to speak. Before he can get a word out, I turn and walk away. As I do, I hear Kimberly in the background. "I don't want *that* ring . . . it's too small." Letting out a little chuckle, I feel that an enormous weight has been lifted.

~55~

Twenty-four hours after Courtney's call, Buck called her back.

"I'll take it," Buck said with a confidence his voice rarely (never) had when handling professional matters.

He had made the decision almost immediately after hanging up with Courtney but wanted to tell his father what he was doing before he officially accepted her offer. Buck had been nervous about telling Larry S that he was leaving the family business, but he knew it was the right thing for him. His Dad and brother were cut from the same mold. Buck's family was close and he knew they loved him, but also knew that his father always considered Larry J to be his junior in more than just name and Buck to be his all-star athlete. Buck's decision to go to law school was an attempt to join their club, but it had really only given him entry to the outside circle.

On Sunday morning, Buck drove to the Denny's where he knew his parents would be having their post-church breakfast. True to form, Larry S and Buck's mother, Patsy, were already sipping their coffee when Buck arrived.

"Bucky!" his mother exclaimed. "What a wonderful surprise. Isn't this a wonderful surprise, Larry?" she asked his father.

Larry S didn't look as excited as Patsy, but he was pleased to see his younger son and invited him to join them for breakfast. Buck accepted both the invitation and the seat the waitress had pulled up to the small table. It wasn't until the food arrived and they had begun eating that Buck finally worked up the courage to tell his father what he came to say.

"Dad," he said cautiously, "I've been offered a job in Los Angeles."

"Doing what?" his father barked, and at the same time Patsy cooed, "Oh, that's wonderful, sweetheart."

"I'll be the head of the legal department for an accessory company," Buck said, emphasizing the head of legal department part and mumbling through the accessory company part.

Just as Buck knew he would, Larry S barked, "An accessory company? Like bracelets and shit?"

"It's called SparkleCourt," Buck said confidently, but wishing the company's name wasn't quite so descriptive.

"Oh my gosh," Patsy gasped. "I've read about it in magazines. Alana Russo's daughter started it."

"Yes," Buck confirmed, hoping, but not counting on, this lending some credibility to the company in his father's eyes. "It's a fantastic offer."

Larry S looked straight at Buck through his narrowed blue eyes. "Congratulations, son," he said before shoving a bite of well-done hash browns in his mouth.

Buck let out a smile with a sigh of relief. "Thanks, Dad," he said, and then looked at his mother and gave her a grateful smile before returning to his own breakfast.

That night Buck returned Courtney's call.

"Oh my God, I'm so thrilled to hear it!" she exclaimed, and her enthusiasm reconfirmed Buck's decision.

It was going to be great to get a fresh start. It was time to get out of Victory. It would always be home, but Buck had to accept that he didn't fit in here as well as he used to. Plus, he had made another decision. He wasn't going to accept that Elizabeth was going to marry Dan. Once in L.A., he was going to tell her exactly how he felt. If, upon knowing how much he wanted to be with her, she still chose her pricklike fiancé, then he would accept it and go on with his life, but he was determined to make one last effort to be with the girl he had wanted for so long.

"When can you start?" Courtney asked.

"How about a week from tomorrow?" Buck asked, almost shocked at how brashly he was charging ahead with this change.

"Perfect," Courtney said. "I'll see you next Monday."

They hung up, and Buck looked around his house. He knew he'd be homesick for the place, but he and Wildcat would find somewhere in L.A. that they would be happy in.

~56~

Friday night I could hardly sleep. I spent the whole night tossing and turning. True, the image of Dan and Defender Bitch postcoitus ran through my head, but the main reason for my sleeplessness was my plan for the next day. I have decided that, like the breakup, I need to tell Buck how I feel about him in person. So, first thing Saturday morning I get behind the wheel of my still-damaged car and hit the road. I make the drive in record time, and by the time I get to Buck's house, my excitement has become almost electric.

I park on the street down a few houses from his own and sit in the car. This could possibly be the most exciting thing I have ever done . . . and I host a live television show! In the few relationships I have had, I've never really put myself out there. I've never decided I was interested in someone before he showed a clear interest in me, and I've definitely never gone straight up to someone and told them how I feel. The tides are changing, though; now is the time.

I flip down the sun visor and glance in the mirror. I look surprisingly well rested considering how little sleep I actually got. Apparently, the adrenaline driving me to my great reveal is flattering. I step out of the car and suddenly feel silly for coming to Buck's house. I shake it off and take a few steps from the car, then stop in my tracks. Suddenly it pops into my mind that I could be setting myself up for a repeat of the day before. What if Buck is currently in bed with someone else? He certainly has every right on earth to be, but what will I do? I take a deep breath and proceed forward. I have to tell him how I feel. If my feelings aren't returned I'll deal with it and go on with my life. My life plan has already crumbled into pieces; one more derailment isn't going to be the end of the world.

I take yet another deep breath and proceed up Buck's gravel driveway. It's almost noon, and Victory is so hot. Even dressed in a tank top and cotton skirt, I am starting to sweat from just the short walk up to the house . . . or maybe it's nerves? Feeling as if there isn't enough oxygen, I step up onto the porch and knock on the front door. The moment of truth has arrived.

"Come in," Buck calls from inside, and I slowly push the front door open.

I've pictured this moment in my mind (in my vision he actually got up and answered the door): Buck will look into my eyes with his own sparkling blues and then he'll kiss me passionately. He'll tell me he feels the same way and then lead me into his bedroom and make love to me all afternoon. I step inside the house and am startled, because nothing is how I thought it would be. Almost all of Buck's possessions are packed into brown cardboard moving boxes, which are stacked neatly at the front of the house.

Wildcat joyfully runs to greet me and I give him a pet as I look around the house, confused. I have a terrible feeling that I've come too late.

"Buck?" I call out.

"In the kitchen," he answers. "Who's there?"

I quickly cross the living room and stand at the door of the kitchen. Buck, with his back to me, is emptying kitchen drawers into boxes.

"It's Elizabeth," I say quietly.

Buck freezes and spins around. He looks shocked to see me.

"What are you doing here?" he asks.

"I . . . I came to talk to you. Are you going somewhere?"

"Yeah, moving day," he explains. "Time for a change."

My heart falls. I am too late. Buck is leaving Victory and probably leaving my life forever. Why am I so stupid? Why did I not listen to Tiffany or figure this out for myself months ago? Hell, why didn't I figure it out in high school when Buck took me to his senior prom?

Our date scared me to death because I was determined not to feel anything for anyone in Victory, but it was undeniable with him. Not only was he beyond handsome and practically a local celebrity, but Buck was interested in hearing what I had to say. Unlike so many of the dates I'd gone on (dates that Charla had always arranged for me since I was too shy to ask people myself), Buck wasn't preoccupied with talking about himself. He listened to me talk about leaving Victory, becoming a journalist, and anchoring the news. When he dropped me off on my front porch, he gave me one gentle kiss and then backed off. I was completely smitten and had to spend the entire summer convincing myself that he was no good. In my mind, I turned him into a football playing meat-head with nothing else to offer. Over the years I guess I began to believe it was true, but as soon as he came back into my life—as soon as Charla brought him back into my life— the truth became undeniable.

"Where are you going?" I ask, terrified to hear the answer.

"L.A. Didn't you know that?" he asks, looking at me con-fused and then continuing to load the box in from of him.

I let out a huge sigh of relief. If this isn't a sign that I'm doing the right thing, I don't know what is. "You're moving to L.A.?" I confirm, part of me not believing it could be true.

"Didn't Courtney or Tiffany tell you?"

"No," I answer, annoyed with both girls for leaving me out of the loop on this.

"Courtney offered me a job at SparkleCourt and I'm giving it a shot."

A smile breaks out over my face. Courtney once again comes through for me. I can picture her and Tiffany plotting this . . . "Plan A."

"I broke up with Dan," I tell him eagerly.

Buck stops packing again and turns to look at me. "Really?" he asks, and then turns around, but as he turns I catch his face curve into a huge grin.

"Yeah. He wasn't the one for me," I tell him. "Say, where are you going to live?" I ask, suddenly curious about Buck's plans.

"I actually don't know yet. I've got to find a hotel that allows dogs until I find a place," he says.

His answer is exactly what I hoped he would say. "Why don't you live with me?" I ask, trying to hide how eager I am.

"Really?" he asks. "Could I crash on your couch with Wildcat until I find something permanent?"

I pause for a second . . . failure to communicate. "Why don't you make my place permanent?" I ask with a little less confidence.

"But you only have the two bedrooms . . . one for you, one for Tiffany . . ."

He isn't getting it.

"Buck," I say almost sternly, and he turns around again to look at me.

I'm not going to take another chance at being misunderstood. I take one step forward and plant my lips directly on his. I start to kiss him and can taste the saltiness of sweat on his upper lip. I wrap my arms around his neck and feel the heat of his body against mine. I don't breathe again until he kisses me back. When he does, my whole body melts against his and I feel that I wouldn't be able to stand if my arms weren't securely around his strong neck.

When we finally pull back, I say, "You could room with me."

"Yes," he says breathlessly, then smiles so widely that his dimples almost extend off his cheeks and his eyes twinkle. "Yes!" Then he kisses me again.

Slowly we fall to the floor and I can hardly breathe; I want him so badly. I have never wanted anyone like this. Without taking his lips off me Buck takes off all of my clothes and then pulls back to look at me. For a split second I am horrified . . . I never let anyone see my skeletal frame in the nude. I didn't even wear my black lace lingerie set because it would have showed through my thin summery clothes. Instead I am wearing boring white cotton underwear! True, in my fantasy this is how things happened, but I never imagined in real life that Buck would be putting my nipples in his mouth. (Oh my God, it feels good.) He kisses every square inch of my body (and I mean *every* square inch) and I am almost shaking with desire by the time he finally pushes inside of me. I groan with pleasure even though I'm lying on the hard tile floor. Every move he makes feels better than the previous and before I know it I'm having an amazing orgasm . . . right there in the spot where I burned his foot with hot coffee!

When we finish (two orgasms for me later), Buck rolls off and joins me on the floor. He lies on his side and grins happily at me. He kisses the tip of my nose and asks, "Did you have something you wanted to talk to me about?"

~57~

Six months later I'm sitting at my desk staring down at the growing bump in my normally concave stomach. The passionate start to our relationship on Buck's kitchen floor left us with a little surprise. Ironically, an unplanned pregnancy was my greatest fear until it happened, and now it feels like the most unexpected joy imaginable. Plus, Buck couldn't have been more wonderful. We had been living together (and loving every second of it) for three weeks when I realized I was late and took a home test. As soon as I told Buck, he was down on one knee.

"Lizzie, I have loved you for over a decade. Marry me?" he asked sweetly.

Of course I accepted, and as soon as I did, he ran out and bought a two-carat emerald-cut engagement ring (which I *never* mentioned wanting) and a three-bedroom house in Santa Monica—with a white picket fence! We got married in the backyard of the house the weekend that escrow closed. Although things happened slightly out of order, I am actually living my ideal life: married to an attorney, an older daughter, and a baby son on the way, a golden retriever romping behind the white picket fence, and a successful career in journalism. Go figure!

It's Friday afternoon and we are finished taping for the

week. I'm going over my files for next week's interviews but itching to get out of the office. Christmas is in a few days and I have about a million things to do to be ready, since we are hosting both families in our new home. Finally, I decide to blow the work off and head to Bloomingdale's to pick up the Chanel Mademoiselle perfume that Tiffany has been relent-lessly hinting for. I can't help but laugh . . . this time last year she was living in Victory and buying knockoffs at Wal-Mart the next town over. Now she's such an L.A. teenager, wearing Juicy velour suits with Ugg boots (lucky for Tiff, she and I wear the same size) and spritzing Chanel. Charla would be proud (and pleased). Just as I am shutting down my com-puter, Kevin walks into my office.

"Have a minute?" he asks, sitting down in the guest chair across from my desk before I can answer.

"Of course," I answer, clicking the "cancel shutdown" button with my mouse.

"Holiday plans?" he asks, completely confusing me. It's not common for the head of the studio to show up on a Fri-day evening to chat about Christmas traditions.

"Our families are coming to town. You?"

"I have no idea," he says, his voice a combination of shame and pride. "My wife takes care of all that."

I smile and laugh, but inside I'm tense with concern about his unexpected visit.

"So," he begins getting to his reason, "there are going to be big changes on the show at the beginning of the year," he says and my heart falls.

Three minutes ago I sat here reveling in the fact that I've finally got it all . . . apparently karma didn't appreciate my gloating.

"Oh?" I ask weakly. I've never been fired, so I don't know what I'm supposed to do or say.

"Look, Elizabeth, lemme level with you. A scandal is going to be breaking in *Us Weekly* on Sunday," Kevin says, leaning forward and lowering his voice. "Thankfully, I've got an old friend over there who gave me a heads-up, and it's going to lead to a total revamping of the show."

I'm literally dying to know what the scandal is, but I'm afraid to ask. Forget it, I tell myself, bite the bullet. "What's going on?" I ask.

"One of the many staff members Renee entertained at the Eagle Lake house has filed a seven-million-dollar sexual harassment suit," he says, slowing over the words seven, million, and dollar.

My jaw drops open slightly and I don't even know what to say. "Who?" I ask, nosily forgetting that it might not be appropriate to force my boss into spreading gossip.

"One of the camera operators, Carlos Dokter. Know who he is?"

I gasp again. "Of course!" Everyone calls him The M.D. "I had no idea," I am completely in shock. Renee was having an affair with The M.D, who is considerably younger than she is and also totally hot?!? Most mornings in the makeup chair are spent listening to the hairdressers and makeup artists talk about how in love with him they are.

"So, it's going to end up in the hands of legal and PR, but Renee is out. The studio and the network both agree that she is no longer the image we want representing us. This company values family and ethics."

As he says it I sneak a peak down at my belly bump. Am I going to be fired for getting pregnant before getting married? We were married before I ever started to show—and before I told anyone at the show . . . except Hope. Would Hope have ratted me out?

"We think you are the one to emphasize this image," Kevin continues, but I'm so focused on worrying that Hope is an evil corporate spy that I don't hear him. "As of the first of the year, you are hosting the show completely on your own."

"What?" I ask, my attention suddenly jerked back to reality.

"How do you feel about being called 'Lizzie?'" Kevin asks.

"Actually, I feel fine about it," I answer, and can't help smiling. My incredibly intelligent husband could never remember "Elizabeth." I guess he knew me and thought of me as "Lizzie," for so long that it stuck . . . and the truth is that coming out of his mouth, I like how Lizzie sounds.

"We think Lizzie has a more approachable sound than Elizabeth," he explains. "So, the show will be *The Lizzie Castle Show*. We're dropping the exclamation point."

"Oh, actually I'm Lizzie Castle-Platner now," I tell him.

Kevin looks up and smiles at me. "Even better. Married, baby on the way—it all reeks of family and stability. Excellent," he says more to himself than to me as he stands up and heads towards the door. "Have a great holiday," he says as he walks out, "and get ready to host your own show the first week back next year."

I reach for the phone and dial Buck as I shut down my computer.

"Hey," I say, and I still feel as excited to be talking to him as I did back in high school.

"Hey," he returns. "I went and bought that Chanel perfume Tiffany has been hinting for," he tells me.

"She's subtle, huh?"

"Subtle like a Mack truck," Buck answers with a laugh. "What's going on?"

"You'll never guess," I tease, and then I tell him everything. I'm so excited that I can hardly form words. Somewhere deep down, I always feared that even all my determination and planning wouldn't work out and I'd never have it all. It still amazes and thrills me that I've managed to pull it off. My life has turned out to be an undeniable victory.